VOLT'S COMMAND

Volt's Command

A HIGH URBAN FANTASY

Harrie Blake

SHB Books

Published by:
SHB Books
Brisbane, Australia
First Published 2023

ISBN: 978-0-6453929-3-7

A catalogue record for this book is available from the National Library of Australia

To the Plantae

1

Live to fight another day

Once upon a time, a bunch of sparkheads ruined it for everyone. Basically, this person, Volt, worked out how to use electricity to power ludere, creating electromagn. This made everyone more powerful, but some went mad and became supervillains. There were lots of wars, and as you know, it was rather static for a while. Eventually, the council of five worked out how to cut them off with magn quotas and a lot of, what Hannah calls, red tape.

Telling It Like It Is
History Assignment
Maxi, Apprentice of Chester

What was I willing to die for? My world narrowed to the mug of coffee in front of me. *Cold.* I shifted in my seat, trying to see if anyone was paying attention. *Spark it.* Swiveling my chair away from the guards, my fingertips buzzed, warming the mug beneath them. Steam caressed my face, and a gulp flooded my system with heat. I exhaled, slumping deeper in my chair.

"Hey Morthwyl, how's your day going?"

I didn't *think* the guards could hear me. Sometimes they threw curious glances my way, and I wondered what they thought about the person sitting alone muttering to herself. The chair swung from side to side as I pushed at the floor of the council foyer where I sat, from opening to closing, checking identification chits. The high vaulted ceilings echoed the quiet back to me. Empty except for the couple of guards near the entrance and my friend, the mural. It portrayed our council of five standing on the cold stone steps of the Apex, monitoring the masses like grandparents left in charge of the nursery. It was also a superb listener.

Morthwyl, depicted in a furred biped form with an impressive head of hair and dark blue robes, stared down his enormous nose at me. He was the most talkative during live events, but his stern expression never wavered during our conversations.

"Busy? Yeah, I get it. Life can be tough." I contemplated the dreams that had passed me by, usually in flames. My muscles tensed, but another mouthful of hot tastiness helped, and my gaze wandered over to Iseret. I had met her in person once. She, in her three-meter-high biped form with long silver hair and dark scales, was unforgettable. I knew if we met again, she wouldn't like me. Morthwyl and I might engage in conversation, but would she even say anything as she ordered my death? Or would she just flick her wrist, dismissing my life like a speck of dust?

"Sup Iseret?" I gave a nervous chuckle, my heart rate spiking. The most excitement I'd had in days. I had been talking to the mural for almost a year and nothing bad had happened to me, yet. My nails unsheathed and clinked against the mug.

"I've heard that you've been busy clearing out nests of illegal magn users. Do you enjoy it? The killing I mean. I never did."

As I took another drink, I frowned. I had not meant to engage in a deep and meaningful with her. But the news this morning showed her striding through a town that had an estimated death rate of eighty people. The last time I had heard of that many people dying was at the height of the electromagn wars. Now they might have been guilty of something, it just seemed unlikely that all deserved to die. It was the killing of the children that was the hardest to stomach.

I shook myself and let my eyes drift over to the golden ones. Either through laziness or some mystical reason I couldn't fathom, they had taken on the same biped form, two meters high, with golden hair, golden skin and dark brown eyes. *And* they were depicted as dressed in white, with gold filigree.

"You've no idea, no idea at all how much damage you have done to fashion in our society, do you?" Rayisa and Tukhunri didn't care. They had moved on from the white and gold painted here. On the news this morning they had framed Iseret, their skin shimmering with a kaleidoscope of colors, in purple jackets trimmed with silver and sequins. Iseret had been in her usual red-and-black armor, her straight white hair tied back as she gave an update on the verdict of death to the camera. Rayisa and Tukhunri stood one step back, sequins twinkling. Sequins. I didn't mind sequins, but I wasn't sure about them as an accessory for killing.

I couldn't help flicking a glance towards the guards at my irreverence. They leaned against a wall, checking their wristbands, and sharing whatever banal thing had caught their attention. I sighed and turned back to the mural. Morthwyl and Iseret probably wouldn't care, but there were enough rumors of deaths, for disrespecting Rayisa or Tukhunri, to make people nervous and the fashion industry giddy.

"Hey Jarweer, how's it hanging?"

If not Iseret, the person most likely to take me out was Jarweer. His yellow eyes stared out of a swarthy face covered in leathery skin and long, dark green hair. He was, as always, dressed in dark greens and blacks. I did not know if I had ever seen Jarweer speak. He lurked. Usually behind Iseret. The story goes he was the one who convinced the others to step in and stop the people farms. He didn't save me, though.

"Out hunting? Been a while, not that you're a camera hog like Morthwyl. Sorry Morthwyl, but you do like being in the spotlight. I'm assuming you'll have a press conference tonight. Remind us all why we need to behave?"

I exhaled heavily. It was hard to argue with the five immortal beings who ruled our world with uncompromising certainty. And I agreed with them in principle. The last thing we wanted was the electromagn wars again. But surely there was a middle ground between murder by psycho magn users and execution by the rule of five.

"What do you think, Morthwyl? Is there a way for us to all just get along without quite so much death?"

The mural's soft orange background, which created a glow around their darker silhouettes, glinted. The blood left my face, but before I could spiral into paranoia, a sound drew my attention towards a tall figure standing at the building's entrance. He stood for a moment, no doubt letting his eyes adjust to the brightly lit foyer after the soft gray of the winter morning. Our gazes connected and ignoring the guards, he did his impersonation of a moving wall and headed towards me. Emanuel Lea, his rough skin covered in thin green hairs highlighting the slime covered muscles underneath, was a friend of a recent mistake.

"I need a scan." He thumped down in the chair opposite and thrust his wristband towards me. It was decked out with all the latest upgrades, not as many as mine, of course. I did like to tinker after all, but in the center sat his physical ID chit, glinting at me.

"Right." I nursed my mug. All citizens had government issued identification chits, however, only three forms required physical verification. But they were important ones, so here I was, sitting in the foyer. "I'll have to verify your identification chit—"

"Yes, I know. That is why I'm here. I said I needed a scan, didn't I?" He pushed his wrist closer to me.

I put down my mug and muffled my sigh. Work was even more tedious sober.

"Which transaction do you wish to be verified for today?" I asked. I could be professional if I had to. My face didn't move, and I worked hard to keep my body relaxed as I pulled his arm towards me to view the chit. That glint. Not a usual feature. He could be using a glamor. But why? I already knew who he was.

"Change of account." My eyelid twitched.

I hadn't stored any magn that morning, so I illegally used the building's electricity again. I was being lazy, really. But it was right there, flowing in convenient little cords in the floor under me. I, of all people, knew to charge at home, but I had taken my time getting ready, which resulted in no breakfast and no charge up. Even as an employee, I had to fill out a form if I wanted to use the building's electricity. Risking death to avoid filling in a form might seem dicey, but in my defense, it was a long form, *and* I needed my supervisor to endorse it. A quick bit of siphoning would not kill anyone, except me if I got caught.

This time I used the magn to scan the chit as I touched it, and my brain caught up with what my eyes had been trying to tell me. If I had been passing the day through my usual haze hungover, I suspect I would have missed it.

"Won't be a moment." What to do? If I turned him in, it would cause all sorts of paperwork and a visit from my supervisor. But if I didn't, and they found out later it was a fake ID, that would be a lot worse. "How's your day going?"

"Just do the check." He sat back and crossed his arms, staring at me. *Sparkhead.* My knee hit the alarm button.

I relaxed and even smiled a little. I hit print on the form

he needed and as the aethercomp spat it out, despite it being directly next to me, I dropped it.

"Oh... dear."

His upper lip curled. We were saved from my improvisation by the two enormous preservation guards heading our way. Guards who, even with my medium-sized form, I could take in a fight. But their dimensions were effective in cutting down chatter.

Emanuel's breath rushed at me. I pushed the chair back and jumped up, softening my knees and using my flat toes to carry my weight. Instead of swinging at me, he dodged past the guards and raced towards the door. The guards, more amblers than sprinters, used their stunners and the entire building trembled as Emanuel crashed, causing new cracks to appear on the floor.

"Got a glamor on, Morgan?" one guard asked, while the other used her body weight to keep him down and put magn-infused cuffs on him.

"False chit." I had an aetherdoc port on my desk for these types of situations, and I touched my chit to its side to warm it up.

"That so?" asked the guard, peering around his partner, trying to see Emanuel's wrist. "Don't see many of them nowadays." He scratched his chin and moved to help his partner.

"No, you don't." I stepped out from behind my desk. One guard kept her knee on his upper back and the other kept his arm still. Theoretically, only certain people could change wristbands which were permanently attached at birth. I squatted beside him and pulled at the wristband to get access to the chip, but my fingers accidentally grazed the wet moss on his skin, making me shudder. I went down on one knee and used both hands to remove the chit without touching him again.

"You're an ignorant piece of static," said Emanuel, his breath almost a hiss.

"True." I frowned at him, but didn't bother arguing. I had learned a long time ago that arguing with the dead was pointless. After the false chit was secured in an evidence bag, I attached a temporary custody tracking chit to his wristband and the guards carried him away. By the time I got back to my desk, the port was ready to go, so I placed the evidence on the tray and activated it. Silence followed. I gazed at the empty foyer and slumped in my chair.

I didn't want to be here, and with Wilbur's death, it felt like I was going to be trapped in this cold, quiet foyer forever. I should have run as soon as he died. But here I was, suffocating in quiet. I had tried singing for a while, but it must have disturbed the guards as I received an order from my supervisor to stop. So, I talked, softly, with the mural. Emanuel, even being the sparkhead that he was, had kept the stillness at bay.

The clock showed it was an hour until my official lunch break, until I could escape into the world of sound. I stretched and took a breath. With a little nudge, my mug was once again full of hot deliciousness and the creak of my chair swinging from side to side gave me some relief.

"Did you see that, Morthwyl? A false chit. Another person for you to kill Iser—"

A singularity of sound echoed powerfully through the chamber as a door to the foyer hit the wall. Shod footsteps have two parts to them. First the striking of the heel and then the soft tap of the flat of the foot. The person heading in my direction was throwing her whole-body weight into a single stomp. I winced and hoped her imposing boots protected her knees. My shoulder muscles relax and my lips twist upward at the sound and energy she brought. A distraction for a few minutes, at least.

I was, as always, a fool.

She wasn't old enough to have achieved independence. Though that could have been the weight of my own years talking. Slumped down in the seat, her wan face stared at me from beneath long dark feathers with green tips.

"Scan?" I had to ask. It was surprising how many people needed directions to the toilets.

"You're Morgan, right?" she asked, sitting further back in the chair and crossing her arms.

"Yes, I'm currently stuck being Warrant Officer Morgan Anastasi. Can I help you?" I frowned. Duskburn was a decent sized city with enough warrant officers that a kid knowing my name was weird.

"I need you to find my scholar."

"Your scholar?" Ah, an apprentice, and if her scholar had abandoned her, there was, as with most things, a process for dealing with it.

"Lifelore Scholar Lenora Chester. She didn't come home last night."

One night hardly equated to abandonment. I sighed, and the kid narrowed her eyes at me. I raised my hand.

"Right, if you're really concerned, I'd suggest you contact the Preservation Service. I can give you—"

"They won't do anything."

"Well, it's their job, and I—"

"She isn't anyone special, and she hasn't been missing that long."

"If it was only last night—"

"She's always there in the morning. It's the only meal she asks all the apprentices to share."

How many apprentices did the poor scholar have?

"Another scholar—"

"The only other teacher we had was Wilbur."

For volt's sake.

I sat back and took another breath as my shoulders tightened.

"You may not know—"

"I know he's dead."

"Right, so…"

"So, I'm here to see you, aren't I? He told me you would help me if I ever needed it."

"Did he?" Why would he do that? "I'm afraid I don't hold the rank of scholar so I can't teach—"

"I'm not here for a teacher. Someone needs to find Lenora, and that someone is you."

"Why me?" With another gulp, I washed away the frustration. "I'm a warrant officer." I gestured with my other hand, taking in the desk and the foyer.

"So what? Was your brain taken when you got stuck here?" She laughed at my expression. "I think it's ironic, really."

I raised an eyebrow, something that always worked well in interrogations.

"Very few people use that word correctly."

"What do you think the council would do if they received an anonymous complaint that one of their warrant officers had a fake ID chit?"

"I'm not sure how threatening me is going to help you get your scholar back."

"Because you're going to go out and use that brain of yours that Wilbur said you had and find her."

"Right. You need to understand that the preservers are an organization with a full set of resources that I don't have access to. I'm unlikely to be of any help." I raised my hand as she opened her mouth. "However, a ... colleague... of Wilbur's still works in the local unit. I'll contact him and ask that Lenora's disappearance is investigated."

A deep v formed in the middle of the kid's forehead.

"Trust me. Despite what you think you have over me, they're going to be a lot more help." I stared at her and thought I saw some give. "There's a form for this." I didn't need to say that. There was a form for everything. "Let's get it started." I found it on the comp and pulled my keyboard towards me. "What's your name?"

Vivian, apprentice of Lenora Chester, was not happy, but I lodged the missing person's report and promised to make a call.

She didn't leave.

"Well, that is about all I can—"

"You said you'd call Wilbur's colleague."

"Yes, I'll—"

"What are you waiting for? Call them."

Hunched down in the chair as she glared at me, I could see a long afternoon ahead. I sent a pulse to my wristband and Amiel's soft hello sounded in the airwaves near my ear. Vivian was scrutinizing me a bit too intensely, but I didn't engage the privacy mode. Let her hear I am being helpful and maybe she would go away.

"Amiel, hey, sorry to bother you, but I've a missing person, a Lifelore Scholar Lenora Chester, that I need some help with."

"Morgan? You haven't missed another check in, have you?" Amiel had always been kinder to me than the others. Not that Wilbur had been cruel, just focused.

"No, not due for another week." I swiveled in my chair. "Nothing to worry about, just have an acquaintance of Wilbur's here that needs some help. Can you?" I asked.

"Morgan, I'm not a help line." The sigh traveled through the aether unfiltered. "What is it?"

A grin pulled at the muscles on my face. For a leader in the Preservation Service, Amiel was a good person. While I wasn't sure how old he was, but despite being brilliant with fire, I suspected that, unless he was about to transition to Dean, he was running out of time. Maybe that gave him a better perspective on life than most of the perseveration asshats.

"Scholar Lenora Chester. She's missing and one of her apprentices is about to lodge the form…"

A soft laugh floated through the air.

"I'll flag it and let you know if anything comes through on the alerts. How long has she been missing?"

"She didn't come home last night, which is strange for her." I considered Vivian and realized how much of my neck I was putting out just because of a vague, and probably unsubstantiated, threat.

"I'll ask one of my team to pick it up."

"Thanks, Amiel, you aren't too bad."

He hung up.

Vivian hadn't taken her eyes off me the entire time. Her face was pale again and her eyes appeared damp and overly bright.

"Amiel says he will allocate someone to investigate it. Trust me, they are the best people to find her."

Vivian's face remained grim.

"Your connector code." The earlier threat wrapped around the words presenting them to me as a present. I left it unopened and gave it to her. She insisted on testing that it worked. Such cynicism in one so young.

She trudged out of the building, and I glanced at the clock. *Static.* Five minutes lost. I marked the desk as closed and headed out to make bad choices for lunch.

I smiled and nodded at the guards as they locked up the building behind me. Despite the drama of the morning, the afternoon had dragged on, one silent moment after another. The guards nodded back at me. A first. Nothing like a shared arrest to build positive working relationships. It was dark early this time of year and an icy wind sliced through my clothes to the thin fur on my skin and I regretted not driving in, even if it meant fighting for a park this morning.

I shrugged into my heavy coat, winding a scarf around me, thankful for the thick fur on my feet. A quick couple of bounces on my toes and I was homeward bound, ducking and weaving through the silent crowd until a small park with a beautiful old tree in its center called to me. A smile forced itself across my face.

"Hey Morgan."

"Hey how's your day been?" I asked.

The tree flicked their branches, shedding more yellowing leaves.

"Shedding. Did you hear about the hedge up the road? Apparently—"

"You're the worst." I stopped under it, letting leaves settle on me. "No, don't tell me. I don't want to think badly of it."

"You've no idea…" The branches waved around.

I laughed. "You've a good night."

"You too Morgan." The tree's branches rustled again, showering me and the ground with leaves.

I was smiling as I continued my meander home. That the plantae held me in affection was the shining light in my life. It was dark enough that most of the hedges and bushes were only up for a few sleepy greetings, but it was nice to hear their peaceful chatter.

Despite the chill in the air, I divested myself of my extra layers and was puffing by the time I reached my street, a sign I really needed to exercise more.

My fingers dragged along the outside brick wall of a converted warehouse until I reached the front door. The protection wards tickled before the door recognized me and swung inwards. Once across the threshold, the wards I reinforced daily sealed behind me, followed by the solid thump of a bar falling.

"I hope you won't get involved. The last thing we need is the preservers or the council's attention."

A door could lock a person in as well as keep the world at bay. The AV was on, and bad dialogue floated through the room as two people awkwardly tried to work out who was sleeping with who.

"What are you talking about?" My smile slipped as I took in my unwelcome housemate, Edwin, lounging, as usual, on the oversized purple couch in front of the AV. I glanced at the second, less comfortable couch, but it was too close to Edwin. It was in the same room, after all.

Edwin's face twisted in an unattractive frown. Today, his dark hair was in a loose style that brushed his shoulders, and his red velvet jacket was trimmed with tassels, and he'd paired it with a deep copper skin tone. I wasn't sure why. I never saw anyone go in or out of his rooms, so I didn't know who he was dressing up for.

"That apprentice, Vivian." Edwin stood up, pulling at his cuffs. No doubt he would be adding sequins soon.

"Vivian? What, you have a tracker on me now? Recording my conversations?"

"No," Edwin sniffed. "She came here first."

"Right, well, thank you for your input, Edwin. You done with the AV?"

"This is going to end badly. Can't you just leave well enough alone?" His weird silver eyes narrowed, and one corner of his lips twisted. "You're like a magnet for trouble."

He stepped away from the couch, so I took that as a yes and flopped down on to it and flicking through the channels.

As I predicted, Morthwyl was just finishing a speech about the importance of the rules when they cut to two Deans advocating for the people's right to have a seat on the council.

"It's not that we aren't grateful for what our five Everlasting council members have done." The Dean stood there tall, strong, her words making the AV vibrate. I snorted. Considering she and her partner, along with a lot of other people, had both had their parents killed by the Everlastings during the war, that was unlikely. "But it has been over five hundred years since the last war, and it is time that we seize our future. We need them to understand that we're grown up now and deserve a voice in our own desti—" The AV switched off.

"Hey." I glared at Edwin.

"This is serious," he said. "We need to talk about this."

"Is it?" I smiled at him. "I disagree. So, if you could go away? And you know, find someone else to torment?"

"You aren't the only one trying to keep out of the limelight—"

I shifted my body in his direction and stared at him.

"What do you mean by that?"

Wilbur and I never got around to talking about what would happen in Duskburn. Then he was dead, and it was too late. He had gotten me a low-risk job where I could be of some use, with guards watching, and created a check in protocol with the local preservation office. He had also had me allocated this old dump of a warehouse to live in with Edwin as a fellow tenant. I had always assumed Edwin was part of the preservation service. That he was here to make sure I played nice, while I was stuck in limbo playing it safe, turning up to work each day and checking in to the preservation office every day off.

"It's best, for both our sakes, if you stay out of it." Edwin headed to his rooms. I watched his tassels swing. Cryptic comments were my favorite.

I turned the AV back on.

"... and this disregard for the lives of people is why we need to make a stand. We're the only ones who can make sure you're represented. It can't just be the Everlastings any-,"

I switched it off again and flopped my head back on the couch. My connector pinged.

"Morgan here."

"You consider us your personal protection service now?"

The voice was authoritative and sharp like an ancient woodpecker hacking at a tree, with my eardrums the tree.

"An acquaintance of Wilbur's—"

"Wilbur Dawkins is dead and whatever influence he might have had died with him."

Preserver Thaddeus Harriden was a sparkhead.

"Master Bridges—"

"I'm aware that Amiel seems to give you more slack than most of those under supervision. However, we'll not be breaking protocol. Amiel might still be my squad leader, but he is in no position to risk his reputation. We don't just sit around twiddling our thumbs, waiting for you to call. We have serious matters to investigate." His voice increased in tempo and volume.

"Perhaps you could assist by putting a trace on—"

"No, Anastasi, I won't be using preservation resources at

the request of a random citizen. You'd do well to remember that you're under our supervision, not the other way around," and with that, he hung up.

"Stupid sparkhead. I hope he sparks out of his mouth." My eyes shut and my head fell back against the couch. I plucked at its edging. Heat pressed against the corner of my eyes, forcing me to breathe.

I tried not to slip into nostalgia. It had been a good life. The crisp smell of the mountain lake, my best friend Seb, and the murmur of plantae for company.

I blinked my eyes dry, sending a pulse of magn. Music played. Upping the volume, I let it flow through me, relaxing the muscles in my throat.

2

A whisper of smoke

My fellow apprentices will die before they make Scholar. The Everlastings might be created by the superverse, but for the rest of us, the knowledge that learning to manipulate energy can increase our lifespans inspires us to study. This led the council to create titles, Dean, Master and Scholar, for those who achieve the level of skill needed to change life expectancy. Giving us all something to strive for and building the learning society I am so proud to be a part of. I plan to be the youngest person ever to become a Dean and thus have the longest existence for a non-everlasting.

The accurate representation of past events
History Assignment
Archie, Apprentice of Chester

My body sank deeper into the couch. With a groan, I shifted so I was on my side and shoved a cushion under my head. I changed from music back to the AV, settling on a show about two best friends smoking Haze and being awkward. I allowed my mind to forget everything else, and the writers even got an occasional smile out of me, until my connector pinged, creaking I turned my head to read the message.

anything?

Vivian

I closed my eyes. Another ping compelled me to drag them open.

I know you've

read this

they rang me

And?

They'll

check it out

The connector went silent. I sighed and tried to get back into the show.

Liar

I winced. What the static was I going to do? Wander the streets knocking on doors?

give it another day

she might stroll in

any moment

my next call

to the preservers

won't be about Lenora

A call that Harriden would be more than happy to take. I rolled over and stared at the ceiling. It was old, full of cracks and dirt, but it did its job of keeping the rain out. I rubbed my eyes. Even if I just asked around, got an idea of what Lenora was up to.

give me a sec,

i'll come over

did you get

your brain back?

For someone who wanted my help, she was being a bit of a smart spark.

haha

we can ask around

see if find where

last seen, not hard

do you think

she is alive

I glared at the phone. How was I to know? The real question is if I said no, would Vivian call Harriden out of spite?

lifelore scholars

difficult to kill

people including masters

killed by council

I picked at the edging on the couch.

channeling illegally?

No

no reason to kill

avoid paranoia

your address?

I whimpered as I pushed myself off the couch. Unable to bear wearing my work clothes any longer, I headed to my rooms and turned on my one pure indulgence, the shower. I hadn't had one in the cabin Wilbur had wrenched me out of, and I figured if I was going to be stuck in this life of supervised service, at least one good could come out of it.

As the hot water dashed across my fine fur, I smiled, imagining it chasing off the stale air of the council building. Eventually I dragged myself out and gave myself an instant magn evaporation which sent me scrambling into a long sleeve black shirt and pants. My hand hesitated at the black winter jacket, but remembering the frosty night air, I shrugged it on.

I admired my color coordination. I did a squat, and it took longer to get back up than I was comfortable with, but the stretch pants held against the flex of muscle, well muscle and a bit of padding after a year of sitting in a foyer, a high functioning matter-maker and watching AV shows.

I tugged at the jacket, making sure it hung down to the top of my legs and clamped one of my own wristbands on my other arm. Satisfied I appeared credible, I padded to the front door, hating myself for taking the long way round.

"Shhhh," I said to the overly enthusiastic front door as I sealed it behind me.

Scholar Lenora didn't live too far away, so I wiggled my fingers in the pockets of my jacket and stretched out my legs. I loved the inherent power of my form, even if it needed serious training. Or a life where I was free to wander around talking to the plantae all day.

The after-work crowd was gone, but I still had to duck around a few slow walkers. I checked the address on my wristband again and realized that the purple concrete façade up ahead was Lenora Chester's. The robin egg blue door was not what I would have chosen, but it worked, if you didn't mind a slap in the eyes.

"Hey Morgan." Winter was creeping in, but the neighboring hedge wasn't asleep yet.

"Hey yourself, you settled for the winter?"

"Yeah, all good thanks. I heard you were in Duskburn. What brings you to the city life?"

"Supervised fun," I laughed and gave one of their branches a bit of a tug.

"Humph, well, you get that here, for sure." The hedge's thin branches, and the few leaves it had left, rustled and settled close together.

"What do…." I sighed. The hedge had drifted off into their dreams. I stroked one of their leaves gently. I preferred the company of plantae most of the time. Except once, in a forest with some sparked off trees, scariest moment of my life.

I moved up the path and knocked on the front door. A wild pandemonium of voices and thumps followed. I struggled to make out the words, but I think it was mostly people yelling at others to get the door, which shuddered as the thuds got louder. There was a moment of silence before its doorknob rattled and it opened to reveal a kid of average height, younger than Vivian, with subtle skin like scales. The most striking thing about him was his hair. I guessed it was the bane of his life by the way the thick mass of tawny fibers struggled against the bonds he had placed on them.

"What do you want?" he asked.

"Vivian." Honoring his desire for brevity.

"It's dinnertime. Come back later." He went to close the door. I visualized myself strolling away, but my mouth had other ideas.

"Vivian asked me to come over." Stupid mouth.

He paused with the door half shut.

"Why?"

"I'm here for your scholar, for Lenora."

"She isn't here."

"I'm trying to find out where she is."

His face scrunched up, and he rocked back away from me.

"Hannah says she is away visiting friends."

Hannah?

"Vivian has asked me to check on her." I smiled comfortingly at him.

"How do I know you aren't a weirdo here to kill us all?"

I dropped the smile. "My name is Morgan Anastasi, and I knew Wilbur Dawkins. Do you remember him?"

The kid grunted in the affirmative but didn't open the door.

Vivian came up behind.

"Archie, who... oh, it's you."

My eyebrows drew together, and I forced myself to take a breath and relax my face. Vivian pushed Archie out of the way and gestured for me to follow her. I stepped through the door and squeezed past Archie, who stood there staring at me.

A tall, well-dressed person with luminous skin entered the hall, frowning as she saw me. Her dark eyes scanned me, taking in my own untamed hair, black attire, and feet, hopefully without any dirt hanging off the fur, before giving a very loud sniff and glaring at Vivian.

"Who's this?"

"Hannah, this is Morgan, Wilbur... recommended... her. I've asked her to help me find Lenora."

"I don't remember Wilbur mentioning her." She scanned me again before turning away from me towards Vivian. "I told you Lenora's away. There's nothing to worry about."

"Then why didn't she tell us that?"

"Why would I lie to you?" They stood there staring at each other. I took a step back towards the door.

"I might leave you both to—"

"No." Vivian swung towards me.

"But if," I waved towards Hannah, "Lenora told Hannah, she'd be away for a few days..."

Hannah crossed her arms and stared at Vivian.

Vivian breathed in, pulling back her shoulders. She turned towards me.

"While Lenora may have told Hannah she intended to travel, I don't think she meant last night. I got a message confirming we were still catching up but that she might be late. She didn't arrive, and I wasn't able to find her. So," she shifted and returned Hannah's glare, "I thought of Wilbur," she glanced at me, "and you."

"A waste of everyone's time," said Hannah, but she moved

backward. Vivian sniffed and led the way into another room. I followed into what appeared to be a living room. I stepped around a stool and hit my toes on a coffee table. My eyes watered and I dropped into a nearby chair, my knees bumping against another table. I took in the four, I assumed they were apprentices, staring at me.

"Who are you?" asked another kid with short, spiky auburn hair and a soft teal hide. She appeared to be a similar age to Archie and was sitting forward in her chair, peering at me the way a cat stares at something tasty. It crossed my mind that going into a stranger's home might not have been the safest thing to do.

"Wilbur… recommended me to Vivian." They all softened at his name, even Hannah. "She's asked me to help get in touch with Lenora."

"Hannah says she's traveling," said Archie, "and that she's overseeing things until she gets back."

"Hannah claims that…" said Vivian, "but I also know that something's wrong."

"You know, how do you know?" asked Archie.

"I can sense it."

Archie sat up straight, sending his hair in a flutter and opened his mouth.

"When was the last time anyone saw Lenora?" My knee bumped the table again, and I forced myself to sit back in my seat.

Archie got in first. "I saw her yesterday morning. She was heading out to visit old people."

"I saw her around lunchtime," said the girl, her teal skin darkening and her eyes, murky pits, staring at me. "She asked me to pick up something for her and said she would see me at dinner."

"Maxi, you didn't tell me that," said Hannah.

"Why would I?" a sneer twisted Maxi's face.

"Why do you think she didn't come home for dinner?" I asked.

"She often doesn't," Maxi shrugged. "I think Vivian is right though, even if she's late, she usually checks my math for me. Everyone else is dumb and can't understand it."

"Hey," said Archie, "I'm getting better marks than you."

"Apparently," said Maxi, "you can't even compare results accurately."

"I'm pretty sure the bigger numbers mean I have better scores," said Archie. "Perhaps we need to get you a special tutor." He sat back with his hands behind his head.

"Oh, like the last one who knew even less than you? If that's possible."

"Does anyone remember who she was going to see?" I realized I probably should have clarified the terms of my assistance. If no one was going to give me any information, she couldn't expect too much from me, could she? I peeked at Vivian and found her staring at me intently.

"Nah," said Archie, "just that she might drop in on a few of the older ones so not to wait for her at dinner."

"I saw her in her workrooms," said Hannah. "She said she'd some friends she needed to visit and would be back in a couple of days." Her mouth thinned. "When she gets back, she's going to be annoyed with us for making such a fuss."

Maxi and Archie glanced at each other, and Vivian scowled.

"Morgan." Hannah rose to her feet. "We're about to have dinner and then we have study to do, so if you don't mind."

Not wanting to burn bridges yet, I took the hint, following her out of the room.

"How is business holding up with Lenora away?" I asked. "Even if she's off helping someone, that means you're without a scholar and you'll need to notify the council—"

"We manage. I don't see it's any of your concern." Hannah opened the front door. "I'd appreciate it if you kept out of our business."

Right then.

Vivian watched me over Hannah's shoulder but didn't object as the door closed on me, and I was once more outside.

The frosty night air was almost as good as a shower. I gazed at the house. They were nothing to me and at the end of the day. The missing person form was lodged and if a body was discovered, at least it would flag.

I headed back home, ignoring the word that flashed on my wristband.

Wait

I pushed more power into my legs and the street passed under the pads of my feet.

"I think we should check out her workrooms." Vivian's voice was close to my ear, and I jumped with a slight squeak.

"What? How?" I glanced back and Vivian stood there with her hands on her hips, her dark eyes staring at me as a chilly breeze flicked her elongated green feathers against her face.

I was pretty sure one tip went straight into her eye, but she didn't flinch.

"Hannah will be busy for a bit and the kids are working out what to have for dinner. We have time to do a sweep of her workrooms."

They say life consists of choices, but what they don't mention is the need to make those choices repeatedly.

Her face was determined. If I didn't go with her, no doubt she would call Harriden, but I also suspected she would go herself. Another death for me to carry?

"What do you expect to find?"

"We won't know until we get there."

I hesitated. I didn't owe her anything, and she was attempting to blackmail me. The dark lines etched around her pale green eyes just highlighted the unwavering intent within them.

A sharp poke got me in the back.

"Do it," the hedge hissed.

"What did you say?" asked Vivian.

I sighed.

"How do we get in?" I asked.

"There's a back way. It's easy." Vivian shifted her weight. "We just might need to be subtle about it, is all."

A sparking break in.

"Right." This was going to go to static.

We pushed off.

I glanced back at the hedge, who apparently had been awake enough to join in the conversation. Several branches waved at me. Shrubbery, always happy to put their two cents in.

I followed Vivian around a sharp bend, the width of the lane forcing me to fall behind her.

The dark narrow lanes created a wind tunnel, not strong enough to cut through my jacket, but just enough that the hair on my arms stood up. At least I hoped it was the wind. I could tell we were heading south, but I blindly followed her through a rabbit warren of small back streets. My gaze flicked around as I palmed my wrist knife and shifted my weight forward.

She trudged up to a basement window and smashed a pane. "No keys, ah?"

"Quiet," she hissed. She fumbled, trying to clear the glass, but eventually it was clear enough for us to get through.

Once inside, Vivian led the way up into a hallway and straight to a door near the back of the building. There wasn't anything special about the structure. The concrete walls and floors were cold, but someone had attempted to warm them up with rugs on the floor and posters of people striking poses on top of mountains. I peered to see if they were feeling the strain of their recent climb, but their faces were in shadow. I bet they were though.

She jiggled the lock of a door, and we entered Lenora's workroom. Lenora's essence permeated it, giving the visitor a sense that all was going to be well. Except at her desk. Her essence, where it should have been the strongest, was absent.

"Can you sense that?" asked Vivian, pointing at the chair.

The smell was strange, reminding me of when we used to

burn the flesh of trees to create fire. That didn't explain the green tinge, though.

"What's that smell?" asked Vivian. "Something happened here."

"Yes." I hesitated to touch the smoke. I activated a magn powered warding around me.

"What's that?" Vivian was staring at me.

"Just my safety gear." I stroked the cuff on my right wrist which housed the ward. It was my second favorite invention. Taking a breath, I stepped closer, keeping an eye out for any wards or signals that the space was still active. The warm air near the chair cooled even as I watched it. Another day and I wouldn't have noticed it at all.

I opened the drawers of the desk and riffled through Lenora's papers while Vivian searched the rest of the room. The slump of her shoulders suggested she wasn't having much luck.

My fingers brushed the top of the desk until they rested against an ashtray with a half-smoked mugwort cigar in it.

"Vivian." I pointed at the cigar, and she frowned.

"Half smoked?" she asked, taking another step closer.

"It didn't burn out. It's been cut off."

"That makes little sense," Vivian's voice broke.

"Unless Lenora was cutting back and only wanted to smoke half a one?" I asked.

"No, no way. It was her one pleasure. She almost treated her cigar time as sacred. I think that is why she usually had them here. She could close the door and just have a moment."

"Did she have a particular time? A routine that she stuck to?"

"It was hard for her. Patients aren't that easy to control time-wise. She'd clear out her schedule around three in the afternoon. Barring any emergencies, of course."

"So, it was a normal day, which we can assume as she lit the cigar, probably settled in to have her one moment alone. If she was interrupted, why wouldn't she have just stubbed it out? Why cut it off cleanly?" I asked.

"When I've seen her interrupted, she just stubbed it out and ran to deal with whatever drama was going on." Vivian stared at the cigar and rubbed her forehead.

"It isn't just smoke." I inhaled and tried to sense even a whiff of anything but wood smoke. "Someone else's odor is in this room. Who else would have been in here?"

"Hannah, but she wouldn't hurt..." Vivian sounded like she was trying to convince herself more than me.

"Anyone else?" I thought she was right the first time, but just because someone jumps in front of you and says pick me didn't mean there weren't other people involved.

"Clients... suppliers... I can't think of any names of regulars."

"Until we have another name and, considering Hannah's behavior... be careful there."

"If she's... maybe she's being blackmailed? I just can't imagine her..." Vivian moved around the room, picking up things she had already searched.

"Maybe." I used my wristband to take a recording of the office. If she was involved, I was dubious about her being anything but a willing participant. She didn't exactly give off a victim vibe. She did, however, make a lot of noise.

Vivian shuffled toward the door, and I grabbed her arm,

shaking my head, pointing to the window. The last thing I needed was Hannah reporting me for breaking and entering. Vivian rolled her eyes but moved to underneath it. She jumped, pulling herself up onto the small ledge. It didn't take much for her to push the window open and swinging a leg out, she straddled it, peering outside.

"Anyone out there?"

"Not that I can see." Vivian shrugged and swung her other leg over before disappearing.

By the time I was up on the ledge, my arms were shaky and my face sweaty. I glared down at her grinning face.

"You alright?"

I used my hand to gesture that I did not appreciate her question.

The creak of the door handle gave me a burst of speed and I dropped to the ground. Lenora's window opened on a laneway which was at least two storeys above the ground, and I jumped before fully assessing the distance of the fall.

Realizing my mistake at the last minute, I attempted to roll, dragging my limbs out of sight of the window. Which gave me a moment to recover my breath and absorb the pain.

Vivian joined me against the wall. We waited and eventually I pushed myself up, limping along, ignoring Vivian's offers of assistance.

Vivian took the lead again, and I hobbled behind as we navigated the narrow streets with the scent of other people's dinners for company.

"What about—"

Heavy meat connected with my shoulder. I reached over,

breaking their wrist and used their arm to swing them into the wall, causing a loud crash to echo into the night. The person collapsed to the ground, and I spun to find Vivian in the grip of a local Blueshroud gang member called Lydia with Emanuel standing, unshackled, next to her. Emanuel's head tilted as he stared down at the crumpled body next to me.

"And here I was, all upset with you for calling the guards on me. Perhaps I should be grateful instead?" He smiled at me. I forced myself to hold eye contact.

"You're welcome." I flashed my teeth and Emanuel's face twisted. Some people found his muscled form covered by a mossy impenetrable hide attractive. Personally, I preferred my males to have more delicacy than a rhinocerotidae.

Lydia, her eyes spinning, shifted her grip and Vivian whimpered. Sparking great, nothing like a thug high on hoarfrost channeling supped up strength.

"What brings you out on this fine night, Emanuel? I thought you would be comfortably set up inside." *Locked up and awaiting a death sentence.* But perhaps it was imprudent to raise that at this moment.

Emanuel's nostrils flared, and Vivian whimpered again. My claws wanted to flex, but I controlled them. Not that I thought I could get out of this without a fight. I just needed a moment to think. Plus, there was the Lydia factor. As large as Emanuel, she was also, by far, the better trooper.

"Unlike you, I have friends. And those friends have asked *me* to make sure *you're* the one staying inside." Emanuel smirked. This was going to hurt.

Lydia took a step to the side, taking Vivian with her. I

thanked the evolutionary pathway that gave me color in my peripheral vision as I tracked Lydia's purple hair, her one vanity.

"The reminder is unnecessary. I'm very fond of staying at home. In fact, we were just heading home. So, if your, err thug, is that the term these days? If she could let go of my friend, we'll be on our way." I rocked back on my heels and spread my hands out in a gesture of peace. The now unconscious body at my feet may have ruined the vibe I was going for.

"See, I think I'd prefer to know that you'll stay home," said Emanuel. "Your word holds as much weight as your little friend here."

Lydia threw Vivian against the wall, and she slid down a crumpled heap of hair and limbs. Lydia stepped towards me. This was not good news. Lydia not only had two arms and two legs that could inflict pain but also a muscly tail, which she liked to decorate with spikes.

I was so sparked.

Emanuel flashed at me, grabbing my head and slamming it down on his knee. I twisted, trying to reduce the impact to a glancing blow, but Lydia reached me, lashing at my ribs with her tail. My body tried to go with the momentum of the blows, but even I couldn't avoid being smashed between them. My head was ringing, and my ribs were on fire.

I screamed. I screamed as if it was my final death cry. I howled, channeling someone who was having their arm cut off with a rusty chainsaw, and added some sobbing in for good measure.

"Pathetic," said Emanuel, stepping back and staring down at me in disgust.

Less convinced by my performance than Emanuel, Lydia got in a few kicks before he called her off. I lay there on the ground with blood spilling out of my head, my body twisted so I resembled a broken doll while I rasped out sobs.

"Static, Morgan. Now you're just embarrassing yourself." Emanuel stood over me while Lydia tilted her head, studying me. He pushed at my head with his toe, and I shrieked.

"I don't know my strength," Emanuel snickered and then spat at me. *Sparkhead*. I played with the moonlight to help emphasize the blood pooling around me and the bruises on my face.

"We should kill them," said Lydia, her tail flicking out and catching me in the ribs.

"Static," I hissed.

"I wish we could," he sighed, like the weight of the world was on him. "More trouble than it is worth, though." He slithered away but not before spitting on me one more time. "Don't you worry, it won't be long before we'll be free to finish this properly." He turned his back on me and Lydia swung their colleague over her shoulder, following him, her tail flicking, the spikes flashing red from my blood.

My eyelids dropped closed and my body went as slack as I could make it, using some of my stored magn so I could still see. A useful trick I had spent years perfecting as a child.

The sounds of dinners being shared had stopped, but no one came. I burned through more of my magn quota to heal the worst of my injuries and expanded my senses to make sure that the Blueshrouds had really left. They were several blocks away and getting fainter.

Groaning, I sat up. Vivian hadn't moved and some of her bones were pointing in the wrong direction.

Static.

I pushed myself to my feet and padded over to her.

My wristband showed I wasn't even at halfway on my quota yet, but still I had used more in the last hour than I did most days. I sat down next to her with a sigh and flooded her with magn. I grimaced as what little magn I had stored disappeared. Healing was always tricky, but the quicker I could do it, the more I could rely on her body's memory. Still, it would have been a lot easier with a power source. Her limbs straightened, and I tidied myself up as I waited.

It wasn't too long before her breathing rhythm changed, and she rolled up to a seated position.

"Hey," I said.

"Morgan," Vivian's head moved in my direction, and she opened her eyes wide.

"Up for a stroll back to your place?" I curled my legs under me and pushed up. Vivian's eyes tracked me, but remained unfocused. "Come on." I reached out my hand and let it rest near hers.

She took it and stood up.

"I thought they were going to kill you," said Vivian.

"Nah, more trouble than it's worth."

Vivian scanned the laneway.

"You...how'd you stop them?" she asked.

"Well, they landed some serious blows, which hurt. I just made them think they had landed the money shot, is all."

"You took a fall."

"I see it more as surviving—"

"What about... well ... they're going to think you're weak?"

"Never underestimate being underestimated." I am just so witty sometimes.

"Why were they after us? Is it because of m—"

"Let's just say Emanuel isn't happy with me. Keep moving. We don't want to stay out here any longer that we have to."

3

Trust me

Hundreds, if not thousands, of people died trying to take out those completely immersed in the electrical current. All had seemed hopeless until the Everlastings, who appear to have some sort of in-built earthing, stepped in. After that, subduing the mad ones hadn't taken long. Though subdue was an understatement, they had in fact obliterated them into atoms and released them outside the planet's atmosphere, just to be safe they said. It didn't take long for everyone to agree that they should rule after that.

Telling it like it is
History Assignment
Maxi, Apprentice of Chester

Vivian pushed open the blue door, and I followed her inside. The living room, lit by lamps, revealed the two younger apprentices sitting on the floor playing a game on a small table. Cozy, except for the names they were calling each other. A comfortable armchair caught my eye, and I flopped into it.

"You kids up to creating something to eat?" I asked. I was running dry. If I was going to question them, I might as well be fed and comfortable.

The two sets of eyes narrowed.

"Why?" asked Maxi, crossing her arms in front of her. "You here to con some out of us?"

"Err, no, I'm just hungry, and if I was going to con something out of you, it wouldn't be food, more like credits and stuff."

Maxi pursed her lips and lifted her chin.

"Hannah says you're a con artist," said Archie.

I hoped one day Hannah's head went to static.

"Hannah is not my biggest fan. Though being fair, it's mutual." I drummed my fingers on the armrest. "She doesn't come across as the warmest of people."

Maxi snorted, and Archie smirked.

"Yeah, she's a bit of a tool. I'm going to make myself a sandwich. Do you want one, then?" asked Archie.

"Maybe some soup? Just in a large mug is fine. Honey and cheese, please."

"Honey and cheese?" his nose scrunched up.

"I can give you the schema?"

"I can do it," said Archie, "it just sounds gross is all."

"I want a sandwich," said Maxi.

"Me too," said Vivian.

Archie rolled his eyes. "Feed yourselves."

He stomped off to the kitchen. I let the armchair take the weight of my head. Vivian was staring at my fingers as I picked at the seam of the armchair, so I folded my hands on my lap and tried not to fidget.

Archie saved me, slamming down a bunch of sandwiches on the table and handing me a large mug. The smell of cheese and honey filled the room. I hummed, taking a sip, warmth filling my body.

Vivian remained standing near the window.

"Perhaps you should sit down, Vivian, or can I call you Viv?" The name Vivian always reminded me of an older supervisor who had a cane she whacked people with for not paying attention. I had often ended up with stripes of bruises, some barely healing before new ones formed.

Archie laughed so hard some sandwich came out through his nose.

"Yeah, call her Viv," said Archie between laughs and re-eating nose flavored sandwich.

"Or Vivi, that's even better." Maxi snorted.

Vivian's neck reddened.

"Vivian," I said, putting a bit of adult into my tone. "You took a hard hit today. Take a seat."

She sat, and we all watched until she had eaten at least half her sandwich.

"You going to eat that?" asked Archie. Vivian didn't get a chance to respond as with a slight pull of magn the sandwich disappeared off her plate and reappeared on Archies.

My eyes widened.

"It isn't aetherlocation," said Maxi, rolling her eyes and Archie smirked.

"But it just appeared—"

The sandwich disappeared off Archie's plate and appeared on Maxi's.

"It is a trick. Anyone can do it." She picked up the sandwich but only got one bite before it was back on Archie's plate. If that wasn't aetherlocation, then I definitely wanted to learn what it was. But one thing at a time.

"So, my goal is to find Lenora, check she's well, and if she is, leave you all alone. Alright with you?" I asked. I kept my face grave and maintained eye contact. Maxi finished two more bites of her sandwich as she examined me.

"Yeah."

"Maxi, you said you saw her just after lunchtime. Is that true?" asked Vivian.

"I wouldn't say it if it wasn't," said Maxi, her expression pinched. "I dropped in, and she said she'd some house calls, so might be late for dinner and then gave me a credit to get a copy of the new chips schema, but I forgot."

"What?" asked Archie stiffening, his voice high and loud. He put both his hands on the table and leaned forward.

"You've the normal schema. I don't know what's so special about this new one," said Maxi, wrinkling her nose. "Chips are chips, after all."

Archie snorted. "You'll never know now." He ripped into his sandwich, glaring at her.

"So, we know she was at her workrooms by lunchtime," I said. "Vivian and I also suspect she had her afternoon cigar before being interrupted."

"No one interrupts her afternoon cigar," said Archie, his eyes serious. "Not if they know what's good for them."

"Yes, I can imagine." With this many apprentices who could blame her. "Something happened that either worried her enough that she cut it short and headed out again or…."

"Or someone killed her, you mean?" Archie's face was calm, but his eyes had a sheen on them.

I shrugged.

"Either way," said Vivian. "We're going to work it out."

I kept still, but I had a bad feeling she was going to regret that promise.

"What do you want from us?" asked Archie. "I'm not giving you any credits."

"Do any of you have a copy of her planner or access to her connector messages?"

Archie turned towards Maxi.

"She used my comp a lot, and I saw her access some stuff." Maxi shrugged and glanced away.

"I don't have a problem with that," I said. "In fact, your nosiness—"

"Not nosiness, accidental knowledge. I can't help if I've an excellent memory." Maxi sniffed and scowled at me.

"Well, your accidental knowledge," I tried to stop my lips curling up, "may be very useful, so if you could…er, show us …?"

She crossed her arms as she flopped back in her chair.

"Maxi," said Vivian, from her slumped position in her chair, her face drawn and voice soft. Maxi glanced at her but sighed and pushed up, making it very clear she was reluctantly dragging herself out of the room.

"Do you think Lenora's dead?" asked Archie.

"If she was, they would have notified you." My knee hit the coffee table again.

Maxi entered the room with her comp in her hands and sat on the floor near me, opening it up on the table.

"Here," said Maxi, turning it so I could see Lenora's schedule.

It was exhausting. I felt like I had a busy day whenever I had to leave the warehouse. Meanwhile, Lenora cared for four apprentices, ran a lifelore clinic and did house calls.

I rubbed my face. Was I fooling myself that I could help with this? Maybe it was better to let Vivian play her card. There might be a fuss for a while, but I doubt it would go anywhere. Still, it would increase their suspicions, which meant I would lose the small freedoms, like the ability to meander home, that I had gained in the last year by being, relatively, well behaved.

Vivian's eyes never left my face and, swallowing a sigh, I noted the names of who Lenora visited in the afternoon.

"At least I have somewhere to start," I said. They all nodded. "About Hann—"

"I don't think we need to tell her anything," said Vivian. "Not until we find Lenora, anyway."

I let out a breath. Now I had seen Lenora's workrooms, I did not understand how Hannah could insist nothing was wrong.

Archie and Maxi glanced at each other and then back at Vivian.

"Agreed," they said.

Archie frowned. "I don't like it, but it's weird she doesn't even want—"

"It isn't normal." Maxi face tightened. "No matter how much Hannah tries to pretend it is."

I rose.

"Something worth keeping in mind," I said.

Vivian escorted me to the door.

"How are you?" I asked.

"Better than I should be," said Vivian.

Ah, right. I suppose I should have guessed that an apprentice of a lifelore scholar would recognize a magn healing.

"That's good, isn't it?" I asked, keeping my tone light.

"Better than I did before something slammed me into a wall?" She glanced at me.

"Self-healing is a powerful thing."

Vivian snorted.

"Wilbur said you were more than you seemed."

Did he?

"Well, I'm still a person like everyone else. I'll try, but I can't guarantee—"

"I know, I'm not a child." Vivian frowned at me.

I tilted my head. "What time does she normally leave for work?"

"An hour after first light."

I blinked. Well, that explained how Lenora fit so much in. I had seen my share of sunrises, just usually from the other direction.

"Right, well, an hour after first light, I'll meet you here and we'll head out."

With that, Vivian went inside. I touched the closed door and the comforting hum of wards whispered back at me.

They might not be the happiest of kids, but at least they would be safe through the night.

I kept to the major streets and enjoyed being surrounded by people going to art galleries, plays, sharing meals at small venues with experimental schemas or something equally exciting. I joined the small group listening to a musician who sat playing a bass viol. Her fingers danced as she drew her bow over the strings, letting the deep sounds purr through the air. The lights from the streetlamps, blurry with evening mist, haloed her. I listened to three pieces before I could tear myself away. The rhythm of my shuffle weaved with the fading music as I dragged myself home.

Sometimes leaving the house is the biggest decision to be made that day, but choosing to go back in can be just as big. When I had been dragged off my mountain, I had been given a choice, contribute or be shackled. I had contributed. But it didn't really feel like a choice. So I reminded myself every day that getting out of bed was a choice. I held my hand a few inches off the front door and closed my eyes.

The fresh mountain air was against my skin. I was in the small room I designed, my best friend Seb waiting outside, and the lake surrounded by mountains stretching out in front of me. The aroma of being surrounded by healthy and happy plantae teased at my memory.

I shook my head, reminding myself that it would be the first place the preservers would search, and pushed air out of my lungs, which turned into mist as it hit the frosty night air. I breathed in through my nose and let my hand touch the door.

Edwin had emerged from his rooms and was once more spread out in front of the AV. He glanced up.

"Have you been in a fight?" His eyes narrowed.

"Depends on your definition."

He examined me, his lips puckering.

"Allowing people to hit you?"

I frowned at him. "That's a very specific definition…"

His face instantly smoothed, resembling one of those marble statues you see pigeons decorating.

"I hope you know what you're doing…" His breath had quickened, and his hand had tightened on the glass. If he broke it, cutting himself, I hoped he could fix it.

"Why don't you relax? This isn't your problem. Now, I have work to do, so…" I headed to the door that led to Wilbur's old office and as soon as the door closed behind me, I sent a rude hand gesture his way and then stood there staring at the polished metal. I mean, Wilbur knew, even before his death, that he couldn't be here watching me all the time. Hence the addition of Edwin to the household. He was part of the supervised service that Wilbur had organized, right? He had to be. Why else would I be stuck here with him?

I switched the light on, and it lit up the dust and mold in the spacious office. I shivered, imagining the mold watching me. No one knew if they were sentient or not, but it didn't stop me from imagining them watching, waiting for an opportunity to spread their spores.

I contemplated the empty chair. Even if I helped Vivian, there was no promise that this was going to work out well for me. I closed my eyes and for a moment, I was on my mountain discussing the weather with Seb. My lips turned up, my body relaxing until a flash of Vivian's smashed body and Emanuel's grinning face interrupted. I growled and lowered myself into the chair.

I turned on Wilbur's comp. The preservation service had done a sweep after Wilbur died, of course, but apparently, he had wanted me to have it. Who knows why or how his twisted brain worked? I had poked around, but nothing interesting had been on it. Still connected with the Aether, it was useful on its own. The plan was to search the list of names and see if there was anything of interest, but first I wanted to find out more information about Hannah, apprentice of Lenora Chester. I found one reference, not in the Aether but on Wilbur's own computer, where he noted meeting her at the Garden after work.

I tried to remember her at the Garden but all I could recall was being hazed, which if I couldn't be on a remote mountain somewhere, it was the next best thing. A quick search on the rest of the apprentices told a grim tale of death. Rayisa and Tukhunri had been busy. Parentless apprentices were being matched to whichever scholar would take them. I grimaced as I remembered Vivian's fear of Lenora's death and the wariness in Archie and Maxi's eyes. Nothing changed. Sometimes it felt like no matter what anyone did, everything just got worse. I closed the comp and turned off the lights.

I stood at the door but couldn't hear the AV. Opening it, I found the living room empty without the usual Edwin fixture in front of the AV. Technically, I could move around Duskburn at night. I suspected they would have preferred if I checked in and out with Edwin first. But tonight would not be one of those nights. Not bothering to change, I wouldn't say I snuck out. I would say I was discrete.

The late-night crowd hadn't come in yet, so there were only three people in the bar. I glanced at the overabundance of fake greenery that attempted to hide the battered furniture and pushed some aside to take a seat.

"Morgan," the person behind the bar was short and strong. She was draped in flowing green fabrics and her skin was a golden hue that glowed and gave a soft warm light to the bar. "Long time no see, we've missed you." She poured a shot for herself and clinked her glass next to mine. I drank.

"Grace," I rasped. "I was going to say I'd missed you too, but you may have burned out my vocal cords."

Grace just snorted and poured me another shot. "If you ain't paying, I don't want to hear you complaining." I took the shot and hoped my tastebuds would forgive me.

"What brings you here? I got the impression after everything with Artemus, you wouldn't be back."

I winced.

"Yeah, well, I wasn't going to, but I'm seeking some information about Hannah. She's one of Lenora Chester's apprentices. I'm not sure if you know her?"

"Yes, of course I know Hannah. She's a protégé of Wilbur's. She still comes in sometimes."

Now, why would Wilbur bring a pupil to a bar?

"What can I do for you, and will you be paying?"

I forced myself to chuckle. "How about this? You answer a few questions for me, and I'll start paying for the drinks?"

"How can I say no to that?" said Grace, pulling out a fresh

bottle she had created with one of her unique schemas, and topped up my glass with something a bit more drinkable.

I established she knew Hannah, who had become a regular, and even knew who Lenora was, but hadn't seen her recently. Familiar with most of the names on the list, she had little to add except to note they were all old meddlers. Hot breath hit the back of my neck.

I rolled my head over and there was one of my less impressive mistakes.

"Artemus," I said, my tongue thick in my mouth.

"If it isn't my little Anastasi. I heard you took a beating today." He scanned me. "Efforts appear to be exaggerated."

I blinked, but couldn't bring him into focus.

"What," I hiccupped, and Grace gave me another shot to help it down, "do you want?"

Of average height with velvety scaled skin, dark eyes and soft feathers for hair, his teeth flashed a brilliant white in a way that I had once mistaken for a personality. Dressed in a white wrap-around jacket, he reminded me of the twin councilors. I squinted and could make out some gold piping on the shoulders.

"Oh darling, there has only ever been one thing that I want from you." He stepped even closer, and I could feel the heat of his body. I shook my head.

"Nope, been there done that, not for me." It was time to leave. "Grace, thanks for your help and for the drinks." I gave her a big smile and shared some credits to her account. More than I could afford, but I didn't want to owe her anything.

"Artemus, it has been... well, it has been something," I tipped my imaginary hat and sauntered towards the door.

I stumbled and Lydia caught me. She held me by both arms, peering down at me.

"I thought we told you to stay home."

"Needed something for the pain."

"Did you?" She smiled at me. "I doubt Grace's water will dull the pounding you got today. As an apology for the hurt, let me help."

Ah, the volt was in it now.

"Artemus, you got any?" asked Lydia.

"For Morgan, I'm always ready."

I coughed as a cloud of smoke hit my face. After attempting to hold my breath, I gasped, dragging the smoke all the way into my lower lungs and felt my body sink, my legs suddenly too heavy to move. At some point I moved, or was moved, to one of the back rooms.

I thought I saw Hannah come and go, but a blue haze enveloped me and I floated. The pipe in my hand called to me, but before I could draw it near it was ripped from my grasp. A crash reverberated through the room and my empty fingers dropped. Hands grabbed at me, my body lifted and turned upside down. I forced my eyes open and saw red.

4

Hazed

A lack of respect is the scourge of our society. Those that are discontent, that want more than their fair share without working for it, need to be watched. Magn-laced pharmaceuticals like hoarfrost are a shortcut to significance for anyone who can't be bothered to study. They are also a primary reason that our preservation service maintains the same numbers five hundred years on. I suspect it is only a matter of time before some of my fellow apprentices reach for the shortcut that will ultimately abridge their lifespan.

The accurate representation of past events
History Assignment
Archie, Apprentice of Chester

I crawled out of bed and saw that first light was in full swing.

Static, Vivian!

I did a quick wash with magn and scrambled into fresh clothes. On my way to the front door, I saw Edwin, passed out on the purple couch. He was fully dressed in his red velvet suit, but had kicked off his shoes. My stomach twisted, but I ignored it, reaching the front door before my feet grew heavy. I stood there staring at the knob.

Just keep moving. You're going to be late. He isn't going anywhere. I peered over my shoulder and sighed.

I shuffled over to him. His copper skin lacked its usual shine, his face slack and body limp.

"Edwin."

His chest rose and fell, but his eyes didn't twitch. I placed my hand on his arm, pushing at it. No response. I frowned at his red velvet jacket. My mind tried to flash some images at me, but I swatted them aside.

He was breathing. That's what mattered, right? Just because I was forced to have him here didn't mean I had to nurse him to health or anything. My feet refused to move.

"Edwin." I pushed at his shoulder again. Still nothing. I growled. He was alive, and I needed to go.

"I don't know if you can hear me, but I have to go."

He just lay there.

I drew down some magn from the house and tried to link it into his energy to give him some more juice for healing, but it wouldn't take.

"Of course, you have to be difficult." I stomped back to the kitchen and pulled out a bowl. Trudging out to the small empty pile of dirt this warehouse referred to as a garden, I filled it with soil and then pumped it full of my magn. He must be weak if he couldn't draw in energy into himself, but I had never met a person who couldn't draw energy from the ground.

I kneeled next to him and put the bowl up against his side, positioning his arm so that his fingers fell naturally into it. Moving up into a crouch, I tried to track the energy flow. It wasn't strong, but it was something.

More importantly, my feet agreed to move again, and I lumbered to the front door.

People were not up and about yet, and the only sound was the occasional splash from the pads of my toes connecting with freezing patches of water. Not even my thick skin and fur could insulate against that, so I pulled on my magn and sent a pulse of warmth down to my feet. If the sun was going to make an appearance today, it was taking its time, with the silver haze of light highlighting the early morning mist that smothered the streets. I quickened my pace. Not that I cared what Vivian thought, and I certainly wasn't aiming to be brilliant or dazzle anyone with my investigation skills. I had let dreams of grandeur go long ago and now my goal was limited to just avoiding an unnatural death, mine and others. Though so far, that goal hadn't been anymore achievable.

A light wind's icy fingers attempted to reach inside my coat, and I shivered, pulling as tight around my body as possible. I peered ahead and made out a fleck of blue, cutting through the murk. I lengthened my stride. For once, I was grateful that the hedge leading up to the house was asleep.

Standing in front of the blue door, I adjusted my coat to

make sure it was straight and knocked. The silence of the morning pressed down on me. I knocked again. A little late, sure, but I didn't think I was *that* late. Opening my messages, I found several asking where I was. I texted back that I was at the front door.

I had checked my wristband at least three times before the door creaked open to reveal a disheveled Vivian wearing a tartan flannel sleep shirt and pants, which were long enough to pool around her tartan slippers. Seriously, all those texts and now I was going to have to wait for her?

"What do you want?" Vivian stood there with her arms folded, glaring at me.

By my calculations, I was only five to ten minutes late and let's be honest, there is a certain ambiguity in using *first light* rather than a specific time.

"I thought we were visiting Lenora's clients today." I glared at the sullen face in front of me.

"Are you sparking me?" she asked. "That was yesterday, static head." I swayed, and she tilted her head and asked with a little less heat. "Where've you been?"

"I...." Where had I been? I had visited Grace and then... nothing but...blue..., *oh static, what have I done?*

"She still isn't home, you know. No one's heard from her, and even Hannah had to admit something's wrong. We let the preservation service know, but they said it was already assigned and basically not to hold our breath." Vivian pulled at her hair.

"Right, I've lost some time—"

"Yeah, I know," said Vivian, stepping back. "And I'll be sending an anonymous tip today, don't you worry—"

"Wait." The chill of the door hit the palm of my hand. I shifted my leg forward. Vivian glared. "You said the pre-servers weren't doing anything. Let's follow this path and see where it leads us." I breathed in through my nose and tried to make my shoulders relax.

Vivian drew her hair across her face and chewed on it, her eyes never leaving me.

"The preservation officer who's assigned to it said that you were not to be trusted, and he wouldn't prioritize it."

Sparkhead Harriden.

"What use have you been?" asked Vivian. She kicked at my foot, and I pulled it back.

"Fine. I'm sure that with me out of the picture Lenora will just turn up," I said to the door. I didn't need this. And who cared if she called in a tip? They wouldn't find anything, maybe. Perhaps it was for the best that I got hazed. Free from this drama, I could focus again on getting home. I was close to being released from supervised service. I could feel it. I just had to hope that Vivian wouldn't ruin it for me.

I spun and marched homeward.

Sparks. All of them.

I tried to imagine another year of this life. Of sitting in that foyer watching and being watched.

What exactly was I waiting for?

I took a step and a scream ripped out of me. I attempted to stifle it, not wanting to bring out a bunch of nosy neighbors and be reported for disturbing the peace on top of everything else, while what felt like a nail attempted to drive up through my foot.

The wall took my weight as I leaned against it, twisting my leg to see what was embedded in my foot. A dark brown husk with a sharp point was embedded into the thick skin on my foot. It hadn't broken through, but would be tender. They thought they were so funny the little sparkers. I pulled it out and glanced around.

It was still misty, and I couldn't make out any plantae that might have dropped this until I spotted a small garden hidden between two houses across the street. Giggles floated through the air. Whichever one did it, they must have put in some serious effort. Though all the plantae had become excellent throwers after the electromagn wars accidentally killed anything that flew.

"Nice," I whisper-shouted at them. The giggles got louder. I threw the brown husk back into their little patch and limped away. I hadn't taken many steps when I heard a clack on the pavement behind me. If they weren't careful, they would be reported to the Boundaries Commission and moved out of the city. People appreciated their right to exist, but there were the boundary agreements for a reason. I reached home, and the door closed behind me, the bolt dropping with a bang.

Edwin was still unconscious, however, there was more shine in the copper of his skin. I pumped the soil full of more magn and observed my quota counter tick up some more.

I flopped into a large armchair, letting my head fall back. My eyes unfocused as I tried to piece together the night before.

"Static."

I sighed and straightened. First things first. I contacted work to let them know I would not make it in today. The last thing I wanted to be is listed as missing and my supervised service level upgraded. I shuddered at the thought.

It turned out that Edwin had called them yesterday and let them know I was extremely ill and might need a few days to recover. I leaned forward, my arms resting heavily on my knees, and watched him breathe.

"I need coffee." Groaning, I waddled over to the maker. By the time I had finished making a couple of cups, Edwin was stirring. He sat up, running his hand through his hair, and I pushed the cup into the other. His gaze, weighed down by his eyelids, cut into me. He took a sip.

"Thanks," I said. "I just wanted to say I didn't go there intending to…" my mouth was dry. I lifted my cup and swallowed a mouthful of coffee. "I just went to ask Grace for some information and hopefully run into Hannah." The red velvet of his sleeve flashed at me as he drank his coffee, making my face and body flush.

Edwin lowered his cup.

"Indeed."

My stomach tightened.

"Well, thanks again." I hobbled to my rooms.

"Are you well?"

I stopped, my hand on my doorknob, and turned back to find his eyes scanning me, paying particular attention to the foot that I was favoring.

"Well, enough." As I left the room, images of blue with flashes of red haunted my mind's eye.

5

Trust no one

It isn't all sunshine and flowers, though. The basic stuff might be sorted, but many people don't like the fact some get to live longer than others. And it takes a LOT of study. I fully get why people take drugs. Live in the moment, amp what you have I say. If you aren't going to be a Scholar, Master or Dean... why wouldn't you supe up?

Telling it like it is
History Assignment
Maxi, Apprentice of Chester

Hot water hit the top of my head, its heat enveloping me. On impulse I triggered peppermint and ginger steam, and it only took a couple of breaths before calm flowed, soothing my queasiness from the loss of a day.

How was the Garden involved? What did it mean that Emanuel was free?

With a sigh I turned off the shower and quickly dried myself. I couldn't be bothered getting dressed, so pulled on a bathrobe and flopped onto my bed.

Breathe in through the nose, hold, out through the mouth. My eyes flicked open.

Spark it.

I tapped my wristband.

I can't believe you.

Were you all in on it?

I regretted it as soon as I hit send. I could usually hold my liquor, but what I drank last night, no, the night before, had hit me hard. And then there was the Haze. I had always found some there. If I could get Haze, and there were rooms for Haze users in the Garden. Grace was running a Haze den, *right?*

If she had deliberately drugged me, what did it mean that she had also been a friend of Wilbur's? I pulled my pillow on top of my face and screamed into it.

Grace had to be playing a larger role. What did it mean that Lydia and Emanuel were regulars at the Garden? Two major users of hoarfrost and that was their local? A half-hearted scream was all I could push out this time. Surely someone would have noticed that the head of research was a friend of a Haze den? Or maybe, like me, they were fooled by Wilbur's veneer of integrity. With him dead, where did that leave me? Holding the bag?

The pale cream of the rendering on the ceiling had small

hairline cracks. My gaze traced them, imagining them slowly spreading until the warehouse was nothing but cracks held together by fine plaster fiber and even the smallest vibration could bring the entire building down.

It hadn't taken long to realize that Wilbur was someone else who cared about the bigger picture. All the conversations I had had with Wilbur, what if they weren't just hypothetical? He had talked a lot about how things need to change, but I had been careful. I was already, because of him, stuck in this city and under supervision. I had often wondered why he kept me so close he had even put me in one of his houses.

If he had been attempting to recruit me, he had been wasting his time. The image of Iseret killing my mother in front of me never really went away. Growing up had certainly been no picnic, and Iseret had saved me from my mother's obsession and control. But leaving me to die had taken the shine off the moment.

I kept the pillow tight across my face and gave one more scream before sitting up. I needed to know. I pulled on my color coordinated top and pants and padded towards Wilbur's office. After he died, I had expected that Edwin and I would be moved on, but instead, the preservers had done a sweep of the warehouse, taking most of Wilbur's things and leaving us alone. I had thought it sloppy that they only took his portable comp, everything that resembled an official document, but left his office, personal papers and the comp untouched.

Unless they had had their orders. But why leave his stuff with me? They always get upset when you use the word prisoner, but I had been under the close, personal supervision of Wilbur Dawkins, the Head of Research. It didn't add up. He must have reached beyond the grave and left it all for me deliberately. I suspected I had been foolish to leave it untouched for so long.

Since I had already checked his comp, I started with his desk, opening every drawer, and pulling everything out methodically, trying to find something, anything, that indicated that Wilbur and Grace were more than just acquaintances.

Three drawers and two filing cabinets later and I wasn't any closer. Why Wilbur had kept paper copies of so many useless things I don't know. So far, I had found flyers for old events, schemas for his favorite dishes, and copies of letters. Most of them were updating details or cancelling things. I had flipped through them until the name Maddalena caught my eye.

Dear G,

I think I have found Maddalena's storage method.

W

I flipped through a few more and saw several of them referencing this Maddalena, unfolding another one.

G,

I will bring the favor to your garden, but we will have to watch out for the light. Not everything can be fixed. Your lover is spinning out of control. Stay focused and keep your garden clean.

W

The few letters I could decipher put cracks in the walls of my world. The light, Lenora meant light, didn't it? So, Wilbur was working with Grace and Lenora wasn't happy about it. I turned the pile of letters over in my hands. Wilbur wouldn't have kept copies of his own correspondence without a reason, and the only Maddalena I knew was my mother. The hairs on the back of my neck stood on end.

"It was obviously wishful thinking on my part to believe you'd taken a nap."

I turned towards the office door and found Edwin leaning against it. While Edwin was irksome, I had never considered him an actual threat before.

"I never asked how you came to work for Wilbur."

The letters sat heavy in my hands and my thumb dragged across the words *stay focused.*

Edwin pushed himself off the door frame and stepped into the room.

"No, you didn't."

I stared at him. He must have had a wash too and had changed out of the red into a purple jacket with green pants, that was much more flattering with his copper skin tone.

"I don't suppose you feel like sharing that with me?"

I had by this point thoroughly disturbed the dust and the mold. The light reflected off the dust as it swirled through the air. I used more of my quota to create a static center with a statue in the corner and drew all the dust, and hopefully a few mold spores, to it. Within seconds, the air was clear.

Edwin smiled. "What do you know? You can do house-work." Edwin's smile slipped, and he exhaled heavily. "Wilbur saved me from a very unfortunate fate."

"He saved you?" The words of the letters danced across my brain. "For what?"

Edwin smiled again, but there was no humor in it this time. "I've wonder—"

The whole warehouse shook.

I shoved the letters into my pocket. "What the—" I stood, stepping close to the wall as the warehouse trembled, just in time to see a large crack appear.

Edwin's mouth was a tight, thin line, and his eyes were completely silver. "It appears someone wants your attention." He moved back into the doorway, bracing himself against the frame.

"Are you really taking time," the warehouse shuddered and the cracks in the walls were definitely bigger, "to do a told you so?" I shook my head. "We need to get out of here."

"I was under the impression, since you've told me often enough, that you'd reinforced the front door so it could withstand pretty much anything."

"It can. I'm just a bit behind on reinforcing the walls as well."

Edwin groaned and stared up at the ceiling. Either that or he was rolling his eyes. The warehouse shuddered, and the cracks widened further, and more importantly, I could feel weaknesses in the wards.

He gripped the door frame harder. "How long do you think—"

"The wards are going to break soon if they keep hitting it with that much energy."

"It might be interesting to know who can bring this much power to bear without alerting the preservers?" The silver in his eyes had intensified and the door frame was warping under his grip.

"Assuming it isn't them, of course."

"I'm pretty sure they would already be inside. Unless you have done something particularly insane recently?"

It was my turn to roll my eyes at him.

"Move it."

The warehouse shuddered again.

"Where exactly?"

My eyes were unfocused as I moved along the wall, drawing in more magn. The rough brick of the warehouse scraped the skin of my hands until the scratchy texture changed to a smooth metal.

"Not that I don't enjoy blindly following you in a mad escape from our house while it's under attack... but I don't suppose you would like to share where we're going?"

I pulled at the door. "Cellar."

As far as I was aware, there were only two people who knew about this exit and one of them was dead.

"What if—"

"I can only sense three people out the front. What about you?" The building shuddered, and I saw a crack widen far enough that I could have put my claw in it.

"Hmm, yes? So about being trapped in the basement—"

I turned towards him.

"There's an exit. Coming?" I struggled to focus my eyes as I simultaneously tracked the movement outside the building, but I could see him squinting down the stairwell.

The tremor was through the floor this time, and one section's wards. I really wish I hadn't procrastinated refreshing them, were so thin I suspected they would disappear with the next hit. I didn't know what part Edwin played in all this, but first things first. Staying alive was the goal, after all.

"Now or never, Edwin. Decide." He rubbed the back of his neck, tilting his head and stared at me.

"If we die today, I just want it on record that I was highly dubious about this idea."

"Noted," I snorted and followed him down the stairs, closing the door behind us. I didn't have time to disguise it physically and using magn would have been like painting it with a neon sign saying this way.

The ward finally collapsed, and the reverberation suggested a wall went with it. We picked up our pace, and it wasn't long before we were in another, smaller, room full of dust and mold. If I survived this, I was going to need some serious detoxification.

"Where's this exit?" Edwin paced around the room, pushing at the walls. There wasn't much natural light, not that it bothered us. I pointed to a small lighter section high on the wall.

"There." It gave just enough light for me to see Edwin suck in a breath. "You could make yourself useful." The exit was boarded up, and I wasn't tall enough to reach it without jumping.

"Err..."

"Warehouse, basement, or the window. I'm afraid we don't have many choices here, Edwin." I was shorter than him, so was trying to find something to stand on. "How about you pull off the boards and we can give it a go?"

"Have you ever—"

"Edwin, just take the sparking boards off."

Once Edwin had pulled them off, I jumped up, and it was quick, ish, work for me to pull myself up into the basement of the neighboring tenement and find myself in another dusty room full of broken bits of bricks, wood and discarded papers.

I was puffing again. This was certainly one way to get exercise. I turned around at the scraping behind me.

He had one arm through but hadn't pulled enough weight forward. He reached out and scrambled against the floor to grip something.

Decisions, decisions. I stepped up over him and hooked my hands under his armpits, pulling him forward.

"Thanks," he grunted. His velvet jacket was covered in dust and had a few tears in it. We would need to clean up before we headed out.

"Here." Once he was standing, I handed him some wood, and we recreated the boarded-up vibe from this side. It wouldn't fool anyone serious, but it might give us a bit more time.

"This is nice." Edwin wandered around the room, admiring the bits of broken wood and dust. He turned back to me with his eyebrows raised. "Can we stay here?"

It wasn't a bad idea. They, whoever they were, would be out in the streets, waiting for us to scamper outside.

"I don't think so. Our trail will be easy to follow."

Edwin winced. "I was afraid you were going to say that." He smeared a bit of dust on the floor with his foot. "I don't suppose you have a place in mind? With a shower and reinforced windows."

I snorted again.

"Sorry. The problem we have is I don't know who is

behind this." I smeared a dirty hand over my face and then tried to use the inside of my shirt to wipe it off.

"I think you're just making it worse."

I glared at him. "I think it has something to do with Lenora. So, we start there."

Edwin shrugged.

"What about the Garden?"

Could it be Grace?

"I doubt the Blueshrouds have the power to pull this off. But you're right, there's something going on there, but I can't see why Grace would suddenly send a full-on assault team. We need to be somewhere else, and we need to find out who is part of this. Investigating Lenora's disappearance answers both problems."

"I'd rather find somewhere safe—"

"And what? The two of us, stuck in a room, afraid to go outside for days or weeks?" I shuddered.

Edwin's face was expressionless, but he followed as I moved through the house. We kept to the shadows while trying to peer out the windows to see what was happening. The street was bustling. A large family strolled past us, filling the space with children's laughter and parents' shouted commands. The light furred children had decided tumbling on the pavements was too much fun to miss while the parents chased after them, trying to keep them off the dirt that had been pounded into the pavement by thousands of feet.

"We could always march up to our front door and ask them politely to not destroy our home?" Edwin wiped his hands on his jacket and then stared at them ruefully.

While we couldn't see the warehouse directly, there

weren't any sounds of collapsing walls either. The amount of magn they must be using was insane and a sick feeling pulled at my stomach. If they, whoever they were, could do this, then what hope did I have?

"Do you think we have a home anymore?" I asked. Edwin's lips drooped. I wouldn't admit it to Edwin, but I was feeling pretty guilty about procrastinating on those wards.

"No, but..." his forehead wrinkled. "Wilbur said accommodation would be provided."

I might have not seen or heard anything, but a tremble in the ground let me know they were still going.

"Yeah, the Council's good like that. They like to know which door to knock on." I stared at his bare feet. "You don't have any shoes." The tenement we were in had been vacant for a long time, and I doubted it had a maker.

"Thank you so much for bringing that to my attention. I hadn't noticed."

"You can't run around in Duskburn without something protecting your feet."

"I can't just make shoes out of thin air," he said.

He was right. There wouldn't be enough matter in the air, but the room behind us was full of bits of paper and wood.

The last thing I wanted to do was use more magn, but we needed to get away from this area.

"What? Are we just going to... oh," Edwin's eyes widened.

Old brain cells fired, making me wince, but I could feel the building blocks of the material in my hand breaking down into its molecules and transforming. It actually took very little magn for that part. The harder and more draining part was to contain it. Difficult without a machine, molecules like to party and were always trying to escape off to a holiday somewhere else.

"I didn't know you could—"

I reached out and ripped off his tassels, throwing them into the molecule puddle I had created on the floor. Edwin's face went slack. He took off his jacket, inspecting the tears. My eyes widened seeing a second jacket underneath.

"You're wearing two jackets?"

"It's winter." He stared at me like I was the insane one.

I blinked a couple of times. Shaking my head, I turned my attention back to the molecular mess in front of me and focused on building a pair of shoes.

"What about sock—"

"Seriously?" I sat back on my heels, taking a moment to breathe, and wiped the fine sheen of sweat off my face.

Edwin grunted but pulled on the dark rubbery shoes with flecks of gold in them and jumped.

"What are you doing?" I asked.

"They're springy." He jumped again.

"Will they stay on?"

"Yes, actually, they're quite comfortable. What's next, a glamor?"

"Not unless you're going to run it. Besides, they are easy to spot in a crowd." I grasped a hair tie from my pocket and pulled my hair back. Another slight difference that might help us remain unnoticed. I handed another one to Edwin, who frowned at it.

"What is that—"

"Could you jus—"

"Fine."

"And I need one of your jackets."

"But I need it."

"Why, you have another one." Edwin's second jacket was a much darker purple and less noticeable.

"It's cold." He sniffed.

"So? You can warm yourself, make your coat thicker or something." I shook my head. "Two jackets."

"I could…" he sighed and reluctantly took off his purple one. This left a green one to match his green pants.

I took the purple one from him. With another pulse of magn, I darkened it to black. I also took a moment to clean us up and with that, we were ready.

A quick scan of the street and I identified a potential couple to shadow. We stepped out onto the street, falling a few steps behind them, far enough back so they didn't feel crowded, but close enough that anyone scanning the area might assume we were together.

"Where are we going?" asked Edwin as he joined me. I shook my head and forced my body to relax, letting my arms swing freely. Within a few blocks, we had left the major streets. I wasn't sure if the smaller back streets were safer, but at least I could control who could see us.

"I would just like to share that I'm feeling uncomfortable about traipsing around Duskburn without knowing what I'm heading into."

I rolled my eyes.

"Uriah's"

"Uriah? Who is Uri—"

"Someone Lenora visited the day she disappeared." If the

preservation service had just done what they were meant to do, I wouldn't be in this mess. I sighed.

"Is that the best place to start? Just in case it's slipped your mind, our home's been destroyed, and I don't think it is too much of a stretch to assume that someone's trying to kill—"

"Lenora's disappearance is the key. Besides being the only thing we've got …"

I zigzagged through the narrow streets until I found Uriah's building. I pushed open the unlocked lower door and crossed a cracked stone floor to a central staircase and peered upwards.

The notes I had on Uriah's residence put him on the top floor. I took a breath and gripped the banister, the metal cold under my hand, and ascended. I could hear the squeak of Edwin's shoes behind me.

"Puffing a bit there," said Edwin. He really was so helpful.

"Thank you for your insightful observation." I said between breaths.

Two stories later, we were standing in front of Uriah's door. I reached out and dragged my fingers across the door, feeling the wards woven into it.

"Be careful," said Edwin.

I flicked him a glance, but continued caressing the door until I found the weak spots. Extending my claws, I stretched their energy into the ward and unknotted it one thread at a time. Wards can be nasty things and you never knew what the backlash would be.

"Err, are you sure that is the best way—" said Edwin.

The ward untwisted. As it dissolved, one strand of energy

flicked out and snapped across the back of my hand, making me wince.

Edwin chuckled.

"Hey, it's broken, isn't it?" I asked as I rubbed my wrist.

The apartment was a single room with a bed and a small desk. Clothes and personal items were strewn across a single armchair and the all too familiar feeling of silence greeted me. I don't know what I was expecting. A note saying he had been kidnapped with the coordinates?

As I ferreted through Uriah's stuff on display, Edwin opened draws and rummaged. Neither of us found anything interesting. I lay down on Uriah's bed and stared at the blank ceiling, running my hand over his sheets and under the pillow, lifted the mattress and kneeled to see under the bed. Basically, touched every part of the room. The whole place resonated with my energy.

"You find anything?" I asked.

"Just flyers inviting people to take part in a local game." Edwin handed one over to me. "The room smells of future death. I get the sense that he is a person coming to the end of his life, not ill, just old."

"Too old to be taking part in local sports events, I would imagine." I glanced at the flyer with a bunch of cheerful people standing in a field. "Well, if Lenora was visiting Uriah, I suspect she came, found he wasn't home and left."

"Very wise and insightful," said Edwin.

I flicked a glance at him. "Do you have a different view?"

"Oh no, the ward hadn't been resealed." He nodded. "Which probably meant we didn't really need to break in. You know if we're searching for Lenora."

I glared at him. "Thank you for your... observation." I glanced around the room again and sighed. "Let's get out of here and visit the next one on the list."

"So," Edwin tugged at the cuff on his jacket. "What I hear you saying is that you want us to go out on to the streets again. The streets that are full of people trying to kill us? Even though we have a nice, easily defendable apartment here?"

"You really want to be stuck here for an indeterminate amount of time?"

"If that would be time that we," He pointed at himself and at me, "were alive and safe."

"I'm still under supervised service. I think the council is going to notice if I don't go back to work."

"If the council comes." He picked up another flyer and put it down again. "That might be a good thing?"

Even he didn't believe that.

"The council doesn't enjoy having to find its citizens."

Edwin sighed. "Who's the next person on the list?" he asked.

"Drudtia, her address is about four streets up. We can take the direct route on the main road or weave through some back streets."

I turned over the flyer in my hand. The graphics weren't great, but there was something appealing about it. Which I suppose was the point. Though, "Watch the fumes fly" wasn't a great slogan.

"Drudtia. I've heard of her," said Edwin.

"You have? What've you heard?" I put the flyer in my pocket and rebuilt the ward. No point leaving Uriah's place wide open.

"Scary."

"Great. Well, let's hope whoever is after us finds her scary as well." I opened the apartment's door and checked the stairwell before turning back to Edwin. "Well? Drudtia's or do you have another idea?"

"Lead the way," said Edwin.

He was right, though, we needed to be careful. I did a scan of the building and found an apartment that was empty. We exited discreetly out of a back window on the first floor. Edwin followed without comment, and I kept us to the back streets, but heading toward Drudtia's. Overconfidence had always been a failing of mine.

6

Life is pain

It is just criminal how Haze, Hoarfrost and other drugs exist. Despite my admiration for the technical capability of weaving magn into a digestible substance, it is obvious to anyone with eyes that they are coming from the council's laboratories, which means someone is a traitor. When I am a Dean, I will make sure that nothing like that happens under my watch. Some apprentices think the council does it on purpose, but that sounds like unsubstantiated nonsense to me.

The accurate representation of past events
History Assignment
Archie, Apprentice of Chester

We stepped into a small narrow lane and found it full of Blueshroud statics. And the biggest sparkheads of them all,

Emanuel and Lydia, stood in the middle of the street smiling at me. A couple of other thugs leaned on either side, flipping knives in their hands like something out of a bad AV show.

"You want to be careful you don't cut yourself," I said, dazzling the crowd with my wit. I smiled at one thug. She snarled back, baring her blunt round teeth, but it didn't hide the fear in her eyes as they dropped to the talons extending from my fingers and toes.

That's right sparker, this time it was them who were going to hurt.

"Emanuel, we'll have to stop meeting like this." I could feel Edwin at my back. I never thought I would say this, but it was comforting.

How the spark was he on the street again? And how much hoarfrost had he consumed? His eyes were like black voids, and he was probably convinced he was invincible. He might even be right.

"You're full of surprises, aren't you, Morgan?" said Emanuel. "Spritely for someone with a cracked skull, who I heard recently had a building dropped on them."

I snarled. "What can I say? I heal fast." I bared my teeth at him and tried to angle myself so I could keep Emanuel and Lydia in view. I had to put one thug just out of my peripheral vision and trust Edwin to monitor him.

"Just makes it more fun," said Emanuel, pulling out a knife.

I should have guessed that Emanuel liked to throw things. He released a small throwing knife at my head, powering it with his hyped-up physical strength and some extra magn to help it hit its target. At least he had stopped talking. I used the air rushing at me to feed my energy and grabbed the knife out of the air, flipping it and sent it directly into the thug near me. The knife spun so its handle hit the thug directly in the head and he dropped unconscious to the ground.

Static, I was good. Who said one person couldn't make a difference?

I ran toward Emanuel and Lydia, extending my claws and using magn to create blades of energy. At the last moment, I twisted, avoiding their attacks, gouging their sides, and slashing at anything I could reach.

"I'm going to end you," hissed Lydia as she whipped her tail at my face. Emanuel came at me from the other side and as I ducked Lydia's tail, I was forced down onto a knee to avoid Emanuel's knife. This was not an ideal position, so I ripped out the back of Emanuel's calf muscle and scrambled back, only to see Edwin being stabbed in the stomach by the other thug.

Oh, for volt's sake.

Lydia jammed a knife into my shoulder. I screamed but pushed myself into it, using it to take a swipe at Lydia's neck with my other hand. She grabbed at her throat, falling backwards, allowing me to bring my attention to Emanuel. His face twisted in a snarl, and he threw his weight forward on his uninjured leg. I grabbed his arm, pulling it down and slammed his knife into the ground, morphing the stones to hold his blade. The split second he spent pulling at his knife was all I needed to slam my elbow behind his ear and knock him out. My other shoulder, which had the knife in it, was numb, but not for long. I ripped the knife out and used its handle to knock out the thug who was attacking Edwin.

Lydia stood there watching me, her tail flicking. She had the bleeding under control but was still using one hand to hold the skin together. She took a step towards me, her tail and knife ready.

I raised one hand. "I'd suggest it's in both of our interests to retreat."

"This isn't over, Morgan," said Lydia.

"What was that? Sorry, you've a bit of a gurgle. You might need to get that checked." I stood there with three unconscious bodies at my feet and stared at Lydia. "So, what's it going to be?" I was so badass. In that moment I wished I could have recorded it, I would have been a star.

She growled at me but grabbed Emanuel and legged it, leaving the other two behind. I hoped she came back for them.

Edwin was curled up around his gut wounds. I reached down, sealing the worst of them, but there wasn't much I could do here. Risking us both, I lifted him across my shoulders. Once I was confident I would not pass out from the pain, I headed towards Drudtia's.

My legs dragged, and each step sent a sharp shot of pain through my body. I tuned out the world and focused on keeping one step before the other. I found a gravel pathway that led up to a house that could have been in a story. One of those stories where the kids get eaten. Between a shoulder with a knife wound and Edwin bleeding out, I didn't have time to worry about what I might be getting us into. I shuffled up the path, leaving a nice blood trail for anyone following.

I placed, dropped, Edwin in the garden near the front porch. The winter flowers kindly murmured their concern and I think some even attempted to heal him. Sadly, they were too small to be of much help. A good reference for those that lived here.

My shoulder was excruciating, and the blood was flowing freely. I slammed the knocker on the front door, glancing back at Edwin, quietly bleeding out in the garden.

The door gradually opened inwards, revealing a person who wouldn't be much off six and a half feet. Her skin was unlined however, a sense of density gave the impression of immense age.

"Finally, I was wondering when you'd get here." Her lips pulled back from strong white bone teeth, and her green eyes shone.

"Right, well, any chance you can give us a hand?" I said, before passing out.

I couldn't believe the person sitting opposite me was any kind of client of Lenora's. Her long fingers, wrapped around her stein, were strong, and she had lifted the jug to fill up my cup with ease. She draped herself over a chaise lounge and sipped on her own drink with her unwavering attention focused on me. I tried not to squirm and glanced around the room. It was decorated in dark woods and deep colors. I wanted to curl up with a warm drink, a good story and forget about the death and destruction that I seemed to create, despite my best intentions.

"Lenora, remember her?" I asked. "She went missing on the day she saw you. You didn't eat her, did you?"

"I don't eat people, not for food anyway." She chuckled. I threw up a little in my mouth.

"When did you last see her?" I asked. Edwin was upright and sitting in a chair with enormous arms, making him appear too tall for it, yet dominated by it at the same time. He was drinking something that smelled overly sweet. Each on their own, I guess. I was just grateful that we were both conscious and no longer bleeding.

"I don't know, maybe three nights ago."

"Here you go Tia. I've made snacks. Does anyone else need a drink top up?"

I watched this new person bustle in and put food down on a coffee table in the middle of the room. His face was also unlined, his dark blonde hair highlighted warm brown eyes, and he exuded a similar level of density to Drudtia.

"Thank you, Alwyn," said Drudtia.

I shifted in my chair. "Alwyn, it's a pleasure to meet you. Do you mind if I use your maker? I find I need some soup, just easier for me to digest—"

"Of course, of course. I can make you some. I have some amazing schemas. Sweet or savory? I have a chili and dark chocolate schema that is to die for."

I smiled. His enthusiasm was hard to resist, even if the idea of sweet soup was just wrong.

"Savory would be great."

Alwyn nodded and disappeared, and I turned my attention back to Drudtia. There was no way I was calling her Tia.

"You might've been the last person to see Lenora," I said, rubbing at my shoulder. It had been healed, but my body hadn't quite forgotten the pain.

"She's a good person." said Drudtia. "Willing to drop in

on the old ones and after the changes in the last few hundred years it's been rough on some. I help where I can."

"I take it you weren't a patient of Lenora's then." I asked. Or she didn't see herself as one, anyway.

Drudtia snorted, "Me? No, I'm what they call a supplier of goods and services."

"You saw Lenora three days ago? Anything different about that day?"

Drudtia tapped on the back of her chaise.

"She was worried about people going missing. She asked me to check if they had returned to the aether. I couldn't feel anything." Drudtia's lips twisted, and she breathed heavily out of her nose. "It was the last time I saw her."

"Do you see her regularly?"

"She often dropped in at the end of her workday. Put some orders in. Check in, share a drink." I couldn't imagine anyone I would want to see every day. Though Lenora seemed to enjoy surrounding herself with people.

"Vivian, one of Lenora's apprentices, said no one has seen her since that afternoon, and we suspect that after visiting you, she returned to her workroom and was taken from there."

Drudtia's face didn't move, but Alwyn, who had returned with my drink, blinked.

"That's not good," said Alwyn, frowning. He took a seat next to Drudtia and let her feet stretch across his lap.

"No, it isn't," I said. "I've also been attacked twice, three times if you count the warehouse, since I investigated her disappearance." I tilted my head. "To be honest, some of those might have been for another reason." I shook my head.

"But the blowing up of the warehouse is definitely linked to Lenora, I can feel it."

"I can give you the names of the others that she thought were missing," said Drudtia.

"She didn't say what she thought might happen, or share what her concerns were?" I asked. Surely, they had discussed some theories.

"The only thing that all the missing had in common was they were all lifelore adepts or scholars."

Oh, for volt's sake

"And you didn't think that after all the years of elec-tromagn wars, that the sudden disappearance of a bunch of lifelorers was relevant?" I couldn't sit still anymore, so jumped up, pacing the room. Edwin put down his cup and got up, but I shook my head and headed back to my chair, perching on its arm.

"Lenora was concerned, yes. I shared her concern, of course." Drudtia gave a regal wave of the hand. Well, I was glad that she had shared Lenora's concern.

"Right, so what did you and Lenora decide to do?" I asked. My shoulders slumped forward, and I swung my leg.

"Lenora said she would call the Preservers and let them know," said Drudtia.

"She left here, went to call the Preservation Service, and then when she didn't turn up the next day, what then?" I watched Drudtia's fingers, tap tap tap, forcing myself to keep still.

"I waited," she turned to me and the green in her eyes became stronger. "I waited to see what would happen next."

"But she was your friend—"

"Lenora knows we can't get involved," said Alwyn, squeezing his eyes shut.

"She knew we had other priorities and can't afford to get dragged into the petty squabbles of the day," said Drudtia.

"Even when it's your friend?" Edwin asked. He hadn't picked up his cup again and sat there frowning at them.

Drudtia and Alwyn glanced at each other, and Alwyn nodded.

She turned her attention back to us.

Drudtia sighed. "We care for Lenora, but with so many friendships and disasters, sometimes we have to make choices."

I slid over the arm of the chair into the seat and put my head in my hands. I counted a couple of breaths and then peered at Drudtia.

"Well, you seem pretty involved to me. It's not like you're off meditating in a forest somewhere." I squashed my mind trying to remind me of the years I spent hanging out with a forest while people died.

Drudtia reached out and grabbed my wrist, causing a sharp pain to travel up my arm.

"What the—"

"I'm just as concerned about Lenora as you. However, do you really think it would help for me to be running around Duskburn pulling up rocks and houses?" She released my arm.

"Ow," was my clever response. "Fine, no, but—"

"What do you want me to do? No matter how much power I can channel, I can't find Lenora with it."

I rubbed my wrist. "You can't—"

"No, I can't locate her."

I picked up my cup and grimaced as the cold soup splashed against my lips.

"You don't like it?" Alwyn asked, his eyes wide.

"No, I mean thank you. I'm grateful for the sustenance. I just prefer it hot." I smiled at him.

"Of course, let me," he reached out and touched the cup, its warmth radiating back through my fingertips.

"Thanks."

"Not a problem, and if you're interested, I have a new raspberry flavored soup, which I think will be a major hit."

"Another time," His face fell, but I didn't feel up to experimenting, "still getting the energy back, you know."

"Yes, of course, next time."

I gave a weak smile back, knowing that a sweet soup was now in my future. Raspberry, it just seemed unnecessary.

"Edwin, how are you holding up?" asked Alwyn, "Is your drink all right? I have some new—"

"Thank you, Alwyn. This is perfect for now."

I took a sip of my now slightly overboiled soup. It was still better than cold.

An hour later, we were still sitting there. Drudtia, Alwyn, and Edwin were rehashing the last few days. On the fourth round of it, I cleared my throat.

I pushed myself to my feet. "I'm going to see what's left of the warehouse."

"I would imagine it's being watched," said Drudtia.

"True, but we need more information." I doubted the

letters could tell me more than they already had. But that didn't mean that there weren't more hidden. "And it isn't here. Maybe something of Wilbur's survived, give us an idea of where to next."

"What about all the people running around trying to kill us?" said Edwin. His skin was back to being the rich metallic copper he favored.

"I know how to protect myself." I frowned at him. "You should stay here."

"He'll be fine," said Alwyn. He rose and patted Edwin's shoulder. "I'll lend you jackets that will provide you more protection than those thin velvet ones. Won't stop anything serious, but it will slow down the occasional knife." He disappeared.

"I like him," said Edwin.

"Because he's making you food and giving you clothes."

"There are worst reasons to—"

"What's your plan? Just amble up and see what they've left waiting for you?" asked Drudtia.

We both blinked and turned back to Drudtia, our cheeks a little warmer.

I cleared my throat. "I'd hope we'd have a little more finesse than that." I gestured in the general direction of the warehouse. "But yes, that is the general gist of it."

"Sounds like a solid plan." Drudtia sat back and clasped her hands over her stomach. "I'll prepare the medicine cabinet for your next visit."

"You're welcome to come along." I wasn't sure if I wanted her to say yes or no.

Drudtia considered me.

"Not that I don't want to help you, but that's not my role here."

"And who dictates the roles?" I cautiously tested my arm's movement and sighed when my shoulder rotated without a twinge.

Drudtia swung her legs off the chaise.

"I contribute in my way."

"By sitting in this house, waiting for injured people to show up?" Maybe that is where I was going wrong. Leaving the house.

"You don't have to rush around to contribute."

"Like providing Lenora the means and medicine she needed to care for everyone."

"Like that."

We stared at each other until Alwyn came back in with two coats, warm and reinforced.

7

What's in a home?

... this red tape thing meant the council controlled the use of electromagn. Which is grossly unfair. If we are going to create good things, why can't we? Why not just control what is used for rather than the amount used? I mean sure the council ensures we have a house, magn to run it and work which, Lenora says, helps to stop everyone being afraid all the time. But it doesn't stop people from being killed.

Telling it like it is
History Assignment
Maxi, Apprentice

As we wandered through the streets, my feet whooshed against the cold stones under them. A long hedge appeared at the next corner.

"Can you just say hello without stopping?" asked Edwin. His coat was open, and his long legs flashed purple with each step.

"I'm being polite." I shuffled faster. "Perhaps that is something you've heard of?"

He stretched out his legs until I had to push actively off my back foot to keep up with him. His stride and my bounding beside him were hardly subtle.

"Would you slow down? We're trying to keep a low profile. In case you've forgotten. Good evening." I greeted the hedge as I drew near. The plantae worked just by existing, as the council pointed out, sometimes with a heavy hammer. Fair enough, a lot less of us would have survived if the plantae hadn't joined together to ground the free flying electromagn at the height of the wars. I envied them knowing their purpose and understanding their contribution by the very nature of who they were. The rest of us muddled along, experimenting, and making a mess.

"Evening Morgan," said the hedge. I never had to introduce myself to them. While they might not move physically like other people, they were well connected.

"Winter settling in then," I had always found talking about the weather to be a safe bet in any conversation.

"Yes, time for sleep soon. You alright?"

I smiled, "yeah, I'm fine. I'll miss you, though."

"It won't be for long and remember, while many of us sleep, we're still around." I smiled at the hedge and ran my hand across their branches and leaves. They gave my hand a little tap. "Stop that. It tickles."

"See you in a few months," I said, laughing, and the hedge gave a mumbled goodbye.

"How does the hedge know you?" asked Edwin, his eyes bulging.

"Why wouldn't the hedge know me?" I stretched out my legs, trying to pad casually along. "Some people find me delightful."

Edwin snorted. "If wild risk-taking is considered delightful."

He never got to hear my witty response as I spotted a couple of Blueshrouds standing on the next corner. I pulled Edwin into a laneway and contemplated the best way to get back to the warehouse.

"Wha—"

I shook my head at him and tried to think. I tilted my head back and gazed upwards.

"Wha—" I put my finger across my lips and pointed in the air. He scowled but nodded.

My claws extended, I dug into the mortar between the bricks in the wall in front of me, just deep enough to allow me to hold on and use the muscles in my legs to push me up it. I climbed, the air rasping in the back of my throat, and with my arms soon shaking. As soon as I was over the edge, my legs folded, helpfully pulling me out of sight from those on the street. I breathed in through my nose and blinked the sweat out of my eyes. Working on my breath control, I glanced around at the empty rooftop and crawled to the edge of the building, peering over the side. Edwin was still climbing. His shoes, he had insisted on keeping the rubbery ones I had made for him, were not helping, so he was relying on his arm strength to pull himself up. It was slow going.

"How long do you think you'll be?" I could hear his breathing. "For someone who was complaining about me stopping and talking to the plantae you're certainly taking your—" He glared up at me. I shifted back from the edge. Some things were just harder with people watching.

I checked my wristband, but no one had tried to contact me so the only thing it told me was that my magn usage levels were high. I couldn't see myself being able to use much, which meant we were going to have to rely on our strength and our wits. Unless Edwin had more skill with it than I had seen so far.

We were so sparked.

A hand appeared and then a foot. His clothes scraped against the brick as he dragged himself onto the roof.

"Er... a little less noise—" I said. His scowl deepened. Something I hadn't thought possible, so I left it. "Next stop, home. Are you ready?" I scanned him, but besides from being a bit worn around the edges from the climb, but no injuries.

"Yes." His breathing was heavy, but he pushed himself up into a half-bent position and we headed across the rooftop.

It wasn't long before the large, unblemished, dark metal roof of our warehouse appeared. I headed towards a skylight in the upper west corner of the roof but was jerked back.

"What's wrong?" I asked, trying to step forward again.

"Besides from you almost killing yourself?" His hand kept a firm hold on the back of my coat.

"Killing myself?" I scanned the roof in front of me but

couldn't see any cause for concern. Inching forward, I reached out my foot to tap the skylight. My foot disappeared.

Static.

I pulled it back under my body and squatted down. Using my fingers, I found an edge. I shivered at the sight of the tips of my fingertips being chopped off as they dipped into the illusion.

Who were these people?

Edwin crouched down next to me.

"Back to Drudtia's then?" he asked.

I picked at the edge and gave my head a quick shake.

"I have questions. First, how can you see through it? And second, can you see a way down?" I asked Edwin.

"I think the more important question is why you can't see it. And if you can't... it's too risky."

The wind whistled between us.

"I'm going down there," I said, my voice cool. No one enjoys being told they aren't capable of something.

"Then you'll die, or at least hurt yourself badly."

"Not if you help me."

Edwin's mouth thinned.

"We aren't leaving," I said, dropping to one knee and trying to use my hands to work out how stable the edge was. "Humph," said Edwin.

I grabbed the edge and gave it a bit of a shake.

"You know this is a mistake."

I swung my other leg over the edge. It was disconcerting to see my apparently amputated leg, but still felt it on the other side of the illusion.

"You're the most reckless person I've ever met. You know that, right?"

I glanced at him over my shoulder and couldn't help the grin that stretched across my face. My leg continued to swing, hoping to hit something I could put my weight on.

"I suspect you're right. Shall we?" I waved my hand over the perfect and not so perfect roof that currently had my leg dangling through it.

He rose with a sigh. "You can't go that way. Pull your leg back up." His face stern, he strode across the roof so I followed, making sure to match his footsteps.

"They left you to report in, did they?" I asked.

The man leaning against the wall jumped up and spun towards us. Most of the warehouse was still standing, but the building had some serious structural issues, including a missing roof. Edwin had led the way, and as soon as my head dropped below the original roof line, the reality of the destruction clicked into focus. Cold had seeped through me.

"Keep back, don't get involved," I said. Edwin nodded, and I stepped into the room alone.

"Morgan, I..."

The late afternoon light filtered through the broken spines of the building. I stood there staring at the person across from me, wondering where this was going to lead. His pant leg was slightly pulled up, and I examined the exposed scaled ankle and shivered.

Artemus smiled.

Nope.

"Morgan, I..." His smile widened. "I just wanted to say I'm sorry about the other night, and this." He gestured to the ruined building around him. "This was not how I wanted our reunion to go." He stepped forward

"I'm sure you had planned a whole thing with string instruments and rose petals."

He laughed, his feathers trembling. "I just wasn't sure if.... I asked to be the one left here, you know." He dipped his chin and gazed at me.

"You realize it was only a few days ago that you blew Haze into my face? What do you really want?" He wasn't unattractive, but the forgive me expression he was attempting to pull off was wasted on me.

"I wanted to say I was sorry. I want to make it up to you." A flush briefly showed in his cheeks, surprising me. "I heard you ask Grace about those people."

"Yeah?" I shifted so my body fully blocked the entrance behind me.

"I know Uriah. He's harmless and often brings food around for kids too whacked out to make it." Artemus' eyes dropped. "He fed me a time or two when I was younger."

I stifled a flare of sympathy. "Do you know where he is?"

"Not specifically. However, I was at Whitpon Pier a few days ago and I could sense that he'd been there. It struck me as strange. He doesn't travel far these days. I think... I think they put him on the ship traveling inland."

"What kind of ship?"

"It's used to move things." His gaze traced a crack along the floor and up a wall before reaching our new skylight.

"Yes, I know how ships work."

"A couple of internal ports are useful to move product from." He stepped backward. It didn't take a genius to realize that he was talking about smuggling. "I'm sorry," and I could see it, a flash of him wanting to be better for a life that we would never have. Then it was gone, and his smooth armor was back in place. "If you ever change your mind, my door is always open to you."

I smiled at him. "Thanks, and thanks for the info on Uriah. I... you just have to know that mine isn't," I glanced at my old front door, "metaphorically, I mean." It was still standing, which was more than I could say about the wall next to it.

A flicker of something flashed through his eyes.

"I hear and obey." He flashed a predatory smile and turned to leave, but lurched to a halt when he caught sight of Edwin behind me.

"Well, Morgan," Artemus raised an eyebrow as he took in Edwin, and his long loose hair, ruffled shirt and Alwyn's purple tailored jacket, exuding debonair. "Not your usual taste."

I turned to find Edwin watching me. His dark hair had a sheen to it I hadn't notice before.

Artemis stomped away, no doubt running back to Grace to let her know we were here.

Static.

"What do you think he really wanted?" asked Edwin.

"You heard him."

"And you believe him?"

"Well, we now have a lead."

"You can't be serious about going to Whitpon Pier on his information?"

"I trust his story about seeing Uriah, but I don't trust him not to tell Grace. And we now know she and her thugs are involved in this somehow."

"What if it's a trap?"

"Why bother? He had us here. Come on, we need to grab what we can and get out of here as fast as possible in case he comes back with friends."

I rushed towards my rooms and found that all my weapons were gone, but my clothes were undisturbed. *Static.* The door to Wilbur's office was gone. As was the comp, everything in the cabinets and even a few of the cabinets themselves.

"They missed the safe," said Edwin.

"What? What safe?"

"The safe, the one in the floor," Edwin pointed at the undisturbed floor.

I perked up. "So how do we—"

Edwin stepped forward and pushed down on a section of the floor. The part he pressed went down, and an entire section of the floor rose to reveal a series of shelves.

"This safe." Edwin picked up a bit of burned wood.

"It's not really a safe though, is it? More a hidden set of shelves."

Edwin ignored me and stood there, frowning as he peered at the bits of wood.

I shoved at the things on the shelves, but the only ones of use to me were a couple of knives with sheaths and a small, highly illegal, electronic interrupter.

"Useful, but not that interesting." I strapped the knives to my wrists and pocketed the interrupter.

Edwin reached around me and picked up a pen.

"I think the pen emits an electric charge," I said. "Maybe wait to click on it at the docks."

Edwin put the pen back. "A midnight stroll near the water, I take it?"

"I'm sure it'll be delightful."

Edwin snorted.

I closed my eyes and took a breath. Technically, Vivian had said she didn't want to have anything to do with me and considering she had probably already done her tip off to the preservers, I really didn't need to involve her in this.

I stepped out into the living and surveyed the damage. What if we weren't the only ones attacked?

How are you and the others?

Have a lead.

I could tell she had read it, but there was no response. *Fine.* If she could read it, then she was probably alright. And if she didn't want to respond, that was also fine.

"Let's go," I said. I had been umming and ahhing on how to get to Whitpon Pier. It wasn't far. Still, it would take an hour if we needed to go all the way out to the lighthouse, and I wasn't exactly sure where this would lead me. Not to mention that the Blueshrouds were hunting me.

I led Edwin through a new gap in the wall to a back street and to an old wooden door a couple of houses down. The automobile filled up the entire space and I smiled as I took it in, my best invention ever. From the outside, it appeared as a gray sedan that would blend into the street.

"I didn't know you had an auto," said Edwin.

I shifted. "Not much cause to use it, still I didn't want to leave it behind."

"That must be the most boring auto I've ever seen. I admit, it's not what I would've picked for you. I would've—"

I touched the auto and removed the glamor.

Edwin exhaled loudly.

"Are you serious?"

"About my auto? Deadly."

"That's a death trap."

"Hey, it moves fast and can hold four or at a pinch five people."

"We're going to die," said Edwin, throwing up his hands.

"Trust me," I said, smiling.

8

Fun in the streets

Of course, life only really got interesting when we worked out how to weave magn through molecules. It is one thing to manipulate them but another to augment them completely. I understand why the everlastings hold on to the knowledge for only those who have proven themselves. Not the thing you want people you can't control playing with. I would hate to think what other apprentices would get up to. Still, I could do great things with it.

The accurate representation of past events
History Assignment
Archie, Apprentice of Chester

Edwin's knees were higher than his waist and he kept a hand braced above his head. The auto was a metal tube, close to the ground and on top of four metal wheels, that I had adapted to be as flexible as rubber.

"See," I smiled at him, "easy fit."

He shot air out of his nose and hugged his door, keeping his face away from me.

"Think of it as going off on an adventure," I said.

I took another sharp right followed by an immediate left as I zigged through the backstreets.

He twisted in his seat to face me. I kept my eyes on the road, but I could see him bringing up one knee close to his chest so he could shift in his seat. He was going to wrench his back if he kept jerking himself around like that.

"Did you just hiss at me?" I asked.

He snorted. "Involuntary response."

"Sure, sure," I took another corner without slowing down. The auto took it effortlessly, but the corner of my lips twitched as Edwin braced himself with one hand on the dashboard in front of him as well as one against the roof.

"Are we in that much of a rush?" asked Edwin.

"Who knows how long Artemus' information is good for?"

"If they are moving people, wouldn't they wait until night? Fewer people around?"

I decreased the connection of the auto's magnbead and let it drop to just under the speed limit. The traffic was building up on the main roads so I kept to the backstreets. I turned the music on, flipping through several songs before settling on a humorous opera.

"Seriously? What's this?" asked Edwin.

"You don't know? It is just one of the most famous arias ever. It's beautiful and funny. My two favorite things." I nudged the volume up a little, conducting the music with one of my hands.

"It's piercing, and please put your hand back on the controls. Perhaps we could have something a bit more soothing? As the guest in your auto, wouldn't it be courteous to ask me what music I might like to listen to?"

"I find it relaxing. Anyway, the driver picks, that's a law that existed before the council."

"Automobiles didn't exist back then."

I waved his words away.

"Driver, of whatever vehicle is used, chooses. Everyone knows that."

"What about the laws of hospitality? Making the comfort of your guest a priority?"

"Vehicles are different. You're already getting the benefit of my driving you around." I was driving sedately enough now that I took the next corner without slowing down.

Edwin's grip on the door tightened.

"You just make up rules as you go, don't you?"

I laughed and navigated some parked automobiles nimbly.

"It might be worthwhile remembering that we're trying to stay alive? In case you've forgotten. Uriah himself is long gone."

I eased the magn down another notch and turned up the music.

"You're right."

The music shut off and Edwin twisted in his seat to face me.

"I'm sorry? What did you say?"

"I said you're right. Uriah isn't there anymore."

"I'm right… wait, I need to record… spark it, I don't have a recording option on my wristband. Can you record it on yours?"

"Record what?" I scanned the next intersection.

"Record you saying I'm right, of course."

I wasn't sure what I thought about Edwin attempting to be witty.

"All right," I said. "No need to make a song and dance about it."

"I don't think you have ever said it before."

"Well, maybe you haven't been right—"

"Don't, don't ruin it." Edwin closed his eyes and rested his head on his seat. I turned up the music just a little too high, but it didn't stop me from hearing my wristband's ping.

I sent a pulse to have the message read out loud.

"Pick me up, Vivian."

My fingers tapped on the side of the wheel.

"You aren't considering—"

"She's caught up in this now. She'll be safer with me." I pulled over to the side of the road but didn't turn around. I created a soothing rhythm with my fingers and tried to concentrate.

"Safer?" asked Edwin, his eyebrows running up his face.

"Despite everything, yes. Better for her to be with us than poking around on her own." I shifted in my seat. To be honest, I wasn't sure about that, but something was telling me that leaving her to fend for herself was a bad idea.

Edwin flopped back in his seat but as he had little room, it ended up being more a collapse of his body over a sharp sigh.

"Might I suggest," he said, "That including an apprentice to this adventure could add another layer of complication that we don't need right now?"

"Send a message to Vivian," I dictated, "on our way."

I kicked the car into gear and did a sharp right. I didn't bother with backstreets this time and despite traffic, it wasn't long before I was pulling up a block away from Lenora's house.

"Accepting the fact that we're going to include her, perhaps forcing her to traipse down a street on her own right now might not be the best—"

"I need to see if someone is watching her. It's an acceptable risk."

"For you maybe," said Edwin.

> *Here*
> *Auto one block down*
> *to your right*
> *Morgan*

I twisted over to the backseat, shifting a variety of things, *why on earth would I have a hat in the auto? I don't even wear hats,* off the back seat of the auto. The only other sounds were Edwin's sighs.

The afternoon sun was suddenly blocked, and I shifted around to see a figure with lank green feathers and non-existent lips staring at me through the window.

I gestured to the back door on the passenger side. The

figure scowled at me. What? Did she want me to get out and open the door for her? I wasn't her domestic.

She huffed and stomped around to the side door, plonking down in the seat behind Edwin.

"What the static is this thing?" asked Vivian, her nose wrinkled. "Are you sure you can call it an auto?"

"A loose definition," said Edwin.

I scanned the street as the weight of someone's gaze scraped my skin. I tried to follow the thread of energy that I could sense, but it unraveled even as I attempted to grip it.

"My creation, who I call Parawar, if you want to be respectful, has a metal body and wheels attached, so yes," I said, "it meets the definition of an auto."

"It's a hand cart with some magn." Vivian's pale skin glowed green. It should have complemented her hair.

"Have you slept?"

A shoulder lifted and dropped.

"Some."

A movement caught my eye, and I adjusted my screen so my back cameras could pick up a wider view. I peered. Nothing. I turned back to Vivian.

"When was the last time you ate? I'm serious." I frowned at the lines around her eyes. Vivian slumped down in her seat and her arms crossed in front of her. "For sparks sake. We're about to crawl around docks and ships. You aren't any good to us if you faint." I pushed the magn bead back into the auto and pulled out onto the street. We didn't have time for this. "Why did you want me to pick you up?" I asked. "Do you have some new information?"

Vivian responded by throwing up on herself.

"Static." I jerked the auto over to the side and before it had stopped, Edwin jumped out and pulled open the passenger door. Vivian vomited again, sadly missing him. He stepped up to her side and supported her, leaning out of the auto while she emptied her stomach of everything in it. Apparently, she had had something to eat, and it turned out to be quite a bit.

The smell of it hit me. My nose tried to retreat, but I took in the dark circles under Vivian's eyes, the green glow to her pale skin, the sheen on her forehead, and grimaced.

"We're going to have to go to Drudtia's," I said. I pulled some more magn. I threw out a healing web and let it settle over her body. Flickers of colors sparkled as it drew magn from me trying to heal her. My wristband vibrating as my magn quota tracker ticked up.

The volt was in it now.

"Shouldn't we take her home?" asked Edwin.

"This isn't natural and I'm not sure it's safe... secure her. We need to move."

He patted the back of Vivian's head and gently settled her back into her seat, double checking that she was fully locked in.

I hopped back in the auto, and as soon as Edwin was in, I sped towards Drudtia's house, arriving with a squeal of tires. Drudtia stood there at the bottom of the steps with her arms crossed.

"Great, you're here," I said. Edwin and I jumped out of the auto, and he pulled Vivian's door open. She was flopped forward against the seat restraint. I moved so I could peer around Edwin to see if she was breathing.

"Who's this?" asked Drudtia.

"Vivian, Lenora's apprentice."

Drudtia's face tightened. She pushed Edwin out of her way and reached out. She dragged her finger through the vomit and brought it to her own nose to sniff.

I gagged slightly.

"I think it's poison. Something with a magn kick," I said.

Drudtia took in Vivian, passed out in the passenger seat, covered in vomit.

"Do you know when she ate it or how much?"

"No. What do you think—"

"Give me a second." She glared at me, and I took a step back and raised my hands, but my eyes stayed on Vivian and the heat of her life dissipating back into the superverse with every breath she should have taken.

"We're going to plant her," said Drudtia.

"Can you do that with a biped?" I shifted from foot to foot.

"Of course you can. That's basic lifelore. Who taught you?" Drudtia unclipped the restraints.

"I'm more of a self-learner." I leaned against the auto and peered down at them.

Drudtia dragged Vivian's legs out and threaded one arm under her knees, the other behind her shoulders, and straightened.

"And you really think it will work?" I asked.

"I wouldn't suggest it if I didn't." said Drudtia, heading around the side of the house. "Just depends on how much damage there is."

"Can you tell what caused it?" I asked.

Edwin and I both kept a step behind her. Once we turned a corner around the house, a tree gathering appeared. There were five plantae. I wasn't sure what their genesis was, but they were beautiful, tall, four times my height. The winter had taken their leaves, but it had done nothing to reduce their beauty.

"A poison," said Drudtia. "I suspect it is all the way through her. Probably been consuming it for at least two to three days."

At the edge of the gathering, I reached out a hand to touch the closet tree, but snatched it back. I wanted their comfort, but not at the price of my arm.

"Right, well, if you don't need us—" I tore my eyes off the trees and took a few steps back.

"I do," said Drudtia as she swung Vivian around and put her feet in a pile of dirt between two trees.

"Right, with you so weak and frail."

It wasn't a good idea to be sarcastic to powerful beings, but at times, my mouth moved before my brain could kick in. Vines pushed up from the ground and wound up around Vivian's legs as the trees on either side leaned over tut-tutting.

"Oh, the poor thing," said one, "Fayrhare, help her out."

Fayrhare's branches reached out and created a support at Vivian's back and the tree's energy flow into her.

"She is on death's door the poor dear," said Fayrhare. "I might need your help, Thorkell."

Thorkell continued to tut tut as their branches reached out in front of Vivian until, between the two of them, and the vines, Vivian's entire weight was supported. My face softened as I watched the gentle energy of the trees flow. It was always beautiful, and I took a deep breath as I saw her diaphragm moving again.

"Alwyn," said Drudtia.

The sound pierced my eardrums, making me wince.

"You hollered." Alwyn appeared at the back door. His smile slipped away. He ran down the back steps to Vivian's side. "What happened?"

"Poison. Morgan and I need to work out what it is. Can you and Edwin work with Fayrhare and Thorkell to get her stabilized?"

"Yes, of course." Alwyn glanced over and past my shoulder. "Edwin, can you go to her other side?"

I twisted to find Edwin standing close behind me.

"Wait, so Edwin gets to hang with Fayrhare and Thorkell?" I smiled at the trees. "It's a pleasure to meet you, by the way." Branches that weren't holding up Vivian waved at me, but they didn't take their attention away from her. I focused on Drudtia, "and I get to... what?"

"Help me test the vomit. Get some samples." Drudtia created a beaker out of the air and threw it in my direction. Impressed, I reached up and caught it. "If I'm going to trace this stuff, I need to do some testing, and that testing is tricky and requires an assistant." The cool thin glass was fragile under my fingers, and I frowned at it.

"You want me to what?"

"Get some samples."

"Ewww."

Drudtia led the way, and I followed her back to the auto.

Ignoring the tracker on my wristband, I pulled on some magn to move Vivian's puke.

"No," Drudtia's voice sliced across the air. I jerked but stopped drawing it in. "It must be collected manually. Any magn could affect the results."

"And this is what you needed my help for?" I grumbled. I lifted my gaze skyward and exhaled. Right now, the only thing I wanted was a shower, to feel the hot water pushing off the stink that seemed to have settled into my fur.

"Hurry," Drudtia's voice making the bones in my head reverberate. "Some things fade, you know."

I ran my clean hand through my hair and tried not to breathe through my nose. I did not have time for this, but I dutifully dragged the beaker through the goop until it was three quarters full.

"Is that enough?"

"It'll do. Come on, stop wasting time." She turned towards the house, this time to a door under the porch. As I stepped through, I found myself at the top of a set of steep stairs, a vast room laid out in front of me.

9

On the road again

I read that there used to be beings that flew around in the air and had sex with the plantae. That seems pretty gross to me, but Lenora says that is why the plantae are all angry at us and if we don't want to end up maimed or dead, we need to be super respectful. I've never seen them actually do anything bad to anyone, so I am not sure if that is true. But I know they protected many people during the wars, so I am happy to be courteous. Except if they throw things at me.

Telling it like it is
History Assignment
Maxi, Apprentice of Chester

The lab itself was the kind that scientists dream of. Well, mad scientists who were a hundred percent sure that the council of five couldn't track them down. I might live on the edge. We all get our thrills from somewhere, but to have copper wires woven through the ceiling beams and live electricity dancing across them was a dangerous game.

Drudtia followed my gaze and turned back to me with a grin.

"Don't worry, I have it all buffered, so we can't take too much. Are you going to fall over if you get a light tap?"

I took the fact that she asked as a sign she was growing fond of me.

"No, I can earth."

"Excellent, I always forget you young ones are sensitive to it all."

I watched a small spark jump from the wire to her skin, like a brief hello. I don't think she even noticed.

"Go put some of that," she gestured to the beaker in my hand, "in a couple of test tubes and smear it on at least three of the dishes. I'm going to have to run some tests so we can see what's going on."

Edwin was probably already back on the porch with a glass of something tasty. My feet shuffled as I moved towards a long bench full of equipment. At the one end, there was a sink and a bunch of glass containers. I hoped there was some good hand wash.

Drudtia took her place in the middle of the room.

"What exactly are we testing for?" I asked. Despite many years of experimentation, I wasn't really into this biological stuff.

"I've a machine which can reverse engineer matter schemas."

"Of course, you do." I gazed at the electricity arcing above me. It was all about trust, wasn't it? Would Drudtia use her powers for good or evil? "So, is that what you do? Replicate healing potions?"

"The healing potions I made... make... for Lenora aren't the kind that can just be replicated."

I poured the contents of the beaker into a smaller glass container and smeared some glass dishes.

"Didn't you just say that your machine could replicate—"

"Only base materials. You can't replicate the effects of magn, so you make the base and then, if you want to add an extra kick, like to a healing potion..."

"Or a poison."

"Or a poison," Drudtia frowned. "I'd also like to point out that you're currently putting the vomit in a small beaker, and I'm pretty sure I told you to put it in a test tube."

Drudtia's hand appeared over my shoulder and picked up the narrow glass tube, handing it to me. I grabbed at it.

"Ouch." I stared down at my hand, now covered in flecks of glass and blood, and this is why I preferred working with metal.

"It's glass, you fool. Don't grip it so hard."

I ran my now bleeding hand under the tap and caught the packet of bandages that Drudtia threw at me with the other. I wrapped it up, which was difficult with one hand, and Drudtia didn't seem inclined to assist.

Once I had sealed it up, I carefully picked up one of the thin tubes with the fingers of my bandaged hand and used a spoon to scoop in some of the vomit.

"That's enough. Give it here."

Drudtia put the tube in a hole of a wooden frame and covered it in a lattice of wires. Reaching up, she pulled down an impressive amount of electricity and infused it into the wires. The wheel under the wooden frame moved and wires glowed different colors and electrical sparks jumped from them to the table. My mouth hung open as my eyes darted from color to color, but I closed it with a snap. I glanced at the front of the table where the real work was happening, my cheeks heating. A large sheet lay there with a rough sketch of a schema. I stepped closer, and I smiled at the increasingly clear schema. I glanced toward Drudtia to find her eyes down as she watched electricity dance across the sheet, her face drawn.

"Not good news?"

Drudtia exhaled and shook her head. "It isn't all bad." Drudtia took a deep breath and slowed the wheel down. Unfortunately, she must have lifted the magn field and some of the vomitus went flying and a bit hit my hand. A symbol of my life. I wrinkled my nose and ran the tap again.

"What does the schema mean?" I asked.

"It means that it is an alchemy-based poison and that we need the magn infused version of it to work out how to block it."

"I get that... but can't you use the stuff that is in... the other stuff..." I pointed, unnecessarily, at the goop over the bench.

Drudtia glared at me, and I took a step back and held up by hands.

"Just asking."

"The magn, what was there, is gone."

"Right, so can you track it?"

"Track it?"

"You know, seek its creator so we can track them down."

"I told you." Her face was grim. "I can't track things through the aether."

I sighed. Right no tracking. Just a lot of sitting.

"So how do we find out who did it, then?" I asked.

"Well, alchemy was used, and the magn has dissipated completely, so it would have to have been done nearby and only a Dean could do it."

"Someone like you, then?" I asked. Drudtia stared at me before turning back, frowning at the bench.

"I'm, of course, capable. However, I've no need for poisons. If I wanted you to be dead, you would be."

I believed her and followed her gaze to the bench. I gagged, but Drudtia saved me when she drew on more electricity and everything that wasn't in a glass container transformed into brief flashes of heat and light.

"I don't suppose you'd do that for me and my auto?"

Drudtia did in the end, after a few more humphs, clean up my auto and my clothes. We found Alwyn and Edwin, as predicted, sipping drinks on the porch. There was also cake.

"Glad to see you're both enjoying yourselves." Drudtia dropped into a chair and glared, but accepted the drink and cake that Alwyn handed her.

"How's Vivian?"

"She's stable. The trees are keeping her alive."

"How long for?" I asked.

"Some of the poison has made it into her blood." Alwyn sighed. "I've slowed it down… but it's very aggressive and they can only keep her stable for a couple of days."

I ran my fingers through my hair, pulling at it, hoping it would increase the blood flow to my brain.

"What happened to your hand?" asked Alwyn.

"Grippy grippy here seems to have forgotten how to hold a test tube," said Drudtia.

"Tia, the least you could do is heal our guest." Alwyn reached out and pulled the badly wrapped bandage off my hand. As he did so, I could feel my skin knitting itself together.

"Thanks." I smiled at him, and his kind eyes crinkled back at me.

"I suppose it could be an advanced Master, but I would consider it unlikely," said Drudtia. I sat back.

"Right, Dean, or almost Dean. There can't be that many in the area? From what I remember, the local ones weren't active and are unlikely to bestir themselves to do something as energetic as this. I'm not sure they're even awake anymore," I said.

"Lost in a good book, no doubt," said Alwyn.

Drudtia reached out and patted his hand. "The best place to be," she said.

Wonderful. I was so glad everyone was happy. Things also seemed to be turning up roses for me too. I doubted Vivian had reported me to the preservation office, Harriden would have been in contact in a second. And if she set up a fail-safe on event of death, I was pretty sure she would have told me about it.

I sipped my drink, now the real question was did I mean a run for it? Or focus on finding who was after me?

"How do we help Vivian?" asked Edwin.

I stifled a sigh.

"I'm sure Drudtia and Alwyn will be fine—"

"I need a sample of the poison," said Drudtia, "with the magn still active."

I stared back at her. "Right."

"So, I can create something to oppose it." Drudtia turned to Alwyn. "They really need everything spelled out to them here, don't they?"

"I'm sure they would have gotten to it." He smiled at me before standing up and heading inside. The plate in front of us was almost empty, and I didn't even remember eating the cake.

"I think we need to continue to follow the Uriah lead," I said. Not that I wanted to pursue any lead. But Drudtia was watching me intently. She said she couldn't track things through the aether, but did I trust her not to hunt me down if I bailed? No, I did not.

Edwin attempted to frown mid bite, which resulted in a lot of crumbs and a slightly confused expression on his face.

"Uriah?" he mumbled. "What does Vivian's poisoning have to do with him?"

"Someone's taken Uriah and Lenora. Someone's trying to kill us, and Vivian. It's hard to imagine it isn't connected."

Edwin and Drudtia both frowned.

"A possibility," said Edwin. "But I think..."

"Find the poison," said Drudtia. "That's the priority..."

They both stopped and glanced at each other.

I took a moment to gaze past the roof's edge at the stars beyond. They always seemed a little brighter in the winter. I wondered what it would be like? To travel between planets, skip through galaxies. Who knew? Maybe with enough time I might work it out.

"… there really are only a few days…" Drudtia tilted her head. "What was that?"

Thumps dragged my attention back, and the small smile that had found my face disappeared. I turned to find Alwyn standing in the front yard, holding two people with a couple of gliders on the ground in front of them.

"Do you know these two?" he asked.

I contemplated saying no. But I wasn't sure where Alwyn and Drudtia stood on killing trespassers.

"Lenora's apprentices," I dragged myself over to them. "What I want to know is how they knew where we were."

"You aren't the only one with Lenora's schedule," said Maxi, her eyes narrow and lips tight.

"And you're pretty easy to follow." Archie pulled himself free of Alwyn, who had loosened his grip, and stood up straight, pulling at his clothes.

"Why—"

"Hannah's missing," said Maxi. She spied the last bits of cake and headed towards it.

"Do you think she's been killed?" asked Edwin.

"Hey, save some for me," said Archie.

"I've been assuming that Hannah is involved in Vivian's poisoning," I said.

"You snooze you lose," said Maxi around a mouthful of cake.

"I didn't have time for dinner either, you know," said Archie.

Archie tried to take a bit of cake sticking out of Maxi's mouth, and Alwyn rushed inside.

"So, what was your plan?" I asked.

Maxi and Archie glanced at each other.

Maxi shrugged. "We're going to find out what happened."

"And find Lenora."

I rubbed at my face. "Someone has tried to kill Vivian, and Hannah is missing. You don't think that's concerning?"

Archie sniffed. "I think you underestimate how much we bring to the table."

Maxi rolled her eyes. "I know he is annoying, but he isn't wrong. We're very good."

"At what? Running around the city at night on bikes?" The last thing I needed was them poking their noses into this. If they were any good, then that just meant they were going to get into even more trouble. "You need somewhere to stay that is safe until we sort this out." I flashed a broad smile at Drudtia. "Archie and Maxi are way too young to be on their own, and I don't know who to trust…"

"Oh, no you don't,"

"You see—"

"Of course, we'll care for them," said Alwyn as he appeared with a plate and an even larger cake than before.

"What? Are you insane? What are we going to do with two apprentices?"

Drudtia's horror was understandable.

"I'm sure we can find something to keep them amused," said Alwyn.

Maxi and Archie appeared to be on a mission to see who

could eat the most cake the quickest. Like flesh beetles on a well-ripened corpse.

"Kids," Drudtia stared at me, "what am I going to do with a bunch of kids?"

"There are only two, and they can help, or you can be their teacher while Lenora is missing." I smiled at her, hoping my face was encouraging.

"And if she doesn't come back, what then? I don't—"

"Is Vivian alright?" asked Archie spraying crumbs.

"No, she isn't well. It's poison, but we have trees who have kindly agreed to stabilize her," said Alwyn.

"What's wrong with her—"

"Has she really been poisoned—"

"Do you think Hannah poisoned her—"

"Is she going to survive—"

"Yes, she's been poisoned. I don't know if it is Hannah, but it could be. The important thing is that right now we can't work out what the poison is without finding the original," I said.

"How do we do that?" asked Archie.

I strode over to the auto and leaned on it. Edwin's head was bowed as he stood close to Alwyn. Drudtia, who had Maxi and Archie on either side of her, stood there with her arms crossed and her lips flattened. If I wasn't getting out of this farce, at least she wasn't either. I smiled, waving at Drudtia, and she scowled.

Edwin nodded at whatever Alwyn was saying and wandered around, saying farewell to everyone.

I opened the door to my auto and collapsed in my seat,

firmly shutting the door behind me. If I closed my eyes, I could almost pretend that this was all over. I pushed the magnbead to start the auto and sat there, tapping my fingers on the wheel, watching Edwin give what appeared to be a farewell speech. I shifted in my seat and turned on the music. The quota tracker hummed in warning.

For volt's sake.

I took a deep breath and tried not to freak out that I was a hairbreadth from a death sentence.

"You alright?" asked Edwin as he slipped into his seat.

I waved my hand and steered the auto around. My eyes were struggling to stay focused and kept checking the quota tracker. How had I gotten so close? I took a deep breath and wrenched my focus back to driving as I left Drudtia's property.

"Hold on," I said. My lips tightened, and I could feel the grooves in my forehead deepening.

"What? Wh- ARGH."

The moon was up, so I ditched the lights, spinning the wheel and careering down a laneway. The wheels on Edwin's side lifted off the ground and his grip on the door tightened, his bones pushing against his skin.

I took a few more sharp turns and everything in the car that was loose thumping around in the back. Finally, I pulled into a deep driveway and turned off the auto.

"What—"

"We had a tail."

"So just camouflage the auto. I appreciate you're reckless—"

"I'm dangerously close to my quota threshold. Unless you suddenly have magn skills I wasn't aware of?"

He glared at me before exhaling and flopping his head back with a thud. The only sound in the car was our breathing, though Edwin must have been puffing the way he was going about it.

We waited for about half an hour before I pulled out of the driveway, flicking the lights on and driving at a sedate pace. Nothing to see here, just a friendly neighbor going out for a drive.

I weaved slowly through the backstreets. If someone was following us, they were good. I pulled into a parking space. We sat watching for movement.

"Ready?" I asked.

"For wasting our time wandering around a dangerous area at night hoping we find a person who has probably already gone, rather than searching for the poison that's killing Vivian—"

"Yes, yes, I get you don't think this is a good idea." I opened my door, stepping out into the icy night. The sharp air on my face was a pleasant contrast to the warmth provided by Alwyn's coat.

A few residences had their lights on, but the semi-industrial dockyard area apparently didn't encourage late night strolls. For a moment, I thought we were the only ones there, but movement caught my eye and I signaled to Edwin. We leaned against the side of a building, keeping still and in the shadows.

There weren't many lights, but I made out a small group

of people, sucking on some smoke tubes, heading down the path to the docks.

Static. There was no way we could approach them without being seen.

"How about that office building?" Edwin's breath brushed my ear, and I turned towards him.

"What?"

He pointed to a building that sat behind the main section of the docks. It was just tall enough that if we got onto the roof, we might have a clear view of the street and docks below. I nodded. Backtracking, we turned down a side street and found a fire door. I scanned the building, seeking a way in, without setting off any alarms.

Edwin opened the door.

Static. While the fire doors couldn't be warded, everyone shuddered at that memory, owners still took steps to protect their property.

I grabbed the back of his jacket and pulled him back onto the street.

"We have visual and weight wards here," I scanned for anything more complicated, but couldn't see it.

"So how do we—"

"With this." I grinned as I pulled out the electronic interrupter I had lifted from Wilbur's office.

"That'll let us in?" Edwin frowned.

"Well, no, but it'll stop the visual wards, and with a bit of footwork, we can avoid the weight ones. Watch." I stood next to the door, attached the interrupter to the building and pressed the button. Like a weight being lifted, if there had been eyes on us, they were gone.

Edwin appeared impressed, but it might have just been a trick of the light. Still, if we wanted to avoid any unpleasant breaking-in conversations, we were going to have to be agile. I stopped a few steps down from the first landing and assessed the situation.

"How are you feeling?" I asked, "Ready and able to do some scrambling over banisters?"

Edwin bounced in the shoes I had made. I wasn't sure how stable those shoes were, but they seemed to be holding up.

He stared down his nose at me, "I'll leverage myself off the banisters to avoid activating—"

"Got it," I rolled my eyes and hooked my foot on the inside of the first banister, pulling myself past the landing and swung back onto the stairs. Moving on up, I glanced behind me to check that Edwin didn't need help to find that he had practically sprung up to the next level. The advantage of long legs, I suppose.

As we climbed, I tried to loosen my throat and draw in more air without making too much noise.

"Do you need assistance?" asked Edwin, a slight smile on his face. I focused on the steps in front of me.

Several flights later, I teared up as the door to the roof came into view. I pushed it open and wobbled out on to the roof. My breath needed time to level out, so I positioned myself to peer over the side into the thick white blanket.

Voices drifted up, and I moved over to the side closest to where they were coming from, but they were muffled, and we were too high to make out what they were saying.

I exhaled heavily. "Right, this was a waste—" The weight of a hand on my arm made me jump.

"You know both your eyebrows are trying to meet in the middle of your face?" said Edwin.

"Presumably you wanted to say something other than criticize my facial features."

"If you could keep them a bit more stable, they'd be less distracting." Edwin shuffled closer to the edge of the roof. "I've something I want to show you."

He peered over the edge.

Then the fog cleared. No, that wasn't right. It didn't clear, but it didn't seem to matter anymore. I could see people rushing around and hear them.

"Only one tonight?"

"Yeah, we've been holding on to him, waiting for the preservers to calm down. They got into a tizz a few days ago."

"I heard about that. Sparkheads ruining it for everyone."

"You try to run a nice little smuggling business and they just have to stick their nose into it."

Chuckles rippled through the air.

"One is better than none. I heard another is about to die, so we need to get him to them."

A grunt floated through the air as one of them swung a long sack over his shoulder and carried it onto the barge. Others passed along boxes, and it wasn't long before the barge pulled away from the pier and headed inland.

I frowned at him. "How'd you do that?"

He frowned back at me. "I do have some skills."

"Not that I've seen so far."

He rolled his eyes. "You know you're not a very amiable person." He turned his attention back to the barge, slowly heading up the river.

"Right, so that's where we go," I said.

"What? On our magn carpet? Or can your auto swim?"

I shrugged.

"How hard can it be to borrow a boat?"

10

Boating and other adventures

Magnbeads are so efficient, allowing everyone, even those not great with the magn, to have access to technology. Which, of course, means they are highly regulated, to the point you can't even move one from one device to another, which I don't need to tell you is sssoooo annoying. I mean, why can't I move my magnbead from the auto to the glider? It would make life so much easier. Instead, if the glider bead runs out, I have to fill in a form to recharge it at a local council charging station, which takes ages! All so I won't, what? Suddenly start running around with plasma weaponry? As if I need a magnbead to run one of them.

Telling it like it is
History Assignment
Maxi, Apprentice of Chester

Edwin entertained himself by dropping a couple of floors at a time. I wasn't sure where this energy had come from or that I liked it, but I swung down behind him, jumping over the last landing and back into the street.

Two coatless figures stood huddled against the side of the building, examining my interrupter.

Spark no.

"What the actual spark are you two doing here?" I hissed. I glanced towards the docks but couldn't see anyone around. I hoped they were on the barge or were headed home.

Maxi held up the interrupter.

"This is seriously cool."

"It can't be legal, though." Archie frowned at me.

"It was Wilbur's and is useless now. But that doesn't answer my—"

"Can I keep it then?"

I frowned at her. "If you're caught with it, there will be questions."

"So, it's illegal," said Archie, his arms crossed.

I closed my eyes.

"Let's focus on why you're here, shall we?"

They stood there staring at me. I glanced at Edwin. His face was expressionless. Helpful.

The sound of the barge pulling away from the docks filled the space between us. I did not have time for this.

"We want to fix Vivian," said Maxi, kicking at the street.

"And find Lenora," said Archie.

I exhaled heavily. "I get it. But your being here isn't helping. How did you get here, anyway?"

I peered at them. Half of Archie's hair clips were gone, and Maxi's face had a number of marks that needed healing or would become bruises in the near future.

"In the boot of your car," said Archie.

"You like your corners, don't you?" asked Maxi. She winced as she touched her cheek.

"Well, I didn't know you were there, did I?" I growled. "How are you going to get back?"

The barge was getting fainter now. I suspected it had cleared the docks and was now heading up the river.

Archie shrugged. "We're coming with you."

Maxi crossed her arms. "I mean, I suppose we could do the hour hike back to Drudtia's on our own, in the dark, with people out to kill us."

I snorted. Good luck to anyone who tried to kill them. If I waited for Drudtia or Alwyn to get them, how long would that take?

My wristband caught my eye, in particular the magn quota. We were about to chase a barge up a river and having some magn would come in handy. I examined the two of them. This wasn't a mistake at all.

"Fine."

Edwin shifted and stared at me.

"Fine?"

"An extra set of hands never went astray. Come on, we need to get moving."

Archie and Maxi

With us

Going up river

Morgan

That's nice

Drudtia

I snorted. Good to know someone cared. I scanned the pier. The inevitable smell of the water, mud and dead fish thickening the air as we got closer. Smaller boats were tied up to the pier and the larger boats anchored further out.

The others trailed behind me like ducklings following their mother to the water. Not an image that warmed me.

"You've a boat?" Maxi's voice rose in surprise.

"I will."

"So you're going to steal one?" Archie's voice flicked high.

I glanced out of the corner of my eye to see Archie frowning at me.

"Borrow."

"What's the difference?" asked Maxi.

I ignored her.

The only sounds were a faint echo of the barge and the lap of the water on the riverbank. I cracked my neck and took a deep breath.

"Come on," I said, and pointed toward a boat docked on the pier.

"Do you even know how to drive that thing?" asked Archie.

"Anyone can drive one of these." As soon as we came along its side, I gestured for the others to get in.

No one moved. I ran my fingers through my hair.

"No one has to be here. The only reason *I* am is someone's trying to kill me." And I didn't trust Drudtia's claims that she couldn't track me down. Still no movement. "Alright, you have two options. Get on the front of the boat, or all three of you can start marching back to Drudtia's."

Three frowns flashed at me, but Maxi stepped forward onto the front of the boat and the others followed.

I pulled the dock line free and took a seat behind the wheel above the half-cabin. A puff of air left my lungs, and I pressed the fully charged magnbead into the on position. A small smile escaping as the motor purred.

"You should ... a clear run of it," said Edwin's slightly disembodied voice.

With Edwin making the fog transparent and I could see the full moon reflected in the dark waters. We left Duskburn behind and swished along the surface of the Blackdwell River, chasing the last sliver of sound from the barge. Edwin stood like a figurehead at the front of the boat, framed by the two smaller figures beside him. His tall, lean body was tilted forward, and strands of his long hair twisted in the air. There is something beautiful about being out on the water at night. Despite the day's events, my muscles relaxed, and I let my gaze take in the moon.

It was too bright for me to see the stars, but I admired how its silvery light did an excellent job of highlighting his body as it flew off the boat. I grabbed the wheel as the boat jerked to a stop. Two splashes followed.

"What the everlastings?" a deep voiced boomed out from the half cabin in front of me. The doors to the cabin pushed back and the nuzzle of a huge blaster held in a large hand appeared.

I jumped feet first into the shallow water. A sharp pain traveled up my leg and I fell forward, landing face down. The pain in my leg distracted me from the freezing river seeping into my clothes.

I kept still, considering my next move. The fog had thickened. I assumed Edwin was currently dealing with his own swim, and hopefully keeping the apprentices alive, which meant that the owner of the boat might not see me. Except he was also stranded on the sandbank.

A massive boom and a splash of water next to my head made me jump up. My once comfortable coat weighing me down as I attempted to drag my legs forward through the thigh high water, my breath rasping against my throat. I flexed the claws in my feet, hoping it would help me get some speed, but all it did was fill them with sand. A boom sounded, and a thunderous hail of water exploded next to me, closer than the first one.

Rethinking my strategy, I sank back down, allowing the icy water to close over me. My fingers pushed into the even colder sand, and I hauled myself forward. More explosions rippled through the water, but they felt further away. With a roll, I freed one ear into the chilly air above and was greeted with sounds of swearing and splashes. Another explosion and the sand under me trembled. The boat's engine revved. I rolled back under the water. The sandbank had dropped away, so I swam until the water became shallow again and I could stand. I drove myself up, my trembling arms relaxing, and shifted my weight into my legs. I checked the river but couldn't see anything but fog. Well, if I couldn't see him, then presumably, he couldn't see me. Bent over with the weight of my clothes, I waded out of the river.

A hand landed on my shoulder, sending me several feet into the air. I landed, facing a frowning and wet trio. Edwin's coat, like my own, was waterlogged. Archie and Maxi were saturated. Their lack of coats might have helped with the swim, but it was going to be a frosty night. Which probably meant they were going to be using their magn to keep themselves warm rather than help me.

"What the static was that?" asked Maxi.

"The owner must have been asleep in the cabin and woken up when I hit a sandbank."

"What'd you do that for?" asked Archie.

A flush warmed me, giving me some relief from the cold air turning my wet clothes even icier.

"If you're alive to complain about it..."

"Are you alright?" asked Edwin, sighing and running fingers through his hair, causing water to flick out across my face, and I winced. "Sorry." He took off his coat and tried to wring the water from it. "Well, how do we get back to Duskburn?" he asked.

I glanced back down the river. Even if the fog wasn't there, I suspected Duskburn's spires were long gone.

"How far do you think it's to the next town?" I asked. He shrugged.

I checked my wristband, and it reminded me I was close to death. The last thing I needed was the preservation service storming in to arrest me. Shivering, wet, and covered in river dirt was not what I wanted to be remembered for.

Static.

"I don't suppose you could be useful and see where we are on your band?" I asked, waving my hand at him. Edwin's eyes flicked towards my wrist, and he shook his head.

"Why—"

"I only have it as an ID chip holder."

"What? Seriously?" I turned to Maxi and Archie. "What about you? Can you map where we are?"

Their faces scrunched up, and they stared at me like I was the crazy one.

"We aren't meant to leave Duskburn unsupervised," said Archie, scowling at me.

"And we can't use magn unsupervised either," said Maxi.

"Which should be pretty obvious." Archie shook his head, trying to get some of the water out of his waterlogged hair.

"Hey" Three voices reverberated across the river.

"Shh." I peered around us. "We don't know what's out here."

"You shouted too," said Maxi.

"Yes, yes, but let's focus on getting out of here first. I'm here supervising, so if you could—"

"It doesn't work that way," said Maxi.

"It never worked that way," said Archie, scowling at me.

"Right, so how do we make it work, then?"

"You have to register as our supervisor." Maxi lifted her wristband and tapped it a few times. "Oh." She frowned.

"What?" I stepped forward and tried to peer at her wrist.

"It's not picking you up."

"What do you mean?"

"I mean, I searched for a supervisor nearby, but neither of you're registered as standing near me." She shrugged.

"Because we aren't scholars?" I asked, frowning.

"No, it doesn't even know you exist."

Static, of course it doesn't.

"That's not possible. Let me try," said Archie. He tapped his band a few times. "This isn't right." He scowled at it. "It must be broken."

I gazed at the path leading from the river to the higher bank. "Fix it later. Right now we need to keep moving, and head upriver."

"We don't know how far away the next town is," said Maxi.

"No, but there is a chance it could be closer than Duskburn."

"A bit of a gamble, isn't it?" asked Edwin. I glanced at him. Interesting that his chit wasn't showing either. Probably a secret preserver one. Maybe I should just get him to ping us out of here. They might not kill us. I examined the motley crew in front of me. But then again.

"You're all masters of your own destinies. But I'm getting off the bank."

Crunches in the dirt followed me. The trees mumbled hello but didn't seem to want to chat and, as always, the grass was silent.

I stood there, my clothes heavy and cold, my arms and legs already tired. I swallowed, trying to work out which way to go.

"Have you changed your mind?" asked Edwin.

"What?"

"About going to the next town."

I stared at him, wishing I could think of something witty to say but only having enough energy left to breathe.

"I'm just working out which way to go," I mumbled.

Maxi rolled her eyes. "The river is a clue."

I shook my head, more at myself than anything, and slogged along the path.

I didn't know how the others were coping, but my damp clothes swung into my skin with every step. My attention narrowed, focusing on breathing and my next step as I tried to control the coldness and to keep my body moving as the clattering of my teeth joined the night noises. The weight of Edwin's hand on my shoulder swung me towards him with a question on my face.

"You're freezing," he said.

"We-ll, a-r-en't y-ou?"

Archie and Maxi were shivering as well.

"It-s-ge-tt-in-a-bi-t-chil-ly," said Maxi, swinging her arms.

Archie's hair had lost enough water to stand up again, with flecks of ice forming on the tips. Whatever warmth the day had brought was long gone.

Heat surged through me, "what the—" it continued to flood me, drying my clothes, and heating the surface of my skin. I stared at Edwin. "Here I was thinking you couldn't use magn."

"I didn't." Edwin rested his hands on Archie and Maxi's shoulders, mist rising off their clothes. Their jaws stopped shaking.

"How then?"

"You don't need to use electromagn to do something as basic as warm yourself."

I blinked. Ludere? Who used that anymore? My fingertips already icing up, forced me to draw from within me whatever small flicker of ludere I could find. It felt eroded, like an old swing squeaking, but eventually the tips of my fingers tingled or trembled with exhaustion. It was hard to tell.

"Ludere?" Maxi sniffed. "Is that even still a thing?"

"What can it even do?"

"Warm us up, apparently." I frowned at them and then stared at Edwin. "Thank you."

Maxi and Archie mumbled thanks as well.

"So can we do it too?" asked Maxi.

"Archaic," said Archie.

"Not tracked," said Maxi. "We'd be free."

"Free to do what? Create chaos?" Archie frowned at her, and she shrugged. "Our society restrictions protect us."

"Enslaves."

Edwin cleared his throat. "Perhaps now is not the time—"

I slapped my hand on his arm. The trees hadn't been overly social so far, just providing a light background noise as they murmured to each other. Now, something other than us had their attention, and another ancient part of my brain woke up. Rusty, it needed a shot of fear to get started, but once it did, it had a habit of trampling over the rest of the brain. I wrestled with it, trying to listen to what it had to say while keeping control of my movements and breathing.

My claws extended, and Edwin closed the distance between us, the apprentices only a step behind.

"If anything comes at us, keep them out of the way,"

I whispered. My heart hitched. A shadow flickered in the corner of my eye. Was it real? Or was I descending into paranoia?

"Mill" his breath was hot against my ear, and the hair lifted on the back of my neck. I understood we didn't want to draw the attention of what was tracking us, but a bit of personal space wouldn't have gone astray. "I can feel it, an old mill, not far," he said.

Another flicker. I waved for Edwin to lead the way. Putting the apprentices between us, I brought up the rear. My legs were heavy, but I gestured for Edwin to keep going whenever he threw a frown in my direction. The outline of the mill came into view, filling the space, death in physical form. Even without Edwin's help, the fog seemed to lean away from the house, allowing enough moonlight for me to see the door. He pushed it open, but I pulled him back and, pushing the apprentices to the side, stepped through.

Careful not to set off my quota tracker, I tried to kick start some ludere. There was a reason the world used magn. Ludere seemed to take more from you than it gave sometimes. My feet dragged my body through the door. I tried not to breathe. The walls were covered in the fine dust of plantae victims. My hair stood on end as thousands of small flares of energy reminded me that the pain of their passing infused their deaths with a greater level of energy than normal, which in our sordid past had both enriched and poisoned all who ate them.

I checked the doors and windows of the small room to ensure they were secure and nothing unpleasant was hiding.

The others had stepped inside but had the good sense to keep their backs to a wall.

"How'd you feel it?" I asked Edwin, yawning. I had pretty good senses, but I hadn't been able to pick up on its presence until it was in sight. I secured the flimsy door and used a little of my ludere to reinforce it. Hopefully, it would slow down whatever was hunting, enough that we had a chance of defending ourselves anyway.

"The grass told me about an unpleasant place, and I realized what it was."

"The grass—"

Both apprentices screamed, and I jerked backwards, huge teeth flashing at my face. I dove to the ground, pulling out a knife I had managed to hold on to.

Static.

I scrambled up and faced an enormous black cat. His head level with mine, his body outweighing me significantly. The cat pulled back his lips, barring his impressive teeth.

Was this how I died? Not the ending I had imagined.

The cat roared, showing off those nice big fangs. The muscles in his haunches flexed, and it jumped, fangs out and claws flared. I tried to roll out of the way, but his massive claws swiped through my shoulder and out the other side.

I pushed myself up, facing it. He swung back towards me, preparing to jump. Puzzled, I touched my shoulder.

"An illusion?" asked Edwin. He was standing to the side with a hand on each of the apprentices. Unnecessarily, as they didn't seem eager to enter the fight. Nice to see they hadn't foolishly wasted their lives by throwing themselves in front of me. Still, pick up a stick or something?

"I don't think so." We watched as he attacked me again, passing through me harmlessly.

The cat growled.

"It doesn't seem to realize that it's immaterial," said Maxi.

"Yes, I can see that."

"Fascinating," said Archie as he shuffled up to the cat and ran his hand through his tail. He growled at him, flicking his tail, which, if it had been real, would have knocked him over. When that didn't work, he circled me, taking the occasional swipe, and growling every time his paw passed through.

"Hey cat," I said, "The attack thing doesn't seem to be working for you."

His growl deepened, and he opened his mouth, trying to rip my head off. It was a strange experience. I could only see glimpses of shadows, but if I turned my head, I could make out the shapes of teeth. Edwin came to stand next to me.

"Perhaps it's a specter?" said Edwin.

"That's my guess. A recent one. Which would certainly explain his confusion."

The cat's growl deepened. He took another swipe at me.

"I need to sit down," I said.

"What? Now we know it isn't a threat. We need to keep moving. This place is not a place to rest," said Archie.

"What if this is just a distraction?" asked Maxi, the color in her teal hide leaching out.

I found a bit of wall and slumped down onto the ground, letting my head fall back.

"Yes, well, I used ludere twice just now. Something I

haven't done in a long time. My arms and legs are jelly." I closed my eyes just as a paw attempted another swipe at my face. "Someone will have to keep watch for a bit while I recover."

A series of thumps next to me told me they had joined me on the floor, however, it was the rustle of a bag that had me opening my eyes.

"Soup?" Edwin held out a small travel flask. Where had this come from?

Maxi's and Archie's eyes lit up.

"I'm starving." Maxi rubbed her hands together.

"Do you have a portable maker?" asked Archie.

The cat's paw threw a shadow between us.

"Hey," I turned my attention back to the cat, "why are you just attacking me and not them?" I jerked my thumb towards the others before reaching out to take the flask. I cradled it. The coolness was expected but disappointing, and I forced myself to take a small sip.

"Here," Edwin reached out and warmed it for me.

"Thank you," I gulped at the fragrant brew. "I think I just need a few minutes' sleep and I'll be ready to go again."

"We can't stay long here."

"Less than thirty minutes, I promise." I finished my soup and handed the flask back to him.

"What if this specter becomes dangerous?" asked Archie.

Maxi stared at him. "You don't know how much it pains me to agree with you," she moved her stare to me, "but we can't assume it's safe—"

"I'll keep watch," said Edwin.

Maxi and Archie examined him.

"The warming with ludere thing was useful, but how much use are you in a fight?" asked Maxi.

"He has moves you've never even seen," I said. My eyes drooped. It didn't matter what was coming through that door. My body needed rest and nothing was going to stand in its way. "If anyone comes, just sic the cat on them." A huff of a laugh followed me as I slipped into unconsciousness.

I was true to my word, and less than half an hour later I opened my eyes.

Edwin was squatting in the middle of the room while Maxi and Archie sat next to the backpack, pulling things out of it and eating them. The clips that Archie used to control his hair were a thing of the past. The tawny fibers reached up and out almost as half as high as he was himself. Maxi's teal hide once more a vibrant color. The spikes in her hair were long gone, and the auburn waves framing her face, were twisted in bliss.

The trail food couldn't be that exciting, but from the expressions on their faces, they were dining in the finest restaurant in Duskburn. They kept pinching food from each other's hands. I watched, trying to work out how they did it. They *said* it wasn't aetherlocation, but so far, I couldn't work out how it could be anything else.

Edwin rocked on his feet but stayed squatting. What was he doing? Going to the toilet? Maybe he had an accident and was cleaning up? He crouched there, running his hands back and forth on the ground. His copper skin was glowing and pulsed with every movement of his hands. Channeling that much ludere and not passing out was scarily impressive. The cat sat next to him, watching, and occasionally reaching out to tap where Edwin's hand had been.

I must have shifted, as they both turned towards me at the same time.

"What are you doing?" I asked.

"Letting them rest."

I examined the mill. The pain and death had become muted. A strange skill to have.

Did the preservation service really assign him to me? He seemed to want to avoid their attention. But if he wasn't from the preservation service, why had Wilbur put us together? I glanced at the apprentices. First things first.

"Right. Shall we head off?"

"You'll not escape me," said the cat.

Sparks, now it could talk.

"You couldn't work on getting the cat to rest as well?" my hand waving towards the cat.

"His name is Jiro," said Edwin, and Jiro's lips curled back to show his fangs.

"Great, you've made friends with him." I pushed myself to my feet and pretended not to see Jiro's paw try to trip me. "Did you explain to *Jiro* that he's dead?" I would not win any personality contests today.

Edwin sighed and sat back on his heels, glaring at me.

"No, I hadn't—"

"Dead?" asked Jiro, his voice booming. He sprang to his feet and paced. "What do you mean, dead? I'm here before you, aren't I?"

"So, you missed that bit where your paw went straight through me?"

Jiro growled.

"I don't know what kind of device you're using that you can avoid my fangs and claws, but that doesn't mean I'm dead."

"So how did you get into this building, then? Or were you always able to stroll through walls?"

Jiro growled and rocked his head from side-to-side, pawing at the ground. He gave a roar and ran outside, through the wall. The ancient part of my brain broke out in a sweat when a howl of pain echoed through the night. I had to stop myself from running around the room in a panic or defecating.

"That wasn't very nice," said Archie.

"You have the grace of an anvil," said Maxi.

"What? Are you all friends with it now? You remember it tried to kill me, right?"

Edwin stood up from his crouch and moved towards his bag. "We need to leave here, and it's getting close to first light."

"I need coffee and food," said Maxi, standing up and peering down her nose at me.

"Sure, let's find you a pastry. Oh, and find Lenora and Uriah who are missing, in case you have forgotten why we're trekking through the countryside at night."

Archie scowled. "We aren't the ones who stopped for a nap."

"Fine, let's get moving then." I jumped up, stomping out of the mill, the sounds of everyone scrambling to pack up behind me. There was no sign of Jiro.

11

Tasty Treats

Some people refuse to create food. They quote an old saying about the circle of life or something, which is why they are referred to as lifers. From what I can tell, it means it is fine to be a murderer. The Preservation Service hunt them down, but I fear they are often not a priority. The thing I find disconcerting is you never know when they will see you as a food source. I wouldn't wish that kind of death on anyone, even a fellow apprentice.

The accurate representation of past events

History Assignment

Archie, Apprentice of Chester

The path along the tree line had disappeared, and we were forced to head down to the riverbank. I squinted, trying to make out any boats. While the sun dragged itself up, fog lay heavy across the water.

Between the sharp rocks on the edge and the overly soft sand of the river, it was hard going.

Maxi stomped up next to me.

"This is a mistake."

I glanced at her. She wasn't even puffing as she bounced along next to me as I labored through the sand.

"Everything in life's risky."

She grumbled. "I'm being serious. Something's watching us."

I considered her. While she usually had a sarcastic comment to offer, this felt different.

"Okay." I scanned the bank. We could probably head back up into the trees, but without a path, it was precarious. While the trees had left us alone for now, but I imagined that would change if we broke a branch.

Maxi drew in a sharp breath, jerking to a halt.

"Ah, the tasty treats have arrived."

I spun to find a mudwan emerging from the fog, heading towards us. A species of river people, this one was living up to every stereotype with carcasses of plantae draped over him. A sparking mudwan lifer, just what we needed. True that not every mudwan was a lifer and true that being a lifer didn't mean the person wanted to eat us, but the opening conversational gambit wasn't promising.

"Nope, no tasty treats here. Just travelers heading up-river," I said. I palmed a knife in each hand, but kept them slightly behind me.

"Travelers, treats, same thing," he smiled at me, and I was, again, confronted with teeth designed to tear at flesh.

"Hello friend," said Edwin, stepping between me and the mudwan, who hissed and took a step back.

"Friends? Hmm, I was promised treats, not friends." The mudwan tilted his head, peering at Edwin, but then he caught sight of Maxi and Archie and licked his lips.

"Treats? We have treats." Edwin reached into his pocket and pulled out some cheese. *How much food was he carrying?* "I'm willing to gift this to you for safe passage and information."

"Hmm cheese..." the mudwan flicked his eyes to us and back at the cheese. "I'm Crollyx." He reached out his hand and Edwin broke off a bit. Crollyx took his time. He lifted the cheese up to smell it and licked it before taking a bite. Never once taking his eyes off me and the apprentices. My stomach rolled.

"Have any boats come past recently?" asked Edwin.

Crollyx held out his hand for more cheese and Edwin broke off another piece, dropping it into the outstretched hand. Crollyx repeated his ritual of staring and licking.

"Yes." He swallowed a bite and gazed at the remaining cheese in Edwin's hand. "Hmm... I'm not sure it's enough of a gift, compared to the other treats you've brought me," his claw pointed at us.

Well, there was a big sparking surprise. I snorted.

"Just to be clear, we're not tasty nor treats," I said.

He snapped his hand into the water and pulled out a small,

scaled person and snapped their neck. I choked as bile rose in my throat.

"This sickens you? Not that long ago you too would've had to kill to survive."

"You know you don't have to, though, right?"

He shoved the rest of the person into his mouth, crunching down.

"Murderer," screamed Archie. He dived towards Crollyx and tried to grab the body of his victim out of his hands.

Oh static.

Crollyx struck Archie across the side of the head with enough force that he was thrown deeper into the river, disappearing beneath the water.

"Archie," screamed Maxi. She dove into the water, swimming towards where he had disappeared.

Crollyx grinned at me, barely swallowing before he was on me, and he wasn't a specter. I swung upward with my knives, but he ripped them out of my hands.

Crollyx's teeth snapped. I twisted to get out of the way, but a fang grazed my neck. *Sparking Sparkhead.* He grabbed hold of my arm but pushed back from me, smiling while he licked my blood off his mouth.

"Delicious."

I gripped the layers of skin at his neck, pulled him towards me, smashing my head into him with everything I had. He let go and staggered back, but didn't stop smiling. With a quick shake of his head, he was reaching for me again.

I tried to block his hold, but he pulled me further into the water. Even though the water was only up to my ankles, the sand was soft and I wobbled, trying to swing at his neck. I bent my knees, preparing to kick out, but stumbled backwards. A spray of hot flesh hitting my face. Crollyx disappeared under the water.

Sparks. I stepped back on to firmer sand, attempting to track the trail of ooze in the water. My gaze landed on Edwin and Maxi, standing waist deep in the river with Archie hanging between them.

"Is he..."

Edwin's face was grim. "He's breathing."

I wiped at the spray of blood on my face and gazed out over the river. The sun had burned off some of the fog and I could make out a barge full of people, and a sizable person standing on the side with a plasma blaster in her hands.

"Hey, you alright?" The holder of the blaster, dressed sensibly in a lightweight shirt and serviceable trousers, was a stark contrast to the rest of the crowd, who appeared to be decked out, ready to party, or considering the time of the morning, coming home from one.

"Good morning," said Edwin. "Your timely appearance has saved us from an unfortunate fate."

"Do you need a lift?" she asked. By her demeanor, I was assuming she was the skipper. She had thick tanned fur, a short tail and the slightly webbed feet of someone whose ancestors had evolved near water.

"If you don't mind," said Edwin, adjusting his grip on Archie. "We'd intended a nice long hike, but as you can see, things haven't gone according to plan."

I wasn't sure that we wanted to get on a boat with someone

who would so casually burn a hole in another person. After all, how did she know I wasn't the one trying to eat him?

We waded toward the boat while Edwin and Maxi kept Archie's head above the water. We had to swim the last part, and I slipped under the water to get some of the flesh and blood off me.

Archie was handed up first, and the skipper kneeled beside him, generously using her own magn to heal and clean him up.

The other party guests stood around, watching us, sipping their morning drinks.

Once on the boat, Maxi rushed to Archie's side. I stood there with my arms crossed, wondering what fresh disaster we had encountered. Edwin dried our clothing and smiled at the crowd.

"Thank you all for your fortuitous arrival."

"Yeah, that lifer was going to rip us to shreds," said Maxi.

"Murderer," said Archie, sitting up. He was pale, his hair a nest debris, but, if he could pass judgement, was probably feeling better.

I opened my mouth to remind them all that I had been about to take that mudwan out. One good kick and I would have taken him.

"You were in trouble there. Got to watch this area. There are a few lifers around. I'll report it, of course, but ..." said the skipper, shrugging.

"I'm surprised they're allowed to live so close to Duskburn," said Archie. Maxi helped him stand. He scratched his cheek, his eyes wide as he stared at the crowd of people gaping at him.

"Just goes to show that things need to change." The party goer had a hot drink in one of his hands and some sort of sweet pastry in the other.

"See?" said Maxi to Archie gesturing towards the speaker. "Everyone knows the system is broken."

The party goer smiled at Maxi.

"Glad to see the next generation is—"

"What brings you all out here this morning?" I asked, keeping my back close to the edge.

The party goer was beige from his hair, skin and eyes. He would have blended into the riverbank but for the vibrant lime green suit with a purple and red striped tie. I blinked as a bit of sun sneaked past a cloud and hit his suit. "We're heading up the river to a rally. Two of our most enlightened Deans are talking outside Evergreen university at lunchtime."

Everyone's bright eyes and matching bunting made my eyes flicker to the water. Evergreen, that was a few towns upriver. Perhaps we could at least hitch a ride until we can work out where our barge stopped. "If we can join you...at least until we can find a town with a barge going back to Duskburn?"

"Of course, you can join us all the way to Evergreen," he waved his hands at his fellow party members, and chairs and tables were shifted to make space for us. Edwin graciously accepted the arm of an attractive female and took a seat. Maxi appeared to have found her tribe and was peppering the speaker with questions. Archie stayed next to me, his arms crossed, pale but well enough to glare at them suspiciously.

"Do you need any healing?" the skipper asked me. I turned to her, warmed by the offer.

"No, thank you, that is very generous of you," I touched my neck. "But I think he only got in a minor scratch despite his best efforts."

"He should be hunted down and executed," said Archie.

"If that was Crollyx, he's a mean one. You're lucky you weren't any further in the water or he would have drowned you for sure." She holstered her blaster in a harness across her front.

Archie swallowed.

"We're not so easy to drown," I said.

Archie gave a weak smile.

I surveyed the party that was kicking off again and groaned. "Can I return the favor and assist you with anything?"

"I'm not up to" Archie peered up at me. "Please don't make me join the crazies." His stiff and uncompromising expression highlighted the pleading in his eyes.

In the end, Archie and I spent the entire trip with the skipper. Apparently, the group had booked her a few days ago, and they had left Duskburn at first light. According to the skipper, the party supported two Deans who were putting pressure on the council of five for a seat at the table. I suspected it was the same ones I had seen on the AV. It made sense to me, in a way, to give a voice to the younger and shorter lived.

After all, what did an immortal person know about the trials and tribulations of a finite life? I saw it every day in inequities, probably unintended, that came from their blanket application of rules. Still, they stopped the Deans from going insane and enslaving us all five hundred years ago. Presumably the Deans had learned their lesson and wouldn't do it again? I snorted, and the skipper turned to me, her head tilted.

"Just imaging the Deans in charge and full of goodness and light for everyone else."

"Exactly," muttered Archie.

The skipper gave a snort of laughter but shrugged. "Still...it's not exactly working, is it?"

Archie frowned at her and I could see he was going to argue, but I caught his eye and gave a jerk of my head. He shuffled back, his arms crossed, staring out over the side of the boat.

The skipper was right. It wasn't working. It was better than what had been before, but bad things were happening now too. The skipper had a maker in the boat's wheelhouse, so Archie made us some food. I had him make me another bowl of soup. I was hungry, but my stomach was still churning.

Edwin's efforts had meant we had dry clothes, but Archie's shirt and pants were stained and had several tears. His hair, with its usual vigor, was now thickened with twigs and algae.

"What's that?" asked Archie, pointing at the riverbank.

I squinted but couldn't see anything.

"What did you see?"

"Something moved."

I scanned as we putted along, trying to work out if it was just a tree branch or something worse, but nothing came into focus.

"Could be anything along here," said the skipper. "Not exactly on the top of the preserver's patrol list."

I huffed and turned my attention to the river in front of us. A stiff smile broke across my face when a town came into view. It had a large dock, and right there in the middle was our barge.

The party was in full swing.

"Edwin, Maxi we need to—"

"Ah," a short woman covered in fine silver scales checked me out, "another one of our intrepid travellers." She smiled at me, showing short sharp teeth that, in another era, might have gone for my throat. "You are so very brave to be out of the city that way." She shuddered.

"I've had little luck with cities, to be honest." I smiled politely back. "Edwin—"

"I'm not from Duskburn myself, but I believe that my life started when I got there." She knocked back the drink in her hand and raised it. It was immediately filled up by someone else, and she cradled the fresh drink to her chest. I peered at the cup in Edwin's hand.

"Nothing intoxicating, I promise." He flashed a smile. "Though I could probably do with a coffee if I was going to keep up with Gaeleath here."

She tittered.

"Morgan." Maxi's voice tapped my shoulder.

I shifted away from them and found Maxi with two younger members of the crowd. I assumed they were siblings. Both had a light red fur, flat faces and while they didn't have my own retractable claws, their nails were thick and would be extremely useful for tricky knots.

"Maxi." I smiled and nodded at her companions. "We need to get ready to—"

"You won't believe what they've been uncovering."

"Won't I?"

"Did you know that more people have died under the council's control than in the electromagn wars?"

"I wouldn't be surprised, though to be fair, the wars only lasted three years or so while the council has been ruling for over five hundred."

Maxi waved her hand dismissively.

"And it's only getting worse."

I sighed. I couldn't argue with that.

"Yes, there seems to have been an increase in executions in recent times."

"An increase? More a mass slaughter. Hi, I'm Hamon and this is my brother, Halueve."

"Hamon, Halueve," my smile was a bit more strained this time. "Nice to meet you, unfortunately we have to—"

"We can't just do nothing?"

"Hmm… I think you'll find that is what most people do."

"Well, I'm not going to do nothing." Maxi's hands were waving around. Drink free, fortunately.

I blinked at the double negative, but I got her point.

"Good for you." I glanced around and could see that Archie had made his way to the ramp off the boat and that Edwin was maneuvering himself in that direction. "Let's get off this boat and go do those things then, shall we?"

Maxi scowled.

"She can stay with us if she wants," said Hamon or Halueve, I'd already lost track of which was which.

"True, so what's it to be, Maxi? Stay here and party or get on the road and see what we can do?"

Maxi's scowl deepened, and she turned her back on me. But I could hear her saying goodbye to her new friends.

The skipper had put the ramp down after a few more thankyous and goodbyes we were on the pier.

My stomach had settled down, but my body's needs were making themselves known. I winced, my heavy bladder making me realize I had missed an opportunity while in the river. Admittedly, I had been busy not getting eaten. The cafés were opening, and the chatter of the plantae rose as the sun burned stronger and more rays fighting past the morning's clouds.

"What's all this noise?" asked Archie.

"How long has it been since you were outside a city?" I asked. "It's the plantae. The sun is up and so are they. Well, some of them are, you're lucky it isn't summer."

"I... yes, of course. It's been a while." Archie scratched his head. "I don't remember it being this loud."

"You just have to turn down the volume, give it a second," I said, scanning the street and saw a café which had a comfortable vibe. "I need coffee and a toilet, and not necessarily in that order."

I strode across the street and smiled at the two people behind the counter. The morning sun glinted in their pale fur, but their eyes were tired. I suspected they were the owners, as they had that air of regret I associated with people in retail. "Coffee and toast, please."

"What kind?"

"Big mugs of creamy coffee and raisin infused toast drowning in butter." I widened my smile, but he didn't raise his eyes from the maker in front of him. "Do any of you want anything?"

"Me too please," said Maxi.

"And me," said Archie.

"Two more slices of toast."

"And another coffee and toast too," said Edwin.

"Okay, four coffees and four slices of toast then."

I liked my soups, but sometimes I needed something heavier. Considering how much exercise I'd been doing lately, I probably could have smashed a plate full of pancakes. But deep down, I knew I would regret it, and there wasn't anywhere for me to lie down and have a quick nap to recover from over indulging.

A few clicks and Edwin was handed the mugs. I had the pile of toast, and a few less credits in my account.

The smell of sweet yeast and cinnamon wafted up, and my mouth watered. Maxi and Archie had found a table, and we followed, putting the coffee and toast down. I excused myself to use the facilities.

As my bladder emptied, I exhaled, my body relaxing for the first time that day. I sat there enjoying the solitude and locked the door. But thoughts of my toast growing cold soon had me weaving between half-awake people waiting to make an order and plonking down in the seat.

I picked up my mug of coffee.

"Hmm…. What's the toast like?"

Edwin glanced down at his own untouched plate. "I don't know, I—"

I picked up a piece of toast and bit down, ripping off a corner, the sweet raisins mixing with the saltiness of the butter making me hum. The melted fat slid down my chin and I tried to catch it with the back of my hand.

"Here." Edwin handed over a napkin.

I ignored it and used my hand to wipe my face.

"Shiny," said Maxi, smirking.

I took the napkin.

"Have you heard anything?" I leaned forward, keeping my voice soft.

"Like what?" asked Archie. His plate was clean without even a drip of butter left on it and he was eyeing Edwin's plate.

"Like a barge arriving and people moving through the town?"

Edwin shook his head. "No, but I did see a well-used road heading out of town, inland, not up the river."

"Only two roads?"

"As you enter the café, you can see the main road heads right out of the town following the direction of the river, but there is a less used one that goes left away from the river."

I rubbed my forehead and grimaced, picking up the napkin again.

"And you think…"

Edwin shrugged.

I finished my toast and sat back with my coffee in my hand and contemplated the two apprentices.

They stared back at me over their own cups.

Edwin checked his wristband and excused himself to use the facilities. I watched him make his way. For a person who said he only had a basic wristband, he certainly checked it a lot. Perhaps he needed to check in. With who though?

"Vivian told us you are under supervised service," said Maxi.

Archie's face twisted. "What did you do to deserve that?"

My forehead creased.

"Nothing. I was minding my own business, living amongst the plantae, when Wilbur came along and ruined it."

"So he put you under supervision?"

"I'd hoped..." I sighed. "To be honest, I just want to go home. But that doesn't seem like it's going to happen anytime soon." They watched me intently. "What I'm curious about is why Wilbur was hanging out with you. So much that he was drinking with Hannah and helping Vivian."

They glanced at each other, and Maxi nodded at Archie.

"We don't really know." Archie rested his elbows on the table and leaned forward over his clasped hands. "But there was something going on with him and Lenora."

"You think they were lovers?" I asked.

Archie's nose scrunched up. "Eww, no," he said, glancing at Maxi who shrugged. "No, I don't think so. They were close, but I didn't get that... vibe. Whatever they had going on, it wasn't always... friendly."

"He blew hot and cold, that's for sure. One moment he would want to be best buddies and then the next he would ignore you." Maxi smirked. "But if you were clever, you took advantage of the moments."

Archie nodded. "Yeah, if he was feeling like it, he would give you anything you asked for."

I stared at them. This did not sound like the cold and reserved Wilbur that I had met at all. Though it did explain some of his decision making. I had thought I was going to be caged up for the rest of my life for a while and then one day he just waltzed in and said it was time for me to be useful and so I went into supervised service. Of course, at first it was just answering queries and shuffling forms, but when I didn't run away, I had been given more responsibility. Each time after a visit from Wilbur.

"Do you think he was sick?" I asked.

They shook their heads. "Nah, it was just the way he was," said Archie.

Maxi nodded, "Lenora told us, she told us all to just wait and watch to see which way the wind was blowing before we engaged with him."

"But he was the head of research in the Preservation service, how…"

"He was good," said Maxi.

"Yeah, superb at chemistry stuff." Archie's face was wistful. "I learned more in thirty minutes with him on a good day than I learned from an entire year with Lenora."

"But he retired before he died, didn't he?"

Archie nodded. "Yeah, but I don't know if that would have stuck, or it was just a rage quit. Something had happened that he was pissed off about."

"He probably would have gotten over it, though."

"Who would have gotten over it?" asked Edwin, sitting down.

I noticed his toast was gone. I flicked a glance at Archie and Maxi but couldn't remember seeing either of them eat it. They were good.

"Wilbur, retiring," I said.

Edwin snorted. "Not likely."

"How would you know?" I asked.

Edwin sculled back the rest of his coffee. "Shall we get moving?"

My fingers drummed on the table.

"Where to? A potential road that may or may not lead tp where they disappeared to?" I shook my head. "I think we need to head back to Duskburn."

"What?" three voices whipped through the café, causing heads to turn in our direction.

Edwin closed his eyes, took a breath, and then opened them again to glare at me.

"We've been in the river, twice, crossed country, been shot at, almost eaten and attacked by a ghost, all because you wanted to find out what was happening..."

"Perhaps I'm just not sure I trust who I'm traveling with?"

"A little late for that, isn't it?"

The warehouse being blown up had thrown me for a loop and led to some poor choices. But that didn't mean I needed to keep making them. And maybe I could be forgiven for not having this confrontation earlier, but there was no way I could be that much of a fool to continue without knowing what part Edwin played in all of this.

"Who exactly are you, Edwin?"

12

Day on the farm

Eventually, the Deans who were hooking into the electricity realized they were less likely to go mad if they paired up with those well practiced with connecting with terra. I certainly wouldn't have made that mistake, it is basic science after all. Of course, they were already slightly mad, so this resulted in a lot of abductions and the creation of people farms. When the earth works started dying, they tried to take the healers, which is when the death toll really climbed.

The accurate representation of past events
History Assignment
Archie, Apprentice of Chester

The town was awake, and stores were opening, but despite wandering around and asking after the people from the barge, we got nothing but suspicious stares.

"We need some transport." I examined the main street and the only road leading inland. I hated to admit it, but Edwin was right. It appeared recently used.

"Over traipsing through the countryside already?" Edwin flashed a grin.

"Haha. Considering we don't know if this road is the right one, then yes, I think we need something."

Something real, something tangible and not these half-truths woven between the spaces in the words.

I glanced down the main street. A bank of public gliders caught my eye. What they were doing in a small town, I didn't know. Probably one of those decisions that seemed good on paper. I inspected them and brushed the dust off a handle.

"Awesome," said Maxi.

"Seriously?" Archie stood there, his arms crossed.

"Err…" Edwin hadn't spoken much since I had confronted him. He sat there, frowning at me. I was about to get up and walk away when Maxi, who had probably been motivated more by boredom than anything else, butted in.

"Wilbur stopped the preservation service from killing him."

"What?" I asked. "How do you know?"

"Wilbur visited us soon afterwards." She shrugged. "He told us he had just saved this person called Edwin from being killed and that he'd quit the service."

"Why were they going to kill him?" I turned to Edwin. "Why kill you?"

"Probably breached his magn quota," Archie snorted.

Edwin flushed.

"Is that it? Is that why you don't use magn?"

"Wilbur told me to not do anything to bring the preservation service's attention to me. I figured it was even more important after he died."

I rubbed at the grooves in my forehead.

"Wilbur would have seen hundreds of people killed for magn usage. Why not you?"

"It was after Nathaniel's death," said Maxi.

The air pushed out of me. Although they were my captors more than anything, even I had felt their grief at Nathaniel's execution.

"Right."

People were gathering near us peering at our empty plates, so we took the hint and left.

And now here we were, back on the street no real clue which way to go. Perhaps I was right the first time. Maybe we should just go back to Duskburn.

"They'll be waiting," said Edwin.

He was right. Duskburn most likely equaled death at the hands of whoever was trying to kill us. Not to mention Artemis, Grace, and a shell of a warehouse. Whichever choice I made it was probably going to be the wrong one. I turned my attention back to the gliders.

"Gliders? On an unsealed road?" asked Archie.

"Any other ideas?" I asked.

They glanced at each other and shrugged.

I had to sign them out under my name, as Edwin's

wristband couldn't even do that, and Maxi and Archie's were banned.

"How do you get banned from using a glider?" I asked.

"Technically, we aren't banned from using one, just from having one registered to us," said Archie, clambering onto his.

"Okay, why are you banned from registering for one?" I tilted my head, watching Maxi jump on to hers. "Both of you."

They squinted at each other and then stared at me. For the first time, I realized they were much more alike than I thought.

"We just lost a few, that's all."

"Forgot to return them."

"How many?" I asked.

Maxi shrugged and Archie wrestled the glider until he was sitting comfortably on it.

I stared at them.

He glanced up and sighed.

"About eight."

"Eight? How do you lose—"

"Not return"

"Not return eight?"

Maxi did a few turns. "The rack was several blocks away."

I shook my head, glad that I wasn't responsible for them, and I hoped that my credit wasn't about to be ruined.

"This is ridiculous," said Edwin, taking a seat. He was overlong for it, so his knees were pushed up above his waist. His glider jumped forward and jerked to a stop as Edwin pressed the brake button too firmly, leaving him wobbling.

I shifted mine around to face the way we wanted to go, jumped on, and then turned up the speed. Maxi's laughter weaved with Edwin's swearing, but we made our way out of town much to any onlookers amusement.

I still remember when the gliders were invented. About a hundred years ago, a scholar had worked out how to create a board that could hover off the ground. I had been envious for a while. It could have been a breakthrough. But no matter what she did, or any other scholar had done, the distance between the item and the ground had to be five centimeters. No more, no less. I examined the unpaved road underneath us and put the glider to maximum speed and held on. I stayed upright even as it threw me around. The undergrowth was still green but covered in the leaves shed by the trees. The trees didn't live closely together here so there was lots of space for the smaller hedges and plants to thrive. I wasn't sure if the trees did it deliberately or whether all the extraverts gathered together in a forest and some chose a more solitary existence. I'd have to ask Seb.

The sound of a crash and the plantae laughing made me jerk to a stop and I almost fell over myself. I swiveled to find Maxi and Archie had stopped and Edwin face down on the road, his glider in three separate pieces beside him.

"Static." I jumped off and legged it back to his unconscious body, exhaling when he groaned and rolled over. "Anything broken?"

"He's not very good at it, is he?" asked Maxi.

Archie flicked on his stand. "It's only a matter of time before were all on the ground."

Maxi snorted. "Speak for yourself."

Ignoring them, I crouched next to Edwin, who growled, which I assumed meant he was fine. The plantae were still chuckling but since we weren't dead, their interest drifted back to the sun and the sky.

"Sparking static." I put the pieces of the glider in a neat pile next to a small stone wall on the side of the road. I would need to report that later or I would lose some serious credits. Right now, however, we needed to keep moving. "Come on."

Edwin sat up. "Can you fix it?"

"Not here." Even with my full suite of tools it probably would be just easier to build a new one.

"I'm not sharing with him." Maxi scanned Edwin's long and now dusty body. "He'll completely throw off my balance."

"Agreed. It's going to be hard enough going as it is." Archie leaned against his glider with his arm crossed.

I glared at them. "What do you suggest? He just run along next to us?"

"Probably take the same amount of time." Archie snorted and Maxi grinned.

I grimaced. This whole thing was feeling more and more like a mistake.

Edwin rested his head on his knees.

I sat on the wall, my fingers catching on my hair as I pulled at it and contemplated dirt in front of me.

"Right." I took a breath and shuffled along the edge of road.

"What're you doing?" Edwin's shoes crunched the road beneath them as he moved next to me.

"Searching."

"For what?" asked Maxi.

"Evidence that someone had been through here." I kicked at the ground, turning over some of the loose rocks on the road.

"Why?"

"If we're going to continue, I need to know that it is for a reason. "

"What are you searching for?" Archie matched my steps and inspected the ground.

"A used smoke tube."

"From the workers on the dock?" Maxi joined us.

"Yes, they were all heavy users of something, and they didn't care about littering."

"Would they have time out here?"

"Maybe? If they did then it would help us know we are on the right path or not."

Archie and Maxi glanced at each other and shrugged. They both scanned the road, pulling tufts of grass aside and turning over rocks. Edwin slumped down on the low wall and left us to it.

I was tired and my eyes blurred as I tried to focus. I kept to the edges of the road hoping that they had maybe flicked one.

"Here." Maxi's voice was over loud with excitement. "A smoke tube."

"And there's another." Archie's voice was flush enthusiasm as well.

Glad they had so much energy after trekking through the countryside all night.

I dropped and rested on my heels, next to them examining the tubes. It was fresh.

"We're on the right path." I turned and glanced at Edwin. "Up to sharing?"

I waved off Maxi and Archie who continued to try and convince me why they shouldn't share. I wasn't going to ask them to anyway. But they obviously felt guilty about it as they kept finding more reason.

I tuned them out and got back on my glider, engaging the dual rider mode that made all their arguments unlikely. Sitting forward, I made room for Edwin to swing up behind.

I peered over to him, he still hadn't moved from the wall and was watching me with a glum expression on his face.

"Ready?"

Silently he dragged himself over and with great care climbed on. Tension oozed from him and I had to force my shoulders down from around my ears.

"Are you holding on?" I asked.

"Yes."

I peered down at his hand resting on the outside of my jacket.

"I meant the handles."

His sigh moved the hair on the back of my head, and he released me to take hold of the handles that had appeared on the side. I shifted forward.

"You focus on holding on and I'll keep the glider upright." I pushed in the magnbead and it started slowly. He was wobbling before we were even moving.

"Keep your eyes up," I said.

"What?" he shouted in my ear. My eyes crossed, but I turned my head so my voice would travel his way.

"Keep your eyes up and let your body relax." I increased the speed again. It didn't drown the comments from the other two, but there was a lot less wobble, and we were traveling faster than hiking or running. I watched Maxi and Archie speed ahead of us and for a moment, holding onto the bucking gliders, they were as relaxed and happy as I had ever seen them.

Their gliders jerked to a halt, and I pulled up beside them but didn't account for Edwin's extra weight. The glider crashed over on its side as soon as it lost momentum. I jumped clear.

"So..." Maxi pushed at the glider on top of Edwin with her foot.

"This might be too much to ask." Edwin twisted his upper body and glared at us. "But perhaps someone could lift the glider off me?"

"Nothing broken then?" I asked.

Edwin snorted.

Archie squatted down and tried to lift it up.

"Mumpf."

"Let me do it," said Maxi, grabbing one end and tilting it up. Unfortunately, that just shifted the weight of it onto Edwin's abdomen.

"Hey."

I grabbed the end digging into him and with the three of us we lifted it up and Edwin scrambled out from under it. The glider's base had a deep indent in it, to the point I wasn't sure it would work again. Another glider down. This was seriously going to damage my rating.

There were a few more trees now but a roof of a building was visible further along the road. I contemplated our gliders.

"We need to hide these," I said.

"Definitely."

"I certainly would, and quickly, too."

"Lots of traffic today."

The plantae had been quiet, perhaps turned off by our noise and erratic movements. I turned to see three medium-sized ulmus trees waving their branches at us.

"Traffic?" I asked.

The trees waved their branches.

"I'm pretty sure I said traffic."

"Oh, you definitely did."

"Apparently she's always been a terrible listener."

I rolled my eyes.

"I heard you. I was just wondering what kind of traffic."

They didn't have too many leaves left but what they did have they used for maximum rustle effect.

"Traffic is traffic."

"What about the word traffic isn't clear?"

"Maybe she isn't that bright after all?"

I stared at the sky, remembering that I only enjoyed hanging out with the plantae when I had nothing to do.

"Was it automobiles or people walking that caused the traffic?"

One of the branches flicked close to my head.

"Snappy, isn't she?"

"Would have thought she knew better."

"She's tired, don't you think she's tired—"

"I'm not tired. I'm just trying to work out if the people we were following came this way."

"You're chasing things now?"

"I thought things were chasing you?"

"Maybe it's both?"

I rubbed my head. They must have all germinated together.

I preferred the big forests where everyone was a different age and time, where it was rare for trees to grow up together and get tangled up in each other's thoughts.

Maxi strode up to one tree and peered up at their branches. "Love the knots in your trunk and branches. "

The trees waved at her.

"Thank you, sapling."

Maxi frowned. "I'm not a—"

"Thank you, Your Excellency." Archie gave a quick bow.

Maxi rolled her eyes. "Oh, for the love of—"

"We're excellent too."

"Extremely excellent."

"Yes, of course you are, beautiful, insightful, observant even." I took a risk and leaned against one of them, giving the tree a pat. "As you seem to know, I'm Morgan, but I haven't had the pleasure of meeting you."

"Humph."

"Now she thinks to charm us."

"Probably wants us to tell her about the transpo that woke us up."

I glared at the others. They had all opened their mouths, no doubt about to ask a stupid question, but they snapped them shut.

"Rude," I said.

"Extremely." The three voices blended together.

"Want me to have a word with them?" I asked.

The trees tutted.

"So clever."

"We can see what you're doing."

"No need to hurt them."

"I'm not aiming to hurt them. They just have a friend of ours."

"Well, you are on the right road."

"There was a transpo."

"It had people in it, and one was sleeping."

I smiled at them.

"Thank you." I transferred my weight back on to my feet as the branches of the tree patted my head. "I know it is hard this time of year, but I'm glad you were awake."

"It might be worthwhile hiding the gliders," said Edwin.

"Yes, perhaps…" I scanned the undergrowth. There were still some evergreen hedges just behind our chatty trees that could provide cover. I reached out and stroked one of their leaves. "Err, excuse me, would you mind…"

After a quick-ish conversation and getting permission, we maneuvered the gliders, so they weren't visible from the road.

"We'll protect them."

"Never fear, they will be here."

"Bodies will rain."

I blinked at the tree. "Err…"

"Sorry, might have gotten a bit carried away." The trees bobbed their branches and chuckled.

"Thanks, well we'd better…"

"Destroy our enemies?" asked Maxi.

"Perhaps it's time to call the preservers," said Archie.

"The only thing they'll do is arrest us."

They scowled at each other.

My eyebrows rose. "Let's just find out what is going on first. How's that?"

"And with no weapons, limited magn and just," Edwin

glanced at the apprentices, "us, how do you want to approach this?"

I ignored his excellent points.

"Let's focus on getting closer unseen. If we can get it, do some recon and find Uriah or Lenora—"

"Have you been watching too much AV?"

I shot him a glare but said goodbye to the trees and headed towards the buildings with their branches happily waving behind us.

"Can you tell if anyone is here?" I asked. Those smoke tubes were only a few hours old, so we couldn't be that far behind them.

Edwin shook his head and Maxi and Archie shuffled along behind us, occasionally muttering at each other.

"No, there's something fuzzy over the buildings."

"Fuzzy... great."

We found a position at the edge of the plantae. The ones closest to the buildings were firmly asleep, so we were careful not to wake them. Four large buildings were scattered across a clearing. I could sense some energy in one, but the rest of the place appeared deserted.

"Let's go," said Maxi.

"Are you insane?" asked Archie.

"What do you think we should do?" She sneered at him.

"Go back, call the preservation office, get help from the town, anything but attempt to—"

I ran. I was pretty sure I heard Edwin swear, but he and the apprentices joined me against the wall of a building.

No shouts, no security troopers.

I had chosen the building with some energy in it, so I carefully opened its side door and stepped into the dark.

The others entered and Edwin closed the door behind us but light snuck through broken boards on a window, giving me just enough illumination to make out the rectangular space we were in. A hallway. Probably not surprising, still, boarded up windows were never a good sign. I ran a hand over the rough concrete wall and rubbed at the concrete floor underneath me. Whatever warmth the sun had brought had not made it in here.

"We should move," I said, gesturing for Edwin to take the lead. I put the apprentices between us and brought up the rear.

"Do you think Lenora's here?" asked Archie.

"If we're lucky," I said.

"We're never that lucky," said Maxi.

We moved slowly with Edwin dragged his hand along the concrete, stopping to examine sections of the wall.

"What do you see?" I asked, my breath puffing out in front of me as its heat hit the icy air.

"I think…" Edwin flattened his palm against the wall but continued to drag it along. "I think there is a slightly different texture somewh…here."

He halted and turned to me. I stared at his hand, watching his fingers trace a section of the wall. I might have missed it, but he was right. There was a door there.

"Okay," I said, keeping my voice soft. "Here's what's going to happen. Edwin, you're going to open the door. Maxi and Archie I need you to stay back and out of the way until I say you can come in. Got that?"

Maxi and Archie's faces were sullen, but they nodded.

"Perhaps there is another way in?" said Edwin.

I shrugged. "Maybe, but the time we spend searching for it might be just as dangerous as going through that door." I stared at him until he nodded. "I'll go first."

A deep breath and a short wish that this not be added to my list of regrets and I positioned myself next to the opening of the door.

"Open it."

The creak was so loud we might as well have heralded our arrival with brass instruments. I jumped through, hoping to take whoever was on the other side by surprise. Instead, hot water dampened my eyes and heat rolled through my body.

People stripped of their ID bands and place in society, in various stages of consciousness, were spread across the floor of the room. I shuddered and swallowed against the sting of bile. How? How was this happening in this day and age?

I scanned the room for security forces but only saw emaciated bodies strapped to the ground. One of them shifted and stared at me.

"Er, hi, are you... Is this what I think it is?"

He closed his eyes. I sighed. I deserved that. It was a stupid question. A couple of other heads turned in my direction, but no one spoke.

If I was going to design a place to inspire doom and despair, then this would be it. In fact, it was almost too perfect. I shook my head as the lights above flickered. Not rhythmically, but with random twitches, whispering of pain. There were puddles of icy water on the floor and dirt dominated the corners. The cracks in the concrete gave no illusion to freedom, instead allowing trickles of water which dripped irregularly in a countermelody to the lights. The designers deserved a bonus.

"I'm Morgan." I kneeled next to him. "Do you know where we are?"

The others shuffled in behind me and stood there, faces grim as they took in the room. I probably would have preferred one of them to stay as a lookout in the hallway, but at least this way, I could monitor them. I turned my attention back to the man in front of me. Everything about him, arms, fingers, toes, was long and thin. Standing, he would reach over three meters tall, but only twenty centimeters wide.

"I appreciate you might not be feeling all that sociable. But there's the possibility that we can help you get out of here. Isn't that worth the risk?"

His eyes opened. "The only thing we've to risk is whether or not our death is painless."

"From here, it seems you've already lost that bet. Do you know where this place is?"

"How can you rescue us if you don't know where we are?" He turned his head away and exhaled. "I... was unconscious when I arrived, and I've lost track of time."

"What is this place?"

His head rocked back towards me. "What are you tourists? Did you just stumble into this place or what?"

"We're tracking a missing person."

"Tourists with a couple of kids. How's that going to help us?"

"What's your name?"

He shifted and inhaled deeply.

"Grollei."

"Hi Grollei," I smiled at him. "Do you know what's happening here?"

"Beyond the fact they are using us to control some serious electromagn flow..." He tried to frown, but his face was slow to respond. "I think... there might be magnets."

I frowned.

"Magnets, huh? Not what I was expecting." I shifted to sit closer to him. "I've more questions. I'll get you, and the others, out of here whether or not you answer them, but it'd be helpful if you did."

He opened his eyes, widening them on finding me so close.

"If you get us out, I'll answer any questions you want." His arm lifted a few millimeters off the floor, but a band of energy resisted any further movement.

"They're bound to the floor by magn shackles," said Edwin. He had kneeled next to another, attempting to lift her hand and studying the resistance.

I pulled at Grollei's arm but couldn't take it any higher. "Yes, I can feel that."

"Did you want me to remove them?" he asked. I rolled my eyes.

"Yes, Edwin, if you can remove these...." I frowned considering his predilection for using ludere. "Will you be able to handle all of them?" I asked.

"Yes, it just might take me a while."

He came over towards me and I reached for him, touching his wrist.

"Call out when it gets too much. It won't help any of them if you topple over before we're free of this."

He set to releasing Grollei. At first I couldn't sense anything but then I drew on my ludere and I could see a thousand lines of ludere spinning from Edwin's fingers, weaving through the magn binds, unravelling them. I would struggle to control that many lines of magn let alone the unpredictable ludere. But it worked and Grollei groaned in relief. I let him do a few stretches before I helped him sit up.

Maxi stood near the door, scowling and her arms crossed. I could feel the anger rolling off her even across the room. Archie followed Edwin, helping those that he freed sit up or roll over if that was all they were capable of. Some of them no longer capable of any movement.

"Do you know the names of the others?"

Grollei raised his arms over his head and his shoulders cracked.

"Some."

"Is there a Lenora or Uriah here?"

"I don't know of a Lenora but Uriah? Yeah," Grollei's face drooped. He pointed to a corner of the room. A small person with fine facial features lay there. His ears were long and narrow, and he didn't have any fur to speak of. I scanned his emaciated body and winced.

"Is he still alive?" I moved over and kneeled next to him. My fingers brushed his shoulder. I avoided putting any weight on them, afraid too much pressure might turn him to dust. "Uriah."

His eyes flicked open and faded lavender irises stared up at me.

"Uriah?" The edges of his lips turned upwards and mine mirrored the movement. "Well hello Uriah, we've been searching for you."

It took him a couple of swallows, but he pushed out, "Me? Why?"

"Well, technically Lenora was searching for you."

"Was?" Uriah's voice was a rough whisper.

"Edwin, do you have anything in that backpack of yours..." Archie, his face drawn and grim, came over, handing me a small flask.

"It's water."

"Thanks," I said. I took the lid off and sniffed. I lifted Uriah's head and helped him take a few swallows.

"Was?" asked Uriah, louder but still shaky.

"Yes, she went seeking you and hasn't come back. You haven't seen her here?"

I handed the flask back to Archie, who continued to wander around the room, helping those he could.

"No," Uriah frowned, gazing around the room like he excepted her to spring up.

Edwin started on Uriah's restraints.

"We know you've been missing for about four days. Have you been here the whole time?"

"Yes, yes, I think so." Uriah slowly shifted his free hand but he wasn't able to do more than drag it across the ground. "I was trying to work out where my friend was. He is, was, a heavy Haze user and then one day he disappeared." He frowned. "I asked at the Garden if anyone had seen him and then woke up here in time to see him die. Too weak for what they were asking of him."

The Garden, again. Not for the first time I wished Wilbur was alive. It might have been a short sparking conversation, but one I really wish I could have had.

"Grollei mentioned magnets?" I asked.

"Yes, giant magnets."

I breathed in through my nose.

"Here?"

"I don't know... if we travel, I'm unconscious for it."

"Right, let's focus on getting everyone out of this room first," I said.

Edwin had released five more and stumbled as he moved to the next one. Archie put a hand under his arm to stabilize him. "Edwin, do you think you can do it?" His sunken eyes stared at me, reminding me why electromagn was invented in the first place. I watched Edwin's now trembling hand reach for the binds on another person. "Static."

As I tuned into my own ludere I was humbled at the volume he was channeling and still standing. I couldn't contribute enough to make a difference, but I could feed him some strength. I put my hand on his shoulder, wobbling for a moment.

Maxi was staring at me. She hadn't moved or said a word since we entered the room. Her fists were clenched and her eyes shiny. I could sympathize with her. The first time I had seen what people were capable of doing to each other, I had thrown up.

I took a breath to stabilize. Edwin's hand stopped shaking, and he released the last two bound prisoners.

We now had nine people, thirteen, including myself, Edwin, Archie and Maxi. Six of them could stand on their own, but the other three, including Uriah, needed help. Wherever we were going, we weren't going fast.

I scanned the ones who could stand.

"Grollei, got enough juice in you to bring down a wall?"

13

Rock meets hard

It is all about control. Supervised service is something that the council reserves for people who don't respect the necessity of contributing to society. To the council's credit, they usually don't care what you do. It could be shuffling the council's papers, creating art or studying. But if you don't want to do anything... Well, the supervisor unit itself is living proof that there is a job for even the most incompetent, uncreative, and socially inept people. I suspect that is where one of my fellow apprentices will end up.

Telling it like it is
History Assignment
Maxi, Apprentice of Chester

Grollei and two others, hope energizing them, shuffled over to a light. Grollei easily touched the ceiling, found the power cord and pulled it down. He and the others drew the electricity into their bodies. They were tired, weak and could only store enough potential for one blast, so we had to get it right.

"That's it, that's all I can take," said Grollei and the other two nodded.

Disconnecting they shuffled toward the closest wall.

"No." My voice rang out. "Not that one."

"What does it matter—" asked Archie, peering at me like I was being difficult.

"It's a wall that leads to another room." I pointed to another side, which had a small, barred window near the top of it. "That one leads to the outside."

There were flushed faces, but they turned their attention to the outside wall.

Maxi snorted, she had spent most of the time watching while Archie had run around helping others. Her face was shut down, her body locked. Her eyes shifted from the people struggling to move and stared at me. I knew exactly how she felt but right now I needed her moving.

"We're going to need help getting everyone out of here."

"I..."

"They need you now. There'll be time to be angry later."

I stared at her, her eyes dropping as she nodded. And then she was moving, helping Archie move those too weak to shuffle away from the wall with the window.

It took three of them working together to collapse the earth under it.

"Everyone out," I shouted.

Those that could move grabbed those who couldn't and

Grollei, with more strength than I gave his frame credit for, stabilized the roof for those critical moments while we dragged everyone into the day, trying not to choke on the dust.

I did a quick check and then nodded at him. "Grollei, run."

He must have had a bit of magn left as he was able to shield himself as he dived from the room before the edges of the ceiling came crashing down.

I double checked again but by some miracle we had managed to get everyone out.

"Morgan." Edwin's voice was grim, and I turned to take in what had once been a collection of empty buildings.

Oh static, how many of them were there?

Transpos spewed forth security troopers and two sedans sat in the center of the compound. In hindsight, I probably should have scanned for an alarm system.

My eyes scanned the others, and then dropped to Uriah in my arms. I swallowed. *Spark it.* I was going to go down helping a handful of people who would die soon anyway.

"I need someone to take Uriah. Maxi?"

She jerked her head and came over to take Uriah from my arms.

"Here, let me help you," said Maxi, her face softening as she took Uriah's weight.

"Edwin, do you have enough to obscure this air, diffuse those energy blasters?"

His mouth thinned, but he nodded. There was a shuffling of people, until everyone was supported, with Edwin and me free to move.

I glanced down at my quota tracker, catching the tremor in my hands. *Sparking volt, just do it!*

There are two ways to use magn. Most people required access to an active electricity current which they could use directly or store for future use. With electricity so easily accessible, most didn't bother storing much, but everyone was taught how to save enough potential in their fat and muscles to get through the day. But there was another way, the way I learned. It was possible, with practice, to weave the inherent electricity in everything with ludere, on the go. The equivalent of handling a live wire. The electrical charge created a feedback loop which had to be perfect, or I would quickly lose consciousness. Useful when I used to have trouble sleeping as a kid.

I had nothing stored in me and didn't have time to go back and connect directly with the electricity in the building, but the electricity called to me. I weaved. Static built, Archie's hair gaining height, and once the energy reached its full potential, I pushed. Buildings exploded away from us, a shower of debris raining down on the security troopers. A grim smile stretched my mouth. *Thanks mum.*

Edwin jumped, "what the spark—"

I turned to him and smiled tightly, my wristband dancing against my skin. The bands shrill sounds even cut through the dust particles exploding in front of me. I spun to find two squads of troopers heading in our direction, firing blasters.

Static. Time to leave.

The dust stayed up in the air, giving us cover, but Edwin swayed on his feet.

Spark it.

I caught sight of the empty transpo only a few meters from us. But even a few meters would be too far, my gaze flicking towards the squads advancing on us.

Right, I needed to-

A large black cat appeared in the middle of the compound and roared. I blinked. *Jiro?*

"Kill them," Jiro's voice echoed across the compound.

A couple of troopers kept their blasters on us while the rest of the squad fanned preparing to meet this new threat. But if I had to guess, Jiro was probably on their side. Still a distraction was a distraction.

"Stay here," I said.

"Where're you going?" asked Maxi. Her teeth were clamped together and her breathing fast.

"We need the preservers," said Archie.

"Don't worry." My wristband continued to jump and squark. "They're coming. But right now, transport." I pointed at the transpo I had spotted earlier.

"Right on," said Maxi. "Let's blow this place... again." She tried to snigger. It lacked its usual cutting edge, but I was glad that she tried.

"That's the plan." I kept my head down and tried to keep automobiles and crates, *why are there always crates*?, between me and the ones shooting at Jiro, who seemed even bigger than before.

I climbed into the transpo, there was no magnbead but I didn't worry about it and just pumped it full of magn, turning it so it backed up towards where the others were trying to stay out of blaster range. More troopers swung their weapons in our direction.

Sparking static sparkheads.

I could hear scrambling as everyone got into the back, so I focused on the troopers now running towards us. I didn't have enough time to defuse or redirect the energy fired our way, so I remembered my training as a child and reached forward, drawing it in. What can I say? My mum liked to test my reflexes.

Rusty I could only draw in the ones coming directly at us and the rest hit the transpo, gouging its sides. Someone banged on the inside. It was time to get out of here.

I threw magn into it, heading towards the unpaved road back to town. A wall of sound slammed into me followed by a sea of overwhelming rage. I turned and saw two people scrambling out of a sedan. My eyes blurred as the emotion and sound rolled over me and a shiver went down my spine. I gritted my teeth and threw a blast of magn in their direction. The pressure of whatever they were throwing at me lessened and I refocused on driving, but not in time to stop it from going off the narrow track. We skidded, and I wrenched at the wheel, trying to get it under control. I took my foot off the accelerator, resting my foot on the brake, turning into a skid until the tires gripped the ground again. The security troopers were jumping back into their transpos and even the ones on foot were close to catching up.

"Hold on," I shouted into the back.

"What do you think we've been doing?" echoed back. They didn't sound happy. I let the rest of the world fade away and focused on keeping the transpo going at full speed along the narrow unpaved road. We were almost half way back to town when I slammed on the breaks.

Spark!

I could hear thumps from the back. A fleet of automobiles covered the road, and my breath rasped like razor blades in my throat. My death had arrived.

The Preservation Service was here.

"Morgan Anastasi," said a sharp voice. My eardrums quivered in remembered pain.

"Officer Harriden, fancy meeting you here." I took in the person striding towards me. There was no doubt Harriden was well-proportioned and extremely fit. His short hair highlighted the structure of his face and the tight shirt the muscles covering his body. Such a waste.

"I might not have the skill of foresight yet, but something told me it was worthwhile monitoring you and here we are." The lack of expression making his face even more striking.

"I'm so glad you did. We were in a terrible situation, and it was the only way I could think of calling for help," I said. "It was just awful, Officer Harriden." I kept my voice soft, tilting my head and maintaining eye contact. His eyes dropped to the blaster holes in the side of the transpo.

"That's going to be your story?"

"Well, it's a pretty good story." I kept up the eye contact and my body turned towards him.

"It's true Officer Harriden," said Archie panting. He halted, standing up straight at my side.

Harriden frowned at him. "What's true?"

"That we were in a dire situation. I kept telling Morgan that we needed you." He blushed. "I mean, need the preservation service."

"Regardless, she's breached quota and will have to come in for judgement."

"See, Archie, your great preservation service doesn't care." Maxi leaned against the transpo, glaring at Harriden.

"Great," I let my teeth flash at Harriden, "In the meantime, I've a load of people who have been tortured and need medical attention. There's also a compound of security troopers complicit in a people farm back up the road." I peered at the burn holes in the transpo's side. "So, you know, priorities."

He glared at me, but called for medics and headed off towards the compound at full speed, leaving a few guards behind.

"Probably burned it all down," said Edwin joining us. He was pale, had a few bruises but was steady on his feet.

"What?"

"The compound, if they don't have time to clean it, they'll burn it down."

I scowled. "Yes, probably." I examined him. "How are you? Do you need the medic?"

"No, I'm better now. Those bonds just took more out of me than I thought possible."

I rubbed my face.

"What I don't understand is how they were getting away with it. I mean, the full force of the service came down on me as soon as I hit my quota. If they are doing something big enough to need terra's earthing it..."

"Grollei talked about magnets," said Edwin. "Maybe

because the magn is passive, rather than active, it isn't registering?"

"Or they're being paid off," said Maxi. The guards glared at her.

"The preservation service isn't for sale," said Archie.

"Everything's for sale." Maxi sighed.

A swooshing sound pulled my gaze to the sky. Two airships, with their small cabins nested under the overly large balloons, landed and over twenty medics headed towards the transpo in a trot. Maybe Harriden's face wasn't wasted on him after all.

Stretchers appeared and everyone was loaded up though there wasn't one long enough for Grollei. One of the medics even came to check on me.

"Morgan Anastasi?" asked the medic. I smiled at her.

"Yes, I'm—"

"Any injuries I should know about?"

"Err…no all good here. I mean, I'm tired and hungry but—"

"When was the last time you ate?" I stared at her. "I'll make a note that you should be fed as soon as possible. And what about you?" The medic turned to Edwin.

"I don't need medical assistance."

"Do you know your name?"

Edwin's eyebrows rose. "Err… yes, it's… Edwin."

"You don't seem sure," said the medic.

"I'm sure it's Edwin."

"Edwin what?"

"Err… just Edwin."

The medic rolled her eyes.

"Helpful." She gazed down at Maxi and Archie, who had taken a stand on either side of me. "What about you two?"

"We're fine."

"Fine."

The medic frowned.

"Where's your scholar?"

"Morgan's supervising us while we find her."

The medic checked her band. "I don't see her as registered."

"We've been busy."

"Right, well, I'll update this. There." She tapped at her screen. She spun around and trudged back to the others, tapping the information into her wristband. We watched the ill and injured get loaded into the airships and then it was just the four of us, and our guards. They took our ID chits. I wanted to grab mine back, but just smiled and let them replace it with the preservation tracker. It was a rather ingenious idea, if I do say so myself. Since IDs couldn't be tracked unless they exceeded the quota, they created IDs with zero usage limits. They couldn't actually track the wearer, of course, something I was very grateful for, but eventually people get hungry and all it took was one moment and the magn flare was lit. My fingers tracked my band. The unfamiliar feel of a preserver tracking chip causing a chill.

"Get in." One of them opened the back door of an auto while the others stood, straight faced, staring at us.

"Right, in the auto then." I dropped into the back seat and turned to see the others being led to a different auto. I hesitated, peering down the road, but couldn't see any evidence of Harriden. The guard securing my door frowned at me, and

I took a breath, dropping my head back on the seat and closed my eyes. Vivian's face appeared.

Static.

As I was driven along, I gazed out of the window, watching the countryside go by and Duskburn come into view. I fidgeted, pulling at one of my claws with my teeth. With the timer on Vivian and Lenora still missing, I hoped Harriden would take the case more seriously now. That did however leave the matter of my own fate still undecided.

They took us back to the Preservation Service headquarters, leaving us in a room with an oversized lock on the door. I flopped down in a chair but stood up again, stalking the edges of the room. The table was fixed to the floor and the only other things in the room were eight chairs distributed evenly around it.

"You've only yourself to blame," said Edwin. I gave him a non-verbal response. He took a seat in one chair, stretched out his legs in front of him. "So, how long do you think we will be here?"

"Until they execute us." Maxi sat in a chair next to him.

"We saved all those people," said Archie, choosing a chair as far away from the others as he could.

"You're a fool if you think that mattes."

"Regardless," I said, gripping the back of a seat. "My magn ball is broken at the moment, so we won't know until they tell us. Though I suspect Harriden will leave us stewing here until he has everything else sorted." I flopped down into a chair, groaning as the night's entertainment caught up with me.

"Is the quota thing really that big a deal?" asked Edwin.

Maxi and Archie swung towards him.

"Of course it is. Surely you know that?" asked Maxi. "It's pretty much why the preservation service exists."

"Who was your teacher?" asked Archie.

"Yes, the quota thing is important." I sighed. "Breaching is punishable by—"

"Death."

I spun the chair and saw Amiel leaning in the room's doorway. His sandy hair had a few more streaks of white, but his face hadn't changed.

He examined me. "Morgan, you look like static."

I laughed. "Yeah, I know. I need a shower, some loud music and a solid night's sleep, in that order."

"Well, considering you're facing a death sentence, you might need to put that off for a bit."

I knew that there was a high chance of this all going terribly wrong, but two things were stopping me from freaking out. One I had just saved nine people from being batteries in a people farm which was no small thing and two-

"Are you even listening to me, Morgan?" asked Amiel.

I blinked at him. "Sorry, the prospect of my death distracted me. Forgive me?" I pushed myself up from the chair and paced. "I went over my quota to save people being used in the farm and therefore I evoke the defense of saving others from the quota charge." Which is what I should have said to Harriden in the first place.

"You went five times over your quota," he jiggled his head. "They're having a hard time understanding how that's even possible."

Volt hadn't had time to think and couldn't have changed that, anyway.

"I was already at my max before I was captured. I had to drain the whole site dry to stop the attacks and get them out of there."

Amiel didn't take his eyes off me. "When they searched the compound, they found no evidence of any major electricity drain." He shifted his weight forward and tilted his head.

"I think it's obvious from the blowing up of the building that I used a lot of electricity." I held both my hands out in front of me. Nothing to see here.

"Hmm... yes the fight, there appears to be several buildings missing from the compound, I'm assuming that is your doing?"

"The captives collapsed a wall but ...er, yes, I took care of the other buildings. Hence the over quota situation we find ourselves in."

"That's very impressive, Morgan, but not necessarily helpful."

Edwin was watching Amiel with a puzzled expression. Edwin being confused wasn't anything new, so I tried not to let it distract me from the problem at hand.

"I've made my choice. I can live with it." I laughed, "Well, I suppose I won't be, will I?"

"You're not dying today," said Archie, frowning at me. I didn't glance at him not wanting him to see the pity for him on my face.

The door opened, and Harriden was in the building.

"So, Morgan, and I believe it's Edwin… Maxi and Archie apprentices of Chester…?" asked Harriden.

"Yes, that's right," said Edwin. Maxi and Archie just nodded.

Harriden examined Edwin. "Family or affiliation?"

"Edwin, affiliated with Morgan Anastasi."

"Wait what?" I stepped forward. I mean, I know we shared the same accommodation but affiliated implied we were working together, or more.

Harriden held Edwin's ID chit in his hand, studying it. My eye twitched as it glinted. *What the static?*

"So, Edwin," said Harriden, replacing the tracker with Edwin's ID. "How do you know this grifter here?"

"Wilbur Dawkins…. connected us."

"Did he now?" he squinted at Edwin and then shrugged. "Well, not for long now."

Maxi continued to impersonate a statue, but Archie sat up straight in his chair. I caught his eye and shook my head.

Amiel cleared his throat.

"Harriden, remember the case," said Amiel.

Harriden stifled a sigh and came over to return my ID chip. "The case," he sighed again.

"What case?" I asked, running my fingertips across the ID's surface, the familiarity comforting.

Harriden thumped into a chair and rubbed a hand across his comely face. "Morgan, how'd you know the ID was fake?"

My face scrunched. "ID?"

"Yes, I've a fake ID identified by a warrant officer, Morgan Anastasi, which passed every test we can throw at it. Except, when we send it back to central, they confirm it as a fake. So how did you know?"

Edwin's ID glinted in my peripheral vision.

"I don't know, really." I shrugged and spread out my hands. "It just lacked… substance."

"Impressive." Amiel smiled at me. It was without warmth but I made myself smile back at him.

"Well, it's useful anyway." Harriden tapped the desk in front of him. "The reality is we don't have anyone else on the ground who can spot them. Which makes locating them difficult."

I would start with Emanuel myself. "So, correct me if I'm wrong," I stopped pacing. "What I'm hearing is that you need me?" I tilted my head towards the ceiling with my thinking face on. "It would be hard for me to assist if I was dead. Just saying."

Harriden's fingers drummed harder.

"It would be wrong for you to be executed anyway," said Archie. I stifled my sigh. I suppose it was too much to ask for him to keep his mouth shut. I was just grateful Maxi hadn't started in.

Amiel sat down next to him.

"When Morgan exceeded her quote of magn, she breached, as I'm sure you know, one of our most fundamental laws. A breach which carries the consequence of death."

"But she did it to save everyone."

"Which is the reason the sentence wasn't carried out straight away," said Harriden.

"Like it usually is," said Amiel, his face grim.

"What next?" asked Edwin.

"A fake ID has been made. We've shown this new fake ID to other warrant officers, and they can't pick up the... lack of substance." Harriden peered at me. "What's concerning is that at the same time these new fakes are found, which can only be identified by Morgan, she also discovers a people farm —"

"If you'd investigated Lenora's disappearance, it would've been you. Did you know that her apprentice Vivian has been poisoned—"

"There's also the question of how you freed the others, as I understand council grade restraints were used on the victims and there is no known way to break them." Harriden sat back in his chair, gripping its arms. "Suddenly we have multiple events, and only one person who seems to have the unique skill to...uncover...it."

"What are you suggesting?" I asked.

He shrugged. "I don't believe in coincidences."

I stared down at him and shrugged. "I can't help what you believe."

He scowled.

"We need your help," said Amiel. "In your official capacity as a warrant officer, of course."

"And then what? I help you and at the end, I'm still executed."

I tried to moisten my mouth. Did they honestly expect me to play the good little soldier and then what? Put me to death as soon as it was over?

"Well, we could always just go straight to your execution." Harriden sneered.

"You could." I leaned against the wall, extending and retracting my claws. I wished I was in an era where ripping someone's head off for being irritating was a reasonable response.

Amiel shot a glance at Harriden, who sucked in his lips like he had eaten something bitter.

"I've been authorized," Harriden cast a sharp stare at Amiel, who nodded. Harriden took a breath and refocused his attention on me. "I've been authorized to suspend your sentence in recognition of efforts in saving other citizens, and for your future assistance in the fraud investigation."

Not that I wanted people ripping my head off, I just wanted to rip off other people's. Was that too much to ask?

"For how long?" I asked.

"The suspension or the investigation?" he asked.

"Both."

"The suspension is indefinite unless you breach the quota a second time, at which point you will be executed without further delay."

My mouth was too dry to swallow. "And the investigation?"

"For as long as it takes," he said.

I snorted, and he frowned.

"Fine, until we identify who is making them or it is no longer an active investigation."

Despite the death threat hanging over me, it wasn't that bad a deal.

"Will I still be required to complete supervised service?"

"Depends on how the investigation goes."

This was it. Save the kid and then get out of this place.

"I want it in a verified agreement, and I want it registered with the council of five." Insisting a copy was sent to the council wouldn't stop them killing me, after all accidents happen, but it made me feel better.

He snorted, "sure."

His head would have been the first to go.

"What about us?" asked Maxi.

Amiel and Harriden examined the two apprentices.

"We'll organize a new scholar for you."

"What about Vivian?" asked Maxi.

"Vivian?" Amiel turned towards her.

"The other apprentice, the one who was poisoned..." said Archie. It hurt to gaze into his eyes.

Amiel and Harriden glanced at each other.

"We'll investigate it, of course," said Amiel.

"After you find the fake IDs," said Maxi a cruel twist to her mouth.

"Fake IDs cut to the heart of our society—"

"She'll die if we don't find the poison in the next day or two."

Amiel turned towards Maxi.

"Let's settle down, everyone. There's work to be done." Amiel turned to Edwin. "Edwin, thank you for ... you're free to go." Amiel smiled at him and strode towards the door.

"What about my affiliation? I'm registered as working with Morgan."

He was?

Amiel paused. "Registered?" He glanced at Harriden.

"And part of that employment is assisting her in whatever way necessary."

My assistant?

Harriden tapped at his wristband. "He's right, Master Amiel. The terms of his service are as an assistant to Morgan Anastasi."

I had certainly never seen any *assisting*.

"And what about us?" asked Maxi.

Harriden and Amiel exchanged a glance.

"As I said, we'll assign you—"

"Morgan has already been assigned," said Archie.

"She's not a scholar," said Amiel frowning down at him.

"True," Archie shrugged. "But she has been assigned as responsible for us until Lenora is found."

Harriden was punching at the screen on his device.

"He's right. How did that happen?" he tapped the device a few more times. "It appears the medic did it."

"She can't supervise apprentices—"

"It won't be a problem. They can stay with Drudtia and Alwyn while I'm working."

I blinked. I was pretty sure that was my voice.

Amiel glanced at Harriden. "Drudtia? Why do I know that name?"

Harriden snorted. "She's a friend of the council, but I don't—"

"When does this case start?" I yawned. What I wouldn't give for a shower. "I'm only asking as we've all been on the go for a day, not to mention in grave need of a cleaning and change of clothes."

Harriden's lips twisted, but Amiel nodded.

"You'll be escorted home and I trust that you will report back here in the morning?"

I nodded. I wasn't foolish enough to do a runner. If I was, I would have attempted it a long time ago.

"And my day job?"

"Harriden, let them know she's been reassigned," said Amiel.

The appropriate paperwork was signed and Harriden and I exchanged connector codes.

"Great," I smiled at the room. "So... about home."

It took another hour to share the details of the attack on the warehouse and register Drudtia and Alwyn's as their temporary residence.

Harriden frowned, I suspected he would be inspecting this afternoon. He was not going to be happy to find out how much damage had been done under the local preservation service's noses.

"Okay," I gave the room a bit of a smile. "Great... next, we need a lift."

We were delegated to a preservation officer with a service auto who ended up driving around the docks for half an hour.

"There it is." I tapped the officer on the shoulder and pointed towards my gray sedan a block away. He pulled over, and we scrambled out. I snatched my hand back as the service auto screeched off.

"How could you forget where the auto was parked?" asked Maxi.

"Blame Edwin, he's the one meant to be *assisting* me."

"Can I sit up the front this time?" asked Maxi.

"And where do you plan for Edwin to sit? On the roof?" She scowled at me.

Archie, whose beliefs, and clothes, had taken a beating, just shuffled up to the auto's back door.

Maxi, watching him, sighed. "Fine. But at least slow down for the corners this time?"

14

Blueshrouds are going to clear up

Every hair on my body, including the thick fur on my feet, throbbed. My jaw clenched so hard that it hurt. Air scraped in through my nose allowing small pockets of oxygen to fuel my body and I took stock. Eyes closed, check, best to keep it that way for now, lying down, check, probably bound, I flexed the muscle in my arm, yep check. Magn stores, check.

I needed more information. At least my magn quota had been reset, allowing me to weave a thin sensory net, a translucent lace, almost impossible to see. I released it and gained a brief picture of a stark living room decorated in basic furniture and dark colors. The image disappeared as an alarm, that appeared to be designed to split someone's head open, peeled out and the binds on me tightened, pushing the air back out of my lungs.

"Awake, huh?"

I opened my eyes.

Gone were the loose, flowing clothes Grace Forge wore at the bar. Now she was dressed in a dark structured jacket and trouser set with bright blue piping on the edges. The weapon, a military grade blaster that could carve up a body, attached to her belt, was a delicate touch.

"Grace, I know I owe you for a few drinks, but this seems excessive."

She smiled at me, and the blood in my veins became a tad chillier. My sensory net had been right. It was a sizeable living room. Its walls were bare of artwork and the furniture was rudimentary, a cabinet, a rug, a couple of black couches with narrow sides, one of which I was bound to and a few narrow-armed chairs where the others sat, slumped forward.

"You think you're so funny, don't you?"

"I have my moments." I pushed at my binds, but my breath shuddered so I settled for rocking my head to the side and watching Grace pace the room. Even that slight movement turned up the dial on the ache. Since my magn was being tracked, I experimented with channeling ludere to heal my head. It became easier every time, if no less tiring. Grace followed every one of my twitches and narrowed her eyes.

"No point sending out a call for help. Nothing's getting out of this room, including you."

I glanced down out of the corner of my eye and saw that my wristband was wrapped, presumably with a dampener. I relaxed and let my gaze take in the return cast of my very own show. Artemus with his chin tucked in and his shoulders slumped. *Sparkhead*. Emanuel, moss man extraordinaire, and surprisingly, but not surprisingly, Hannah, Lenora's not so worried apprentice.

I focused on Emanuel.

"How's the leg?"

He stepped forward with violence etched in his face, but Grace placed her hand on his shoulder and his expression smoothed under the pressure of her white knuckled grip.

"An easy fix," said Grace.

"Right, no harm done then."

"The problem is," Grace let go of his shoulder. "The problem is, Morgan..." She moved, brushing the hair back from my face. My muscles tightened.

Archie and Maxi were shifting in their seats. I tried to signal to them not to do anything foolish. I think Maxi rolled her eyes at me. Edwin hadn't lifted his head.

Grace punched me in the temple.

"Ow, what'cha do that for?" I couldn't raise my arms to touch my head, but I was pretty sure she had broken the skin.

"I want to talk to you about our problem, not watch you make moon eyes at your lover."

If my face hadn't been distracted by the pain, I would have frowned. Artemus' gaze shifted to Edwin, his eyes narrowing. Grace slammed her fist into the side of my head again.

I gazed up at her, tuning out the rest of the room.

"Better." She settled back on her heels. "My... our problem, Morgan, is you can see the fake IDs. What'd Wilbur do that made them identifiable?"

It was a good thing that my face was already numb. She slammed her fist into my temple again.

"Grace, if you want me to remember anything, lay off."

She landed a couple more blows and my vision blurred.

"Just kill her," said another voice, "All problems solved."

I didn't need to turn my head to know that Lydia had entered the room.

Grace stood over me, staring down. "I want to know the how first." Her eyes narrowed and lips thin. Death by preserver might have been less painful.

"Morgan, I asked you a question."

I blinked at her. Everything hurt. What would I know about why Wilbur Dawkins, the former head of research, created fake IDs? I had hardly been his confidant.

"He left a loop in the glamor," said Edwin.

Now he decides to regain consciousness.

"How?" Grace moved closer to him.

He shifted around in his seat, trying to sit up straighter. "A small one, hard to see, but something he could use to keep track of them."

"Edwin, isn't it?"

"Yes."

"This loop, your idea?"

Grace loomed over him.

"No, it had nothing to do with me. He told me about it so I could..."

"Could what?"

Edwin shrugged, but his eyes flicked towards me.

"Is this loop common knowledge?" asked Grace.

Say yes, say a bunch of people know and they will take it to all quarters of the compass and across the aether.

"No."

Oh, for Volt's sake. Archie and Maxi stared at him with puzzled expressions on their faces. Understandably as he had probably just signed their death order as well.

"Are we really going to believe him?" asked Artemus, staring with disdain at Edwin. I glanced towards Emanuel. He hadn't taken his gaze off me the whole time. He gave a small smile, his gaze tracking what felt like blood trickling down the slide of my face.

"I doubt Wilbur told him anything," said Hannah. "If Wilbur had done anything to those IDs, or any of the material he supplied, I would've known about it."

Maxi and Archie stared at her. I suspected they had a lot they wanted to say to Hannah, but there was no expression on their faces.

I lay there feeding more ludere into my body, my brain unscrambling. Interesting that Hannah felt she had his confidence. Wilbur had played his own game, and anyone who didn't realize we were all just pieces in his puzzle was a fool.

Grace stood there, shoulders back, legs wide and arms loose.

"I want to be satisfied," her voice rose, "that these fools won't expose the whole thing." She took a breath. "I want to know what they know." Her voice reverberated around the room.

"I could get it out of them," said Lydia.

"No, the information from your methods has questionable veracity."

"I could drug them," said Hannah, her voice going high at the end.

Grace swiveled towards her. "What kind of drug?"

"It's a new one made of magn infused hyoscine. It drops the inhibitions, but is enforced to ensure that what they say is real, not fantasy."

"Does it actually work?" asked Grace.

"It claims to have a ninety percent accuracy," said Hannah.

"Do it," said Grace.

Hannah headed towards the maker sitting on a cabinet. Maxi and Archie's eyes tracking her every move. Halfway there, she paused.

"What?" asked Grace.

"It takes a bit of time to work."

"How long?"

"It's most effective after an hour."

"Fine, start the clock and I want someone in this room monitoring them the whole time. How they got out of the compound is on the list of things I want to know." Grace strode from the room with Artemus and Emanuel following, leaving Lydia and Hannah behind.

Lydia stood over me, smiling her most unpleasant smile. She flicked my head.

"Hey."

"You know what I think?" asked Lydia.

"No one cares what you think," said Hannah from the

corner of the room. The beakers in her hand clinked as she filled them with liquid and weaved magn through it.

Lydia flicked my head again.

"Not that there's anything in there, but if there is, you're going to be spewing your guts."

Hannah's gaze slide towards me and she smiled. Her expression twisted and cold.

"Remember, Grace wasn't into the whole torturing thing?" I asked.

"Grace wants answers, and she isn't squeamish," said Lydia.

Something the side of my head could attest to. I drew in more ludere attempting to reduce the internal inflammation and bruising. Lydia smiled misinterpreting my trembling fingers.

So far, everyone had been ignoring Archie and Maxi. I wasn't sure if I should be grateful or worried.

"Need me to hold his head?" asked Lydia, moving up behind Edwin.

Hannah grinned and took a few steps towards him. "Yes, if you don't mind." She cradled one beaker while Lydia wrestled with Edwin.

"No..." Edwin tried to turn away, but Lydia's fingers pressed in against his head and pulled it back while Hannah forced the liquid down his throat. Her magn infused his system and Lydia pushed his head away, turning to me with a grin. His head wobbled and for a moment, I thought he was going to pass out again.

Hannah didn't even peek at her fellow apprentices, moving straight to me.

"She'll need to sit up," said Hannah.

I kept my eyes on Lydia but didn't move.

"Just pour it down her throat. She'll be fine."

"It'll be harder to swallow. Which means either she won't absorb enough for it to work, or she will choke, or both," said Hannah while Lydia got a dreamy expression on her face. Hannah frowned. "Regardless, Grace won't be happy."

"Fine," said Lydia.

I found myself wrenched upright and clenched my teeth against the pain in my head.

"The great Morgan Anastasi, trussed up like a baby." Lydia spat on me.

"Great?" I asked, my voice shaky as the binds around my arms and chest restricted my breathing. "You think I'm great?"

Lydia's fist connected with the same side of my head that Grace had been pummeling before. I closed my eyes and tried not to throw up.

"Lydia," Hannah exhaled heavily, "I need her to swallow." She reached out and grabbed my hair, holding my head, which had sagged into an upright position while Lydia put her hands on either side in a vise and tilted my head back. Hannah released my hair and pushed open my mouth while pouring the contents of the beaker down my throat. As I expected, it went down like glass.

"Static, is she whimpering?" Lydia's lip curled, and Hannah shrugged while she checked our pupils.

"I don't know what the fuss about her is." Hannah laughed. "It's going to take an hour, at least. I'll let Grace know. You stay with them."

"Aren't you going to do the other two?"

For the first time, Lydia turned in their direction, examining them as potential threats.

"They know nothing, trust me," said Hannah. "I've had to listen to them all day, every day, for years. They're useless." She headed toward the door.

Archie and Maxi's faces were carved from rock.

Lydia snorted as she positioned herself near my head. If she was going to stand there for the whole hour, I hoped her feet hurt.

Edwin was pale and struggling to breathe, but he was scanning my binds.

"You alright?" I asked.

Lydia spun, raising her fist. My breathing freed as the restraints binding me disintegrated. I took hold of her arm but didn't have the core strength needed to go from horizontal to vertical in one move. Scissoring my legs, I tried to create the momentum needed, pushing myself up, struggling to keep hold of Lydia's arm. Her tail swung at me. I dodged it, but it broke my grip.

"Thank you," said Lydia, grinning at me. "Thanks for giving me a reason."

Her tail hit my rib cage. I swiped at it with my claws extended but missed and stumbled sideways. I tried to pivot so I wasn't jammed up against the couch, but she was too close. Her tail flicked my ribs again while her hand reached for my neck, and I fell back onto the couch. Then she was on me, the weight of her large body suffocating.

Static she was heavy, especially as a dead weight. I tried

peering around her and could make out Maxi standing there with a large metal tray in his hand.

"Thanks," I grunted, trying to push her body off me.

Maxi put the tray down and she and Archie dragged Lydia's unconscious body onto the ground. I lay there, trying to get by breath back and checking to make sure none of my ribs were broken.

Maxi glared at me. "We need t—"

I held my finger to my lips and listened, taking the absence of footsteps running towards us was a good sign.

"Can you bind her?" I asked Edwin. I had an unpleasant flavor in my mouth, but whatever Hannah had used didn't seem to have had much effect on me. Except to make me thirsty.

Edwin's face was pale, his mouth a thin line, but he squatted next to Lydia and nodded.

"I've rebound them."

"Rebound, as in the same ties? I thought you made them disappear. These are just ours but untied? How's that possible?" Archie crouched next to him and tried to touch the bind of energy now wrapped around Lydia.

"Ludere and magn work differently for everyone—"

"No, they don't. That is why we study—"

"You study one way, it's not the only way." Edwin rubbed the back of his neck. "Is this really the time for this conversation?"

Archie obviously felt it was, but I stepped in.

"Focus people."

"How do we get out of here? Do we contact Drudtia and Alwyn?" asked Maxi.

"Well, since we're consulting with the Preservation Service, I suggest we call them in to clean up this mess."

I nudged Lydia with my foot, but she was out for the count. Maxi appeared to have quite a swing on her. Or a lot of rage that needed working through.

"They let out that moss man last time," said Edwin.

I frowned.

"The big creepy guy from earlier?" asked Maxi.

"Yes, he's been arrested for having a fake ID but somehow..."

"They would have only released him if they didn't think he was involved." But Archie's voice wasn't as confident as it had been a few days ago.

"They're probably all in on it," sneered Maxi.

I shook my head. "Doubtful. I'm going to roll the dice, gamble on Harriden not being involved."

"I'm not sure the meathead would have the imagination for it." Edwin chuckled at his own comment.

My eyebrows rose.

"Meathead?" I wasn't Harriden's biggest fan, but from what I have seen, he was a, relatively, competent officer.

"If you go for that kind of muscle-bound soldier, thing, sure."

I smothered an unexpected burst of laughter. "Are you alright?" I asked.

"Am I alright? I have twice been abducted and bound, twice made unconscious and now forced to drink some disgusting home brewed poison. No, no, I'm not alright." Edwin's attempt at a whisper sizzled the air.

I blinked. That was the most verbose I had ever heard

him. "I'm not sure I can get us out of here without setting off my quota limit again, which would mean death. For me anyway."

"Ridiculous quota rules." Maxi glared at Archie like they were his fault.

"They aren't ridiculous. They stop people from misusing power." Archie glared back.

"They just find other ways."

I picked up Lydia's legs and dragged her behind the couch, out of sight from anyone entering the door.

"At least that is one less way," I puffed.

"You're a fool if you think it makes a difference," said Maxi. Easy to say for someone who hadn't been alive to see the death and destruction of the electromagn wars.

Ah, to have that much certainty about life again.

"Well, this fool is going to hide behind the door until they get here, if you want to join." I let the wall support my weight.

I thought it strange that Emanuel had been released. But I had to trust that they would not make the same mistake twice.

I unwrapped the dampener on my wrist.

abducted by blueshrouds, with apprentices

grace forge leader

sending coordinates

assistance needed

I took the time to make it clear that the apprentices had been abducted as well, just in case he was hesitant to rush over just for me.

The others joined me against the wall behind the door, and we watched the clock. Each shift in time that took us closer to the hour suggested by Hannah was linked to the relative tenseness of my muscles.

"No need to stress about it, either he comes in time, or he doesn't," said Edwin.

"You're telling me not to stress?" I peered at him a bit more closely. "If Harriden doesn't come, there's a good chance I'm going to die."

Edwin snarled. "Harriden? You give him too much credit."

"The point is, I wanted to avoid the fighting, hence the call for help."

"I don't think you're going to get your wish."

"Why?"

"They're coming."

Archie and Maxi tensed.

I couldn't hear anything, but I trusted Edwin's senses.

"How many?"

"Two, Hannah and the moss person."

"Emanuel? Well, it appears we get to have a rematch." I hefted the tray Maxi had used so effectively on Lydia while I examined the apprentices. "I need you to stay out of the way, but if you see a chance to cause a distraction without getting yourselves killed…"

Their expressions grim they nodded. Edwin's face had shifted from his preferred metallic copper to a shiny pale green, I just hoped he stayed upright.

The door swung inward, and I saw the tip of Emanuel's shoe. I threw my weight into the door, smashing it into him. It cracked on his skull, but he barreled through.

He snarled. "Morgan you—"

I bashed Maxi's tray across his head and exhaled in relief when he slammed down on the floor. Edwin threw binds over him securing him.

I turned my attention to Hannah, who stood there frozen, staring at me, her mouth hanging open and face white. The edges of my lips turned upwards, and I stepped towards her. She ran.

15

It's a new day

Harriden arrived, taking a safety-first approach bringing an entire squad with him. My chase ended with Hannah running out into a courtyard overflowing with preservation officers in the middle of arresting blueshrouds. First glimpse of us and they tried to detain us as well.

Harriden watched smirking but at least he had stepped in when they brought out restraints.

"I hadn't realized how big the gang had become," I said, watching bartenders, cleaners, and administrators being divested of weapons, and a surprising number of brass knuckles, before being escorted into the service's vans.

"I don't think anyone did." He seemed subdued, or at least less arrogant than usual.

I was sure that the preservation officers would share their victorious story over a drink or a dinner that night.

He examined me. "It seems you can't even make it home without causing a ruckus."

"Oh, you mean busting this case wide open, that kind of ruckus?"

Harriden snorted. "We'd have gotten here. Though I was surprised to find an entire stack of IDs in what appears to be that apprentice's workshop. Makes me wonder if the missing scholar was caught up in—"

"Workshop? Can I see?" I straightened.

"I don't think we need your help with this one. Boxes of IDs ready to go is enough for us."

"But we also suspect Hannah poisoned her fellow apprentice, Vivian. We need to check it out."

"Poison?"

"Come on Harriden," said Edwin, entering the conversation, "Vivian? The one who lodged the missing person case you ignored? That was poisoned?" Edwin sniffed. "Spark it, keep up Harriden."

I glanced at his green tinged face. His pupils dilated.

Harriden scowled. "And you think it was this Hannah, the other apprentice, who created the poison?"

Maxi and Archie had joined us as well and stood there, arms crossed, scowling.

"Obviously," said Maxi, glaring at him.

"I saw her weave magn through a liquid," said Archie.

"Magn through liquid?" asked Harriden, his smile condescending, "That's Alchemy level work."

"I can only say what I saw." Archie's lips were thin and the betrayal in his eyes bright.

Harriden dragged a hand over his face. "Fine." He turned and strode towards the building.

"Come on," I said. Maxi and Archie kept up with me, but I pulled Edwin back a few times as he crowded Harriden's heels.

Hannah's workroom wasn't as dramatic as Drudtia's. A maker, an aethercomp and over a hundred jars full of solutions were the only items in the gray and white room. I picked one up while Harriden sat down in front of the comp and tapped his preservation ID against it for access. Privacy was something that happened to other people.

"Static," said Harriden.

"No luck, eh?" I asked, smirking.

"Probably doesn't like you," said Edwin. "Like most peopl—"

I huffed and kicked him in the side of his leg.

"Ow."

"Maxi, Archie, help me search for the jars with the markers Drudtia gave us," I said.

"What markers?" asked Maxi.

Right, they hadn't been there for that discussion.

"Here." I forwarded the details about the markers.

"Got it," said Archie.

"Of course you got it, we both did," said Maxi.

I cleared my throat. "Vivian?"

They nodded and wandered around, examining the jars in the room.

I sent a message to Drudtia.

found workroom

searching for poison

be ready

"Won't the schema or details be on the comp?" asked Harriden, whacking it on its side.

"A live sample would be better. Let's just take them all back to Drudtia and she'll be able to—"

"You aren't taking them anywhere. They're evidence and might apply to our fraud enquiries. What if one of those is linked to how they made the IDs?"

"So, you're going to let a young person die just in case one of these is relevant?" I grumbled and handed a couple of jars that seemed promising to Edwin. I checked my band again. Nothing? Seriously?

"I can't just let you take them away." Harriden stood up and turned towards us, the scowl etched on his face again.

"I think I have it," said Archie, holding up a jar.

Maxi scanned the liquid and nodded at him. "Nice work."

Archie cradled the jar as if it was the most precious thing in the world.

"There you go, no need for the meathead here to worry," said Edwin.

"Meathead?" Harriden faced Edwin. I was pretty sure that Edwin was still under the influence of Hannah's concoction. His colors were off, and so was his mouth.

"Come on Harriden, just one to save a life?" I asked, stepping forward, attempting to divert Harriden's attention to more pressing matters at hand.

"I want to know more about this poisoning," said Harriden.

"I mentioned it back at … never mind, I'll send you a full report. As part of our work—"

"Your part in the case is over—"

No, it sparking wasn't. There was no way I was going back into that foyer. Not yet anyway.

"Almost over, you never know there still might be more…" I spread both my hands out in front of me, making sure my claws were retracted. I could feel Edwin take a breath, but Harriden nodded, so quitting while ahead I grabbed Edwin's arm, pulling him towards the door.

"Archie, Maxi, let's go." I glanced back at Harriden. "You saved a life today."

Harriden ran a hand over his hair but turned back to the comp. With Archie and Maxi leading the way, I dragged Edwin out the door, ending up in the main courtyard where I had to convince an officer to give us a lift to Drudtia's.

The gravel crunched under our feet as we fell out of the service auto. Technically, we had all fit, but we had been a bit closer to each other than any of us felt comfortable with. Still, if Archie had picked up the correct solution, we were returning conquering heroes. Well, except for the fact we didn't know where Lenora was or exactly what was going on.

We strode up the front stairs and I lifted my hand to knock, my arm swung downward as the front door opened to reveal Alwyn. His face might not have been able to show lines, but his eyes were full of worry.

"Did you find it?"

"I hope so," said Archie, showing the jar.

"I'll let Drudtia know. Come in." He stepped back and

waved us across the threshold. Drudtia was sitting in front of the AV in the living room.

Today we go to Duskburn, where we find Ebarin and Ohith, Deans, who despite having seen their own parents killed by the everlastings, have been steadfast in their support of the magn regulation. But times are changing, and they are now gathering support for reviewing the council's membership. Here they are meeting with their local supporters.

The camera swung around to show two people standing in front of an enthralled crowd, listening to every word Ohith was saying. I was pretty sure there were people from the boat in the front row.

"I'm not saying that the Everlastings haven't been helpful." An image of the five everlastings, their faces cold as they stood on a balcony gazing down at a crowd, flashed up. *"They stopped the war, and we will always be grateful for that."* The camera swung back to Ebarin and Ohith. *"But unintended consequences to their decisions are resulting in missed opportunities for those whose lives are shorter than theirs and the overly strict application of outdated laws. We need—"*

Alwyn turned off the AV.

"Well?" Drudtia stared, arms crossed, and both eyebrows raised. "What took you so long?"

Was long the right word?

By my calculations, we had been gone less than twenty-four hours, been captured twice, recruited to assist the preservation service, and found a jar containing Hannah's poison.

"Maxi and Archie compared it to the markers. We think

we have it." I pointed at the jar cradled in Archie's arms, and he displayed it for those in the room to see.

"All the markers?" She rose, reaching out her hand to him, and he passed it over. Drudtia grunted as she took it. "Good work, Archie, Maxi. Edwin, I might need your help." And with that, she turned and left the room, and Edwin followed her.

Good work Archie? What was I? The sidekick? I wanted to point out that I had done most of the heavy lifting, but spelling it out felt like having to tell someone you are beautiful.

"Do you think Vivian will get better?" asked Maxi.

"We got back in less than twenty-four hours," I said, shrugging. "I'm hopeful."

"Where'd you find it?" asked Alwyn.

I sighed. "It was Hannah." My body creaked as I lowered it into the chair. Alwyn handed over an oversized cup with what smelled like soup. I sipped it and my face scrunched up, lukewarm. I spun a bit of magn through it to bring it up to a drinkable temperature and took another sip and hummed.

The corner of Alwyn's eyes attempted to scrunch, and his lips lifted at the edges. "Too cool, was it?"

"Hot is better."

Alwyn shook his head.

To be fair he had been experimenting with flavors again and this one was a watermelon and olive combination. I could understand why he had served it cold. It was still better hot though.

Archie paced. "I can't believe that Hannah..."

"She obviously poisoned Vivian but why?" asked Maxi, her face drooped.

Archie frowned, "and what about Lenora—"

"I don't know," I said, taking another sip, watching them. If Hannah was working with the Blueshrouds, it would be foolish for me to assume that they weren't involved. Despite their expressions of surprise.

Archie paused his pacing and turned towards me. "But why—"

"Do you think Lenora is still alive?" asked Maxi.

"I think there's a possibility," I said, finishing my soup, groaning as my body used the nutrients to repair itself. I stretched out, my muscles creaking.

"Let's go find her," said Archie.

"We will. As you know, Edwin and I are assisting the preservation service," I gestured to Edwin, who had returned, "I'm hoping to—"

"Finding her is not their primary concern." Maxi glared at Archie. "So much for your precious preservation serv—"

"Maxi, that isn't helpful."

"Vivian." Archie and Maxi jumped up and ran to her. Maxi stood a little back, but her eyes checked her face. Archie immediately wrapped his arms around her.

"Vivian, how are you feeling? I'm Alwyn." He smiled at her. "You must be starving."

Vivian smiled back at him. "Alwyn, from what Drudtia said, I owe you a lot. Thank you for caring for me while I was unconscious."

"Not at all, not at all." Alwyn's eyes swept the room. "Come on, I think we all need a proper meal."

Alwyn's version of a meal was rather bizarre. He obviously enjoyed experimenting and, well, let's just say none of us would forget what we ate that day. Vivian was still too weak to go home and with Hannah arrested and Lenora still missing, Archie and Maxi needed to stay here until Lenora was found or they were placed with an alternative scholar.

"We'll just leave them here for a few more days," I smiled at Drudtia.

"Good thing you'll be here to supervise them then," said Drudtia, smiling back sharply.

"Oh, well, I was thinking Edwin and I should head back to the warehouse, to search—"

"Are you an actual fool?"

"I didn't think so."

"You're going to get attacked again if you go out now."

"But all the blueshrouds—"

"For sparks sake Morgan, do you really think—" Drudtia threw her hands in the air.

"Morgan," Alwyn rested his hand on Drudtia's shoulder, "While many of the blueshrouds are off the streets today, I suspect Drudtia is right. There are more or others, just as dangerous out there."

I sighed. "Maybe."

"Drudtia's right, we'd be foolish to go out today. Tomorrow we can go into the preservation office and use that meathead to help us."

Drudtia and Alwyn's eyebrows shot up.

"Ignore him. Hannah gave him a truth potion of some sort. For some reason, it only seems to make him say bad things about Harriden."

"Why didn't she give it to you?" asked Drudtia.

"She did." I shrugged. "But it didn't seem to have any effect."

Drudtia and Alwyn exchanged glances.

"I still feel queasy," said Edwin, rubbing his stomach. I hadn't noticed him slowing down at dinner though and his face was back to being copper.

"Stay here," said Alwyn. "At least for tonight."

I sighed.

Vivian was given her own room with special infused healing woven into it. Archie and Maxi refused to leave her and set up cots in her room while Edwin and I camped out in the living room. I suspected that Archie and Maxi's bed were also infused with something as they went straight to sleep with none of the bickering that I expected.

I lay there stretched out on a narrow bed in a strange house, listening.

"Are you listening to me breathe?" he asked.

"It's the only noise in the room, so it's hard to miss."

"Stop it. I need rest."

"Rest away."

"I can't rest if you're lying there listening to me breathing."

I exhaled loudly. "I can't help hearing sounds."

"Go to sleep."

"I can't."

"Why not?" He huffed.

"I'm in a strange house, in a large room with multiple unlocked doors."

He shifted and I felt his gaze touch me.

"Nothing is going to get past Drudtia's wards. Even the council of five would struggle to get in here."

"Even the council of five?" I asked. I adjusted the sheet and quilt trying to get comfortable. "And what about Drudtia? Who, or more importantly, what, is she?"

"They, Drudtia and Alwyn, are..."

"Are they Deans too?"

"In a way, they're a type of immortal, but it would be more accurate to say they're..."

My blanket slipped, letting the cold of the night sneak under. I shifted it higher. "Still there?"

"Yes, I just don't know what the word is."

"Right."

"I suppose the best way to describe them would be a multiverse everlasting."

"Wait..." A scowl settled on my face. "Then... one, why are they helping us and two, how do you know them?"

"I don't know, and I don't."

"Then how do you know what they are?"

"Alwyn told me when we were stabilizing Vivian."

"So, he just said, oh by the way, I'm a multiverse everlasting?"

"I asked him what brought them to Duskburn, and he said they were seeking someone, but it was complicated and there were multiple dimensions involved."

"And..."

"And what?"

"What else did he tell you?"

"Nothing. We were busy helping Vivian."

"Did you ask who he was seeking? How long they're in

Duskburn? Where else they had been?" I rolled over on to my side. "Did you ask any questions?"

"It didn't seem appropriate." I could hear Edwin shifting.

"Really? no questions?"

I heard Edwin shift again.

Un...sparking... believable. Images of Vivian being planted, strange foods and arguing apprentices swirled in my mind. I closed my eyes but Edwin's face appeared, staring at *me* like I was crazy.

Next thing I knew, the lightening of the room was pulling me back to consciousness. I sat up and ran my fingers through my hair. Edwin was gone. A shower would be good right now. I gritted my teeth as I used some of my stored magn to clean myself up and watched my quota tracker ping up a couple of notches. I was a long way off it being an issue, but any use made me nervous.

I found everyone in a large room at the front of the house with curved windows and a view of the garden. A long table ran down the center and Edwin and Archie were guzzling and shoveling food while Drudtia and Alwyn sipped drinks watching. The maker was being used by Maxi, so I took a spot next to her.

"What now?" asked Maxi. Seemed she had a taste for a rice dish this morning and the sweet tang of its aroma made me double guess having soup for breakfast.

"Edwin and I report for duty at the preservation service and help find Lenora."

"And what are we meant to do?" asked Archie, staring at me.

"You need to be here." A frowning Drudtia was visible in my peripheral vision.

"Great," said Maxi. "We do nothing. Lenora might be in trouble."

"No offence, but what can you do? Vivian's still recovering, Hannah is arrested, and you're both too early in your studies to be of much use." I was pretty sure both of their eyes teared up at that.

"Are you sure we should go in?" asked Edwin.

"Besides my not having much choice? It's still better to work from the inside with their resources—"

"We don't know who's involved."

"Which is why we need to go in."

"You think the Preservation Service is a part of all this?" asked Archie, frowning.

"It doesn't sit right that Emanuel was released," said Edwin.

I sympathized with Archie but no one's perfect. "It's a possibility," I said.

Archie slumped in his chair.

Drudtia tapped the table, and Alwyn rearranged his cup and saucer.

"How's Vivian this morning?" I asked Drudtia.

"She's still resting but is on the mend," she said.

I made a flask of soup and left them to finish their breakfast. Her door was open, and I rested against its frame.

"Hey," she said.

"Hi yourself," I took a few steps in but stayed standing. "How are you?"

"I'm better. Thanks for finding the stuff." She ran her

fingers through her hair. She was still pale but her breathing was back to normal.

"Archie brought it home." I shifted my weight from one foot to the other.

Vivian frowned and played with her blanket.

"What about Lenora?"

It was too much to hope she would not ask questions.

"I don't know. I found Uriah, one of her clients, but she wasn't there."

"Are you going… are you going to keep searching?"

"I'm working with the preservation service now, so yes." And if working with them and finding her releases me from supervised service, all the better.

"And bring her back."

I frowned down at her. It wasn't a promise I could make, but my lips moved of their own accord. "Yes and bring her back."

Vivian smiled and relaxed against her pillow.

Stupid mouth.

"Thank you."

I stood there for a few moments, but Vivian had fallen back to sleep. With a sigh, I turned and left the room. It was time to get ready for our first day of work.

"Spark it." I stopped in the front doorway and gazed at the empty yard.

"What?" asked Edwin crowding behind me.

"No auto."

"Err…so we hike it?"

"It would take an hour, at least, I'll—"

"Problem?" I turned to find Alwyn coming to check out the traffic jam at the front door.

"No auto." I exhaled heavily.

"Oh," Alwyn pulled at his beard. "Well, do you want to borrow mine?"

I perked up.

"That'd be great." I scanned the property, trying to find a garage. Alwyn grinned and turned back into the house with a spring in his step.

I frowned and shared a glance with Edwin.

"I agree. This will not be great at all," he said.

I chewed the corner of a claw and forced myself to retract them and put my hands behind my back. Something started up and then Alwyn came around the side of the house in a glider that had a side mobile attached.

Edwin groaned.

"I'm not sitting in that thing," he said.

"You want to drive the glider?" I asked.

He frowned at me. "I won't fit in it."

"You can drive if you promise not to crash it."

I sat on the glider and Edwin squeezed himself into the sidecar. His knees jutted out, and I laughed at the disgruntled expression on his face. But at least we would get there in one piece.

Minutes later, with a minimal amount of heckling from other drivers, we arrived at the service's headquarters. It took time to find a park, and set up some protection wards, but the last thing I wanted to do was to lose Alwyn's glider. The way I was going, I would soon have vehicles parked all over the city.

I took a breath and tried to calm my nerves. I could get through this case, find Lenora and, who knows, maybe make a positive difference for once. A vine covered the cement barrier in front of the square gray headquarters, making me smile.

"Hey," I said.

"Hey," said the vine.

"Anything interesting happening today?"

"Hmm."

"I'm Morgan."

"I know. I'm Freddy." A tendril of the vine reached up and tapped my hand, making me smile. I stroked a leaf.

"Hope you keep safe this winter."

"Thank you. I've survived many before and I'll survive this one too. The council helps, you know."

I patted their leaves and then kneeled and poured some of my breakfast on the ground near one of their roots.

"Thanks," the vine leaves fluttered at me before settling down to sleep.

"I both love and hate winter," I said.

"Why love?" asked Edwin.

"The air is beautiful, clean, crisp and feels good on my skin. But the plantae are quiet. I hate the quiet."

"Yes, I know..." Edwin drawled. "So, are we going to stand out here all day?"

"I'd have thought the potion would've worn off by now?"

"Potion?"

"You know, the truth thingy that Hannah gave you? The one that made you say all those things yesterday?"

"The only thing that potion did was make me nauseous. Wait, why didn't it affect you?"

"Why say all those things to Harriden, then?"

"Because I wanted to."

I snorted. "Let's focus on my not getting killed today?"

"You think hanging out with your future executioners is going to stop that?"

"Yes, we're going to be helpful."

"How? We've already handed them the blueshrouds."

"It can't just have been them. They were the distributors. There's no way Hannah—"

I stopped. Maybe this was a mistake. Hannah couldn't have done it on her own which meant-

"Excuse me," said a sharp voice, and I turned to find people dressed for business glaring at me.

"Sorry," I stepped aside.

"Why not?" asked Edwin.

"Someone within the council's research centers would have to be helping them or someone near the council..."

Edwin stood there watching people file past us.

"I would've thought that was pretty obvious." He shrugged and stared at the door of the building. "Do we go in?"

I rolled my shoulders. "I don't know if we have a choice at this point." A push on the door and we were in another foyer. This one was a lot less grand than mine. I huffed but peered around. Cold. Grey. Overuse of white. Unlike the council foyer, though, it was noisy. A short line of people stood in front of the front desk, so we joined it.

"I don't like this place," said Edwin.

"It's a preservation office. It isn't designed to be liked."

We stepped up to the guard on the front desk and displayed our chits for inspection. It crossed my mind that Harriden might have been a jerk and not listed us, but we were waved through.

I stood there peering around until I saw the travel shute we needed. It opened as we approached, and I keyed in the destination given to us.

"Ready?" asked Edwin.

The doors closed, and we descended to Harriden's floor. A smile sneaked across my face.

16

Life's an illusion... then it is pain

I tried to rub my eyes, but my arm was caught by something. Seriously? Again? The cold concrete scraped my cheek as I moved, but I shifted enough to see Edwin sitting upright in a chair, straining against his binds.

"If you're going to get us out of here, now's the time to do it," said Edwin.

My brow wrinkled.

"Break your own." I took in the room's shabby concrete walls. "This is getting ridiculous. I don't suppose you know where we are?" I sniffed but couldn't pick out any identifying odors.

"I saw something, a person, a person in a robe."

Why the sparks would someone be running around in a robe?

"Like a bathrobe?"

"No, a ceremonial robe." He frowned at me.

I gazed up at him. "Male, female, scales, fur what?" I asked.

"I couldn't see … there was a golden light…"

I tried to think, but could hear people approaching. With my arms bound behind me, I twisted and tried to flex my stomach muscles, but they didn't respond. Ungrateful, that's what they were. How many times had I gotten up off the couch and stretched them out? I exhaled, blinking a few times, until my eyes cleared to take in the sight of Grace and that sparkhead Emanuel stepping through the door. *For volt's sake.*

"What're you doing here?" I asked.

Grace gazed down at me and laughed. "Need a hand?"

I glared at her. Emanuel lifted me upright, and I had to suppress my instinct to thank him. He, or Lydia, had undoubtedly been the ones to push me over.

"What are you going to do with us?" Edwin asked while I focused on flexing the muscles in my arms and legs to bring some feeling back into them.

"It's time for you to die in a tragic accident." She smiled, patting my head. I couldn't stop the growl from escaping. She stepped into my personal space. "Just like poor Wilbur." The crazy in her eyes was magnified as her face dominated my field of vision.

"Grace Forge the mastermind." I pulled at my binds, regretting not taking the time to learn Edwin's trick.

"Mastermind, I like that," she smiled. "Not an inaccurate description."

"So, what? Wilbur fed you hoarfrost and haze all these years?"

"Yes, well, I would have thought that was obvious." Grace frowned at me, and I flushed.

"But why would he help you?"

Grace sighed.

"He, like all of us, wanted to recreate the world. Until he got cold feet and well..."

"You killed him?" I didn't really care by this point, but it was strangely satisfying to have the answer.

"He became a liability."

"But what about the IDs? How could you do those without him?" I wanted to scream at her and demand their names.

"He's not the only one wanting changes and let's just say that the fake ones were still useful for getting the monthly minimum income."

"All this... for money?"

"Money?" Grace snarled, "Money is nothing without power. We were trying to redress the issue of balance."

"By creating a people farm?" I said, gagging.

"Sacrifices must be made in pursuit of—"

"That's static and you know it—"

"What I know is that I'm going to live a lot longer than you will." Grace chuckled and spun on her heel. "Emanuel, see to it."

"What? Wait." I pulled at my binds.

The thud of the door added a kick to Emanuel's smile.

"Static, Edwin, can you do anything with these binds?"

"I can't—" He slumped back against the closet wall. "Can you..."

I stifled a scream. *All for nothing.* I closed my eyes and let my head drop forward.

"Time to see if you know how to fly, Morgan." Emanuel dragged me up while sneaking a few punches and kicks in. I swayed, woozy and unable to fight as he applied a magn blindfold. I could hear someone else grappling with Edwin as they dragged us away.

The chair had been replaced by an aviator's seat and the sounds of an airship hissing. My arms were strapped with the controls out of reach. I guessed that a crash was in my near future.

Edwin smiled sadly at me.

"I can't believe this is happening to us," said Edwin. He was strapped in too, but his binds were loose enough for him to twist in my direction.

"Neither can I. It seems farcical, really. I mean, how hard is it to keep Grace and Emanuel locked up?" I tested how much I could move, my fingers straightened and relaxed again.

Edwin dropped his head back on the seat and closed his eyes, exhaling. I attempted to slump and just stared at the slowly approaching Duskburn and contemplated the end of my life. I was a bit bitter that after all the effort I had made to stay alive over the years. it was going to end at the hands of a petty criminal like Grace.

"If I could save us, I would," he said, rolling his head towards me. I met his gaze.

I shifted as much as I could and angled in his direction. His face had never shown much expression, but now it was lined and drooped. I gazed into his eyes.

Weird. He obviously could save us, all he had to do was release the binds.

"You can't?" I asked. I examined his face. The color of his skin was back to copper, his long black hair was loose. But his eyes were green. Edwin could change many things about his coloring, but I had only ever seen his eyes be copper, silver, or obsidian. Green was just wrong.

He sighed again. "It appears to be hopeless."

"We'll just have to hope that Harriden arrives in time to save the day."

"Do you think even Officer Harriden could help us?"

I stared at him. *Even Officer Harriden?* What happened to meathead? And why ask me?

My attention was drawn to Duskburn's spires, which were getting closer. Presumably they were going to crash us within sight of the dirigible landing area. There were at least a dozen crashes every year, a gust of wind at the wrong time, badly maintained equipment. Fortunately, most people walked away, except for the airship crash that Wilbur Dawkins had been the sole passenger on.

I glanced at *Edwin* again. Drudtia and Alwyn's had been real. No one would make up a strawberry and black pepper blood pudding soup. Freddy was real. I had still had my leftover soup on me. It must have been from when we got to the Service Headquarters. An image of my hand punching in the code given to us by the guard on the front desk of the preservation headquarters flashed across my mind.

The constant prompts for me to save him must mean they thought I had unknown powers or something. Perhaps the blowing up of the other compound and freeing everyone had been a mistake. One of many. So, what to do? Burn through my magn quota? Even I couldn't pull enough juice to break council-grade magn binds. Plus making things explode wasn't all that helpful in an airship.

The airship's sounds weaved around us, but I sniffed and realized that I couldn't smell anything.

"Edwin," my eyes watering. I pulled on my memories of some of Alwyn's schemas, "Oh Edwin, I can't believe this is happening." I couldn't quite get enough water going for a tear down the face. I stretched my hand towards Edwin, though the binds kept us from touching each other.

"Can you think of, is there any way we can get out of this?" he gazed into my eyes. "I just, I just want us to get out of here, together."

I was going to give their script writer a severe talking to.

"Edwin, I'm sorry. I'm too weak. I'm afraid, dear Edwin," I tried to hide my gagging from whoever was watching and hoped they took it as a fearful swallow, "that this is the end."

It was a gamble, but I breathed and sent a heartfelt resonance to the world. I twisted even further away from the controls of the airship. I might have imagined it, but I thought *Edwin* gritted his teeth.

"I'm exhausted too, if you could just push at the binds..." his voice was soft. Push a bind? Who was he? Not that bright, obviously. "If you can release it enough for us to..." he tilted his face, so he was gazing up at me.

I glanced at the image of Duskburn, now filling the view.

"I'm afraid it's useless. If we had to die, I'm glad we're

together. And at least we know—" I brought my gaze back to him and gave a small smile, "at least we know we'll be avenged."

Edwin's eyes narrowed. "A small comfort, besides do you think it will work?"

I sighed, "it's probably the only thing I have faith in." I kept my body facing him, rested the side of my head against the seat, and let my eyelids drop. The whoosh of the airship disappeared, and silence descended.

My eyes opened to find myself in a small sitting room. I smirked. I had been *sparking* right. They were playing mind games.

Binds cut into my skin, and I pressed my arms and legs into the chair to allow blood to flow. The room was empty except for the haze of green tinged smoke. I tried to breathe as little as possible, but I could taste charcoal on the back of my tongue. *Lenora's chair.* The taste, the color was the same. Perhaps I should pay them for ferrying me around to their locations?

I extended my claws and was ripping manically at the chair's arms when the door pushed open. The blood pumped through my veins in a crescendo. I scrambled at my magn but it evaded my control which is the only reason the person in front of me didn't explode into a shower of blood.

"Aaaaaaahhhhhh," I stretched against my binds, making my chair jump. I screamed again.

Artemus ran to me and pulled back my head, shoving a device up each of my nostrils. With his hand covering my mouth, it only took a couple of breaths before the blood crescendo faded and I sagged in my seat.

"When I saw you at Grace's, I knew you had to be involved with the ID fraud. But I must admit, I didn't think you would stoop this far." My stomach turned with nausea. Regret snaked through me and grabbed my throat. I swallowed, trying to focus.

"I admit I've been working for Grace, but when I realized what was going on... I'm... helping... Harriden."

"Harriden? How do you know him?"

"He busted me for handling Haze years ago and well, he let me off for some information and well..."

"You're a snitch—"

"We don't have time for this." Keeping a hold of my arm, he used a device to release the binds. My arms and legs were jelly, and it took a few goes to stand. "Hurry," he whispered. I glared at him but pulled myself together and followed him from the room. As soon as we were in the hallway, I could hear it.

He flattened himself behind the pillar, pushing me against the wall. Thuds and shuffles that signaled throughout time, the tread of a security troopers echoed down the hall. I glanced back but there was only the room we had left and a dead end. We were *sparked*.

"Can you get in contact with him?" I asked on a breath that barely moved the air in front of my face.

He nodded. The steps were louder now.

"Get back in the room. If they find me, and we're lucky, they'll take me away."

His lips thinned, but he didn't move.

I grabbed his arm and wrenched him around so the security troopers would see me first. "Go."

Shapes came into view, moving towards me. I closed my eyes. Not for any strategic reason, just to avoid that awkward moment as someone approaches. I wasn't up to dealing with whether to stare at them or pretend something else was interesting, when in reality they had my undivided attention. The footsteps speeding up and shouting let me know when they saw me. They grabbed my arms, I was lucky I didn't bruise, and tied my hands behind my back before dragging me off. Every step away from Artemus made breathing easier. It seemed like luck was on my side, after all. And then, as was luck's want, it turned around and slapped me.

The security troopers pushed at some double doors, and I found myself back in a lab. A two-story high room made up of sharp metal edges, clean surfaces, and lab coats.

"Morgan." Amiel stood in the center.

"Are you serious?" my body sank, and the security troopers grunted but kept me upright. Amiel's face appeared sad, but his eyes were cold and calculating as he examined my slack face.

"Things needed to change," he said.

"True, but—"

"Nathaniel's death showed me how little time we truly have..."

Something clicked in my brain. Wilbur had worked the scientific arm of the council for decades while Amiel was active in the preservation service. Nathaniel had been set to follow in Wilbur's footsteps until he was caught experimenting. Grace stood there smirking next to him.

I wanted to scream. All I had wanted to do was keep my head down and get home. I had accepted that Wilbur and Amiel were just doing their jobs and had never held their role in putting me in supervised service against them. I had felt sorry for Amiel when his son Nathaniel died. *Sparker.* I think I even gave him my condolences.

"I just don't...." They hefted me up again as I attempted to slide to the floor.

"This must be the Morgan we've heard so much about." Dean Ohith's voice resonated through my body and my eyes widened as I took in her, and her partner, dressed in lab coats. "Wilbur had high hopes for you."

Sparking static, what hopes? Was I right? Did he know? Who did he tell?

"Sorry to disappoint," I snarled.

"I didn't say we shared those hopes," she smiled down at me. "Still, it doesn't mean you can't be useful." She turned to Amiel. "Wilbur thought she was something special. I'd like to see the effects of our everlasting fumes."

I could live with special.

"Strap her in," said Amiel, and I was lifted and strapped to a gurney.

I could have fought back, I suppose, but what was the point? It was death by the council or death by Amiel and Grace. I closed my eyes.

Spark them all, they deserved what was coming to them.

"Hook her up," said Amiel, each word out of his mouth a slice across any chance of survival.

Someone strapped a ventilator to my face and hot, thick air pumping through it. I kept my mouth closed and breathed in deeply through my nose, hoping that whatever Artemus had shoved up there was strong enough to handle a direct assault. I listened to the gentle rhythm of my blood.

"Why isn't anything happening?" asked Ohith.

"I'll knock her out so it can work faster." Amiel's voice floated over my head and a needle was pushed into my neck. Hot blood crawled down my neck until it hit the floor with a splat. I tested the straps and someone's hand pressed my arm down into the gurney, reminding me of my mother. I focused on breathing in through my nose.

Volt, just stay awak—

A sudden pressure on my back and concrete scraped against the meaty palm of my hands. Bits of dirt and blood that weren't mine encrusted them. I opened my mouth to drag in some air, coughing as dust and smoke filled it. I scrambled to my feet, trying to breathe through my nose and cough at the same time. Unsteady, my eyes watering and my nails only half extended, I faced the room.

Oh static.

A massive space covered in dirt and surrounded by glass walls greeted me. Clean and well-dressed figures fogged the glass where their noses pressed against it peering at us through the thick green smoke.

I focused on this side of the glass and the two wide, stocky people who were attacking Edwin. They may have only come to his shoulder, but they easily outweighed him. They were also armed with axes that were shooting sparks. The one on his right swung his axe at Edwin's knees while the other went for the shoulder. As the axes descended, they skidded against something. They weren't stopped, but their momentum redirected away from Edwin. The one on the right had overextended and the new direction pulled him off balance. With him distracted, I ran up to the one on Edwin's left. He had gotten his axe under control and was going for another swing. I came up behind his arm and grabbed it. Using his own momentum, I angled his swing towards his body, in particular his leg. He screamed a lot. The other headed my way. I stepped around so that I was between him and Edwin but kept the other in my peripheral. Just in case he got the blood flowing under control.

I didn't have time for anything fancy. I stepped towards the attacker, blocking his swing with one arm and jabbed my fingers, nails extended, into his throat. He barely missed a breath, and his free hand punched the side of my head. I blinked and opened my eyes to see an axe rapidly approaching. I used every muscle in my legs to propel myself backward. The axe swung through the space I had recently occupied, and I landed with my weight forward and grabbing the once more over extended arm, propelled the axe into the attacker's foot. With a lot of ruckus, he joined his colleague on the floor. I just hoped they were slow healers.

"You alright?" I still did not know what fresh horror we had stumbled into. I kept my attention on the two attackers bleeding out on the floor. "Edw—"

Edwin punched me in the back of the head. It was a good

punch for him. But landing a decent punch takes practice. I spun around and even through the haze in the room, it only took one glance to see the crazy in his eyes.

"Edwin, it's me, Morgan."

He came in swinging and even with no technique, it took some fancy footwork to avoid him while not hurting him.

"Edwin, come on—" I jumped back to avoid a kick and my brain knocked for my attention.

The sparking smoke.

The glass walls didn't allow for electricity points. I grinned. *Nice try sparkers.* Everyone has their thing, and while I had built my skills in various areas over my life, there was only one thing that was my thing. And that was channeling magn from pretty much any source available. Air, dirt, it didn't matter, I could use it. However, channeling magn while in the middle of a fight was not for the faint of heart. And I remembered that even I couldn't connect with magn when I was high on the smoke so I kept my mouth shut and breathed in through my nose, trying not to feel grateful to Artemus.

I didn't want to do anything too foolish so I drew just enough magn to cleanse the air that Edwin was breathing. Edwin kept swinging, his eyes wild, but for once his ineptitude saved him. It was in the middle of my dodging a badly placed punch that his eyes cleared. He wobbled, glancing around. A door in the glass wall had opened and a squad of troopers were heading in our direction.

"Edwin, breathe, I need—"

He grabbed my arm and all my magn was sucked from my body.

17

Inside and out

A cross-eyed cat greeted me, and I swallowed a shout and tried to push at Jiro's head, but my hand passed through him.

"What..." I blinked but my eyes struggled to focus but I saw Edwin recklessly leaning against a tree.

I pushed into the soft dirt, stepping through Jiro, but overlapping the specter made my brain try to run away and I slipped. My knees striking the ground on the edge of a large pit.

Static.

I labored to my feet, twisting my body weight away from the hole below and eventually my unsteady legs lead me towards Edwin

"You alright?" I asked. We were on a small hill with a collection of buildings, and shadows scurrying around them, visible below.

Edwin's head dropped forward. "No." He lifted it to stare

at me. His eyes had bled to black, and his copper skin had taken a green tinge again. "I almost killed you… twice."

"I'm not saying the punch to the back of the head didn't hurt, but you didn't get close to—"

"What about on the airship?" He sighed.

My eyebrows crawled upward. "Airship?"

"Yeah, we were in that airship, and you begged me to save you and I—"

"Edwin—"

"I don't know what happened, I just couldn't connect, that's never happened to me before—"

"Listen—"

"And then we crashed, and then there were the people attacking me and then I was attacking you…"

I sighed and reached out resting my hand on his shoulder. "It wasn't me."

"You said the punch hurt."

"Yes, in the room, with the punching that was me, but not in the airship." I removed my hand and found I was wearing a loose black top and pants, not my coat with pockets. I glared down at the sparkheads below.

"But… you said that you I—"

"Edwin… can you really imagine me saying whatever that person said?"

The copper of his skin darkened, but a slow smile broke across his face. "I wondered why you were asking me for help rather than barking orders."

"Ha-ha, that should've been your first clue."

He turned back to the buildings below us. "I'm sorry about the punch."

"Hey, you got us out of there...how did you do that by the—"

"We have to get back in."

"But you've made all that effort to get us out. It seems a shame to waste it." I swayed and reached out to steady myself on a tree, wincing, ready to apologize for not asking first, but the tree ignored me.

"Go back," said Jiro.

"Sorry to be rude, but I need some help." I gave the tree a pat and let them take some of my weight.

"Great, well you and Edwin head back in then and I'll—"

Edwin frowned. "No, you need to—"

"I'm not ready to die. And that is all that is waiting for us there, death. So, what I'm going to do is regroup back at Drudt—"

"We can't leave her to be tortured."

"I agree. If Lenora's in there, bad things are happening to her. I'm not saying we abandon her, I'm just saying—"

"Not Lenora, Syl," Edwin thumped his tree. I raised my eyebrows and shuffled away from him. The last thing we needed was a tree teaching us a lesson. Edwin caressed the trunk and mumbled an apology. The branches never even moved. *What the static was going on here?*

"We can't rescue everyone—"

"They're cutting out parts of her body and burning her."

"Her?"

"Syl, the everlasting they've captured." Edwin gestured at the hole behind us and which all the trees were leaning away from. I touched the filters in my nostrils. Jiro paced around the edge, occasionally stopping, and sniffing a section.

"Burning?"

"To create the smoke, the one that was making everyone go insane, it's from burning Syl's body."

Sparking what?

I threw up, my hand automatically grabbing the closest tree.

"We don't have time for you to be all sensitive," said Jiro.

"Edwin just told me I inhaled a part of a being. Forgive me for being grossed out." I spat, wishing I had some water to clean out my mouth. "If they're willing to burn people, this is way beyond something I can fix."

"Oh, so that's it. It gets hard and you tap out?" asked Jiro.

"Gets hard? They are burning flesh and using it to mind-control people." I pushed myself off the motionless tree and tested my legs.

"When you're literally inhaling it, how can you run away?" asked Edwin, his hand curled up in a fist.

"I'm not saying we do nothing. I'm saying that the two of us—"

"Hey," Jiro flicked his tail through me as he paced past.

"The two of us, and a being who refuses to admit he is dead—"

"I'm not dead," said Jiro. "Just have a temporary corpore-alization challenge."

"As I was saying, we"—I circled my hand— "can't do anything but get captured again. If we want to help, we must let someone know."

"Who?"

"Amiel—" I sighed and leaned against the, hopefully, non-responsive tree again.

"Exactly. If he's in this, who else is?"

"Artemus—"

"Artemus? Just great—"

"He's contacting Harriden."

Edwin paced between the two trees. "How is that going to help? He could be deep in this too—"

I sighed. "Whatever you think of Harriden I doubt he has anything—"

"How do you know?" asked Jiro. I turned to find him examining me.

"I know a rule follower when I see one."

"Do you?" Edwin sniffed, "Even if the meathead isn't involved, wouldn't he just tell Amiel?" Edwin shook his head. "I'm going in. I can't abandon her. Join me or don't."

Edwin headed down the hill, with Jiro following. The silent trees covered the hill but didn't quite reach the residence. Which was going to cause a problem. Not to mention all those moving shadows.

"Static, you can't just stroll in there. Do you even have a plan?" I said to the back of his head.

His shoulders hunched but he kept moving.

I followed, grabbing at his arm, forcing him to stop.

He turned towards me. "I'm going back in."

"A couple of minutes of thinking won't hurt. First off, how did you get us out of there?"

"Aetherlocation."

"Only Everlastings can aetherloc."

"Well, this is awkward..." Edwin gave me an uncomfortable smile.

My eyes narrowed. "This is not the time for humor."

"I wasn't being funny, but the situation is. Someone with a sense of humor would know that."

"I have a sense of—" I took a breath. "You, the being who lies around all day on the couch watching the AV... you're an everlasting."

"Yes."

"So, just use your powers and take them all out," I gestured towards the buildings.

"I told you. I can't connect."

"But you got us out."

"By using your magn, not my own, anyway I'm more the original version of an everlasting."

"An original version? I didn't realize that there were different versions."

"We're, in essence, the same, but years of study and skill—"

"I'm not surprised you skipped out on the study."

"I've been asleep. Wilbur found me and hid me. Syl wasn't so lucky."

"Syl?"

"She must have been sleeping too, but this time, someone else found her and had a stronger stomach than Wilbur."

"They've been searching for sleeping everlastings? And what? Once Wilbur found you, he couldn't stomach cutting you up?"

"If he was involved in this, then yes."

"Oh, I think we can assume he was involved. But why

doesn't Syl just kill them all? I'd assume any version could cause some damage."

"Magn'd magnets," said Jiro.

"What?" I turned towards his voice, only to find him once more in my personal space. My foot shifted back, but I forced it under my body.

"Magnets, powered by magn." Jiro's voice dripped with contempt.

"I know what they are, but what do they have to do with this?"

"They've her surrounded so she can't transform, think, or move." Jiro frowned. "You don't really know what's happening, it's all through a fog. Except when they extract some of the matter out of you."

"Out of you?" I asked.

"I remember it being extracted," he sighed. "I remember a person, a young male, taking it from me."

"No smoke?"

"No smoke, just magnets."

"Nathaniel, I bet you anything it was Nathaniel," I said.

"What? Amiel's son?" asked Edwin.

"Sparking Amiel, Wilbur and Grace." Even without Syl's smoke, I could feel the beat in my blood building. Fueled by the image of people shackled to the floor. Their life being drained away for no other reason than someone else's insatiable desire for more. Drugs, fake IDs and, for what, the unattainable goal of immortality? How deep did the corruption in the preservation service go?

It was never going to sparking end.

A branch dropped in front of me, and I gazed up at the tree we were next to.

"They took without asking." It was a tall tree, hundreds of years old, with deep roots, which gave their voice a deeper resonance than their younger cousins in the city. The tree's branches moved, but there wasn't any breeze.

"Err... yes, I suspect they did." I shuffled away from the angry vibes vibrating from it. "Just to be clear, you know it wasn't us, right?"

"You're Morgan."

"Yep, that's me." I tittered nervously.

"We'll clear the path."

"Oh... no need to do that." I didn't even want to imagine the carnage the trees would cause.

"We'll clear the path." The trees in the grove spoke in unison, making me shiver.

"How about this?" I tried to slow down my breathing. "I'll, we'll, get this Syl out—" The trees hissed, causing me to swallow and try to get some salvia back in my mouth "—and if we need help, we'll give you a yell." In the still cold air, branches waved above me. "But no need to go around killing people in the meantime."

"We'll clear the path."

"If we need you to." I took the movement of their branches as an acknowledgement. "Edwin, can you make it so I can see what's going on? Like you did at the pier?"

The air in front of me shimmered.

The residence came into focus. With a large main house, a few outbuildings, a shed and a security gate, the only thing strange about it was that there were no plantae. It wasn't just an absence of trees or hedges, either. Not a spec of grass or vine had entered that space. Unless the owners had won a serious property dispute at the Boundaries Commission, the plantae were keeping away by choice. I considered asking the surrounding plantae, but considering how riled up they were, I wasn't sure how much I wanted to involve them. A conversation for a later time, perhaps.

I scanned the people moving about. A fountain in the middle of the driveway obscured one building and a mural depicting an everlasting using their enlightenment, while all the other minor figures stared on in awe decorated the wall of the main house, summing up the entire problem.

"Troopers," said Jiro, from his position next to me. He raised his front paw, pointing to a group of nine people, dressed to kill, and heading in our direction.

"Err... would you mind terribly if I climbed you? Just to work out what is happening?"

One of the larger branches of the tree, I probably should have asked their name, dropped, and I used it to climb up. It only took a bit of height and I could make out three other groups, again of about nine each, heading out, each in a different direction.

"Thorough," I said, jumping back down to the ground.

"How many?" asked Edwin.

"Four squads, about nine in a squad, and I think at least twenty troopers, probably closer to thirty, are still in the building."

"What? They're all just standing around for you to count

them?" asked Jiro, his lip curling back and exposing one of his long incisors. I smirked.

"The automobiles you sparkhead." I scanned the ground, seeking rocks and other useful things to hit people with.

"What about the automobiles?" asked Edwin.

"She's guessing," said Jiro.

I shrugged. "They've seven transpos, all designed to carry up to eleven people and their little squads of nine." I reached down and found a nice long rock and used magn to shape it. I reached for my stored magn potential and found my body empty. Edwin hadn't been joking when he said he used my magn. He had drained me dry. I exhaled, centering myself and letting energy from the very atoms in the ground and air fill the well inside me. Once I had enough, I shaped the stone into a long knife.

Jiro, watching me, licked his paw.

"Can you feel yourself?" I asked, "I mean, are you actually licking yourself or are you just trying to hide that your tongue is passing through your paw?"

"I exist," said Jiro, petting the ground. "It's you who can't interact with me."

"Me and the walls of buildings…" His eyes narrowed. I raised my hands in front of me. "Just saying."

"Perhaps we can focus on the nine heavily armed people heading in our general direction?" asked Edwin.

"Jiro, do you think you could interact with them?" I asked. There may have been a little snark in my tone.

Jiro cleaned his claws with his teeth. I took that as a no.

"Fine…" I thought about what I had seen. The squad was well trained. But they were hunting something, us. Perhaps

Jiro could be useful after all. "How about this? Jiro, if you could let them all catch glimpses of you..." Jiro put down his paw and stared at me. "It'd be good to get them focused on what was in front of them. Edwin..." I frowned at him. His trick of making things easier to see was useful, but I wasn't sure if it could work both ways. "Can you make it... make it harder for them to see?"

"What do you mean? Make the area foggy? I can't—"

"No, more that it is just difficult to focus, like the opposite of what you do when you make it clearer for us to see long distance."

"I suppose, so I make it hard for them to see and you..." He stared at the sharp stone knife in my hand.

"Jiro gives them something to focus on. You make it hard to see details, and I skillfully track them down and knock them out."

"How much skill's needed if they're blind and distracted?" asked Jiro.

I huffed. "There's an art to doing it without the others knowing. The last thing we want is for all four squads to be heading in this direction."

Edwin and Jiro weren't the most cooperative of team-mates, but we got something of a plan together. I climbed the tree again for another quick scan. It was harder to see them now they were amongst the silent and unmoving plantae.

Jiro disappeared and Edwin climbed another tree, keeping his feet hidden from view. I tucked my top into my pants and stretched my legs, bouncing on my feet to warm up.

As much as I hated it, it was my turn to create silence. I weaved my way through the unmoving trees and meagre undergrowth. Shadows flickered, and the world narrowed. Even smells were muted and only the sharp smell of metal cut through it.

Pete.

"Aye."

Some movement here. If you see something, kill it.

"Aye." The trooper's response was almost inaudible. Time to turn the tables.

I shifted my weight forward and rolled through the pads of my feet until I was behind him. All I needed was a line of sight of his equipment and I would be able to—

A tree next to him shot out a branch with a sharp end, jabbing into the side of his throat. *Static.* I wasn't happy about it but I didn't want to waste him being dead either. I sent a pulse of magn through a small crack on the side of his wristband, temporarily creating enough feedback to avoid any alarms.

"What happened to waiting until I called?" I kept my voice low and soft. "I can knock them out with their equipment. Just give me a moment, okay?" A branch of another tree patted my head.

I kept moving, my face grim as I took my position behind another squad member. She shifted and her eyes went wide. I tracked a pulse of energy travelled towards her wristband.

Static.

I jumped forward, using my body weight to slam my fist into the center of her body, knocking her out.

Sparking static.

The worst was I could *feel* the trees saying *I told you so.*

I used an old trick to detach the trooper's wristband and

scrambled up the nearest tree. My breath sounded overloud, so I relaxed my throat and stilled while I imagined them watching, waiting for me to make a mistake.

"The others are subdued," said Jiro into my ear.

My brain fired orders, and I wrestled with it to get it under control. "What? How?" I rasped, removing my stomach from my throat.

"The trees subdued them." Jiro pushed his nose through my ear and I grimaced.

"Err..." I let my head fall forward into the tree I was hugging. "I'm not sure that answers my first question."

"All those near us are no longer a problem."

"Temporarily not a problem?" I asked hopefully.

"No longer a problem." Jiro jumped down to the ground, sitting and examining his paw. I exhaled and joined him.

More death.

"There are still the other squads, though."

Jiro chewed on one of his claws.

"Where's Edwin?"

Footsteps tramped over the ground in our direction. I winced. He was frowning and appeared tired, but his eyes were bright silver, and his skin was back to being a normal copper color.

"You okay?"

Edwin nodded, but his face was grim. "Yes, mercifully, the trees didn't see me as a problem." A branch reached down and patted his head. He tried to hide his wince.

I hated to do it, but they had acted in our defense.

"Thanks for... clearing the path."

"Path is cleared," the tree next to me said, their voice very close to my ear, which did not help my nerves. "Are you all okay?"

"Yes, we are well." I lay my hand against the trunk next to me. "Thank you."

"Happy to help, Morgan." I suppose I shouldn't be surprised that they knew my name. But I didn't have time to exchange introductions with an entire forest right now.

I glanced at Edwin and Jiro. "I will come back and visit properly, but for now, we need to get moving."

"Save our heart."

I blinked.

"We will," said Edwin.

"Okay... anyway, the other squad members outside the range of these trees are likely heading in this direction." The knife I had made might still be useful, so I created a small sheath from some dead leaves to hold it against my wrist and then headed towards what I hoped was the direction of the residence.

Edwin rubbed his face with his hand but followed. My eyes were twitchy, torn between seeking shadows or sharp branches. I sped up, just giving quick hellos as we slipped through trees. The cover given by the plantae finished and there was a large, cleared area to cross before we reached the fence around the property.

"They're coming," said Jiro.

"How far away?"

The cat shrugged. I was both annoyed and impressed. I had never seen a cat shrug before.

"Can you go invisible and scout around?" I asked.

"You see only what I give you permission to see," Jiro sneered.

"Great, well, can I see less? Thanks."

Jiro sharpened his claws with his teeth, or whatever specters do.

"If they have blasters, we won't make it over the wall," said Edwin. "Even if I can thicken the air."

"You're right." I glanced at the wristband I had taken. "I don't suppose you have any metal?"

Edwin's lips curled up, and he held out his hand. My eyes widened and my stomach rolled as he pulled a strand of metal out of it.

"What are you doing?"

"Copper, here." He handed me a thick piece of copper wire.

"Is that... your flesh?" I asked.

"No, I used my essence to assist with the transformation, but it isn't... me."

I swallowed but took the flesh metal from him and kneeled on the ground. "Jiro, at least let us know if they get in blaster range, will you?"

There was no avoiding it. This was one I needed a decent amount of magn for. I drove the wire through the stolen band and drew magn down into it. I held it just above the soil and kept feeding it more and more energy. My eyes closed, I focused on pushing it out, following all the invisible aether connections between the team. Those closest got the worst of it, but at least they would only be unconscious, not with a branch through their neck.

A symphony of buzzes echoed back through the trees, getting increasingly faint until there was only silence. I pushed the wristband deep into the soil beneath me and allowed all the excess electricity to roll off me back into the earth. My breath shuddered, the band around my lungs loosening. Jiro was no longer lounging, but pacing in a circle around me.

"That's not possible," said Jiro, stopping in front of me.

I used my hands on my knees to help me stand.

"What isn't?" I asked. The copper wire was useful, but I wasn't sure how best to carry it. In the end, I wrapped it around the top of the blade on my stone knife. I checked, for the millionth time, my quota limit. Halfway there. *Static.*

"The electricity through the aether, that's not technology we have—"

I glowered. "We? Who's we?" My eyes flicked to the side and widened as I saw Edwin running over to the wall. "Static."

I followed him, hoping that I had in fact, taken out all the blaster-wielding security troopers. Edwin and I flattened ourselves against the wall. Our breath sounding like sirens.

"Since when did you become the reckless one?"

He grinned.

"Just don't throw away your sense of caution completely." I rested my hand on his arm. "Ready?"

"Do we have a plan?"

I shrugged. "Keep going up."

18

Magnets and death

"Thanks for coming back."

We made it over the top to find ourselves behind one of the smaller brick buildings. It seemed ideal. Except for a tall grumpy Blueshroud with purple hair, a lashing tail, some burn marks on her wrist and a blaster in her hand.

"Didn't want to miss out on the fun and excitement." I couldn't help the grin that spread across my face. There is a certain joy that comes from knowing everything is out of your control.

Lydia lifted her blaster and my vision narrowed.

"Nice," I said, "Is that one of the new plasma blasters? I didn't realize that they were in production yet?"

"Shut – up," she snapped, her teeth clicking.

"Is it safe to bite down that hard? You might hurt—" Lydia fired, and Jiro appeared between us, roaring as the energy hit him. I dived to the side. The clean and empty space might make its homeowners proud, but it wasn't of much use to someone seeking cover.

I pulled magn and channeled it through the wire on the knife, creating a lightning arc and whipped it towards Lydia. By the scream, I got a bit of skin. I was also going to get a bunch of people coming to check out what was happening.

Lydia snarled. "I'm gonna rip you to pieces—"

I swung the knife again, trying to knock the blaster out of her hand. Instead, I hit the wall next to her, which smashed down. Her body crumpled beneath the building's weight. I stood there panting.

Static, please no.

I imagined a world where Lydia wasn't angry and full of violence. Maybe it existed or could have. But I had made sure we would never find out. I swallowed the hard lump in my throat.

"A wasted life," said Edwin frowning.

My feet were stuck and I couldn't tear my eyes away from the hand and tail that were peeking out from under the rubble.

"I didn't mean..." I gazed at Edwin. His hand was a comforting weight on my shoulder.

"She—"

"Keep moving," snarled Jiro.

The volume of voices and footsteps had increased.

"Do you know where we're going?" I asked, shaking my head and tearing my eyes away from Lydia's body.

"Yes," said Edwin, he pointed to one end of the building just as half a squad came around the corner. The other half came from the other direction. I sighed. The killing just never seemed to end. In seconds we were buffeted by intense waves of energy and any parts of the building that remained standing exploded, showering us with debris.

On one side of me, I had Jiro jumping and twisting in the air as he snapped at the energy streams that only he could see. On the other, I had Edwin working to thicken the air enough to defuse the blasts. I took my lead from Jiro and pulled the energy into me, choosing how they entered my body, converting it to magn. I'd never drawn in live concentrated energy being thrown at me before. Blisters formed on my skin, and I was soon panting.

The troopers advanced and, using as little magn as possible, I fed it into Edwin's copper wire.

"Get down," I shouted as I spun, flinging out a wave of power that knocked everyone in its wake unconscious. Except for Jiro, who was like a large kitten playing in all the energy being thrown around. "Edwin, where're we going?"

A trooper reared up in front of me, swinging his knife at my neck. I stumbled back but captured his arm. I head-butted him and in the moment it gained me, I punched him with the hand holding my knife on the side of his temple, he dropped.

Edwin turned back towards me. "Are you coming?"

I rolled my eyes. "Forgive me for..." I glanced at the unconscious bodies littered around us. "Saving you?"

He gave a small smile, but it didn't reach his eyes.

"They're hurting her."

Jiro took the lead. We followed him past the building into a tunnel that burrowed into the side of a hill.

"You just won't die, will you?" A section of the wall moved and Emanuel stood in our path.

"That's literally the plan," I said, smiling at him. My knife was still in my hand, and I fed magn into it.

Emanuel sneered at me while checking out Edwin. His eyes skipped Jiro, so I assumed the cat was going incognito.

With the magn I had absorbed from the plasma blasters still rolling through me, it didn't take much for the copper around my knife to spark.

Emanuel clocked it and his lips drew back in a snarl, his weight shifting forward.

"This is going to feel good," said Emanuel, launching at me. I raised my arm, ready to whip him with the same wave of energy I had used so effectively before.

"Morgan, no, the tunnel," Jiro shouted, directly in my ear and while I was trying to uncross my eyes, Emanuel reached me.

I stabbed at him with my knife, but he swept it aside and it flew out of my hand. His hand wrapped around my throat while the other pounded into my side. My head ringing, and my imminent death in front of me, I extended the talons on my hands and feet and ripped out his throat and stomach.

I lay there. A rotten odour coming from the sludge oozing out of his body. His weight was considerable and made it difficult to breath. My claws were still extended but I could feel the heat, the energy leaving his body and knew I had another death to add to my list.

"I might," I turned my head to the side to get some air and keep my face away from the ooze dripping off his body. "I might need some help."

I stared at Jiro who sat there staring at me, his eyes narrowed.

It took all of Edwin's, and my, strength to get me out from under Emanuel. I stood there shaking, covered in gore, glaring down at him. I'll never know why he didn't use his blaster. Afraid of bringing the roof down on us? Or just so egotistical that he thought he could take me out without it.

"You had to do it," said Edwin.

"I know." Maybe, but when would the killing stop?

"Clean up and get moving," said Jiro. In a daze, I obeyed.

Jiro bounded ahead, but my feet were heavy. I'd promised myself I wouldn't be responsible for other people's deaths again, but the count was rising.

Eventually, we found ourselves in a cavern composed of magnets. In the center, a five-meter-long fossilized tree with gaping holes in their bark, was laid out on the ground. I swallowed and let my eyes move to the six people strapped to the floor in a circle around it.

Lenora! Her skin was stretched taunt and covered with bruises and sores.

"Why—" I asked, choking.

"They're feeding the magnets," said Jiro.

"How?"

"Magn flows and is amplified through them."

I kneeled next to Lenora and touched her unconscious body.

"Edwin, can you release her? Their binds?" I asked.

He frowned but crouched down with me and touched her

wrists. His shoulders hunched, and he panted. But no matter how much I pulled, I couldn't move her.

"It must be the magnets," Edwin gasped. "They're keeping me cut off from the ludere."

"Use my magn…"

Edwin dropped his head. "It doesn't work like that."

I swore.

"Even if you could break the binds, it wouldn't matter," said Jiro. He sat watching us and even his shoulders were drooping. "She's too deeply woven into the magnetic field." Jiro swung his head towards me.

"No," I said.

Edwin checked on the others. They were like Lenora, alive but unconscious.

"They're all at the point of death," said Edwin.

"Don't even try it," I touched Lenora's neck, "I can feel her heartbeat and see her breathing."

"Her body's going, but her brain…" Edwin kneeled next to one and pulled back his eyelids.

"There has to be some way to save her," I said.

Edwin just shook his head and pushed himself to his feet. He shuffled into the middle of the room and gazed at the tree. His hand reached out and gently brushed their branches.

"We can't save them, but we can save Syl."

I gazed at Lenora, an unwelcome hot wetness in my eyes and I swallowed.

"Fine, while you work out how to save *Syl*. I'll save Lenora and the others on my own."

Jiro padded over to my side and sat down with a huff next to me.

"She's gone Morgan," said Jiro. He lent forward and snuffled Lenora's face. "This is nothing but an empty vessel, waiting to be converted back into the elements of the superverse—"

"I appreciate you're having your own existential crisis, but it doesn't mean that—"

"The only way to get Syl out of here is to remove the anchors," said Jiro.

Deep and irrevocable lines formed in my forehead. "And by removing the anchors you mean..." my hand rested on Lenora's shoulder.

"We need them to stop feeding the magnets," said Edwin.

"Oh, so you're going to kill them then. Is that it?"

Lenora had deep, dark circles under her eyes and most of her hair had fallen out. Strands lay scattered around her.

"We need to do it all together," said Edwin, "I can take out the three on this side and you can—"

"You're willing to kill unconscious people who haven't—"

"They're already dead," said Jiro.

"I'm not killing six defenseless people," I began drawing on the well of magn within me.

"What are you doing?" asked Jiro.

"I'm going to free them." My throat was tight, and I breathed in through my nose, closed my eyes and wove an energy field like a web around their bodies and slowly, subtly reduced their connection to the magnets.

"Morgan, stop," Edwin's voice lashed out.

I didn't need to use much magn for this, I just need to

keep weaving energy between theirs and the magnets. The magnet's grip was waning. It wasn't a sharp flick, but a gentle pop of release, and then they were free.

I opened my eyes and grinned triumphantly at Edwin and Jiro. They stared back at me, their faces empty. I smiled at Lenora and my body stiffened. I could feel my breath lock in my chest and then there was nothing but me, Lenora and the *no* echoing in my head.

Every wick of moisture had been removed from her body. Her eyes were white, and her skin was mummified as if she was the fossil, not the tree. It took all my strength, but I raised my head. A live tree was now surrounded by six mummified bodies. And the hum of the magnets was silent, crushing.

I tried to breathe through my nose, but my throat was so tight it blocked any air from getting to my lungs. I swayed.

"Stop it," said Edwin. He grabbed my shoulders and shook me. "We don't have time for this."

"He's right," said Jiro.

If his plan was to provide me with a distraction, it worked brilliantly.

"Let me tell you what you can do with *right*. You can take right and shove that static up your sparks until you have static pouring out of your sparking heads. That's what you can do with right." I shrugged off Edwin's hands and leaned forward. As soon as I touched Lenora, she crumbled into dust.

"SPARK."

I wiped my face but just smeared Lenora's dust over it.

"Spark."

I stood, swaying, empty.

"Wake the tree up and get her into a form that can move," I growled.

Edwin kneeled next to the tree. I couldn't see, but I could feel enormous quantities of ludere flowing through him. Jiro settled next to him, almost leaning on him.

"I thought you couldn't connect—"

"The magnets have been—"

"Right." I held up my hand. The deaths of the people in this room was now embedded in my subconscious. I examined them creating a vivid memory to be called forth later in dreams.

The tree disappeared and was replaced by a bimodal female with bark like skin. Large gashes were visible with puss oozing out. She had two eyes, one nose and a mouth which was currently open and screaming. She lunged towards me.

"Syl." Edwin dove between us and grappled with her arms. The dark swirls on her hide spun, mirroring her agitation.

"Win? What? Did you do this to me?"

Win?

"No, they wanted to do it to me too, Syl." He pulled her into his arms. I shuffled and glanced away. I wondered what stopped Wilbur in that moment. He had found his power source, but instead of capitalizing it, he hid it away, created a fake identity and cut himself off from his co-conspirators. He must have known he was signing his own death warrant.

Syl pushed back and her eyes flashed green, darting around the room, and examining the five people, and Lenora's outline of dust, laid out on the ground.

"Who're they?" Her hair, which rivaled Vivian's with its layers of green, fell forward over her face.

"People who died to bring you back." I tried to keep my voice calm. Syl glared at me. "We need to leave this room. Now."

"Morgan's right. We need to get you out of here." Edwin reached out for one of her wrists again and led her towards the door, with Jiro following them. And then it was just me and the dead.

I didn't want to leave them alone, with no one to remember. I also didn't want them to end up in some preservation storage unit. I crouched next to each one and took an image on my wristband in the hopes I could give their friends and family some peace. My thumb pressed down on their dried out remains and each of them in turn scattered to dust. I softened the stone of the floor, and it welcomed them. A farewell whispered between my lips, heard only by me.

The others hadn't gone far. Once out of the room Syl had refused to move until Edwin had explained everything, which seemed to take some time with Jiro interrupting every couple of seconds.

"We don't have time for this." I turned to Syl. "Syl, people are using sleeping everlastings for power that can't be tracked. Jiro, have you seen any other people being held against their will?"

"No, just here and where you were."

"Great, so let's—"

"Who?" asked Syl.

"What?" I asked

"Who's on this council of five?"

"Everlastings—"

"No, which everlastings, what are their names?"

I rolled my eyes, for volt's sake.

"We need to get out of here first and do history lessons later."

"Jiro, what is the fastest way out?" I asked. Jiro's head swung around. I wasn't sure what it was, but something had changed, and my brain had firmly put him back in the threat category. "If you don't mind sharing."

He grumbled but stood, stalking down the hallway. I followed.

Edwin shifted his weight between his feet. "Syl, we need to—"

"I want—"

"I don't care," I said over my shoulder.

Footsteps followed me and with Jiro providing directions, we avoided security. My relief grew until we came to a set of large, and familiar, double doors. My stomach dropped.

"I thought you were leading us out?" I hissed.

"I'm showing you the fastest way."

"How's going through a lab full of blueshrouds, Deans and corrupt preservation service masters going to be faster than a side exit?"

Jiro snorted.

"What's happening?" asked Edwin.

"Jiro's led us to the sparking lab, is what's happening."

"It's outside of the hill," said Jiro.

I snarled at him.

Edwin frowned. "Why did you do that? We need to get Syl—"

I tried to step back, but Syl had moved at the same time, and I was thrown forwards. The double doors gave way under my weight, and I found myself back in the lab. At least this time I had a knife.

The two Deans, Amiel, Grace and about twenty of Blueshroud muscle, turned towards me drawing their blasters. The Deans took in Edwin and Syl, but their gaze seemed to miss Jiro.

"Can't see me," said Jiro.

I tuned him out and focused on the static in front of me.

Grace smiled. In fact, they all did.

Absorbing the magn of three blasters had hurt. Twenty might be a bit much, even for me. I was still within my quota for now, but it was going to take a miracle for me to get out of this without dying by someone's hand. Diplomacy first.

I focused on Amiel. "Let me help—"

Grace's smile twisted into a snarl. "Kill her—"

"No." Amiel stepped forward and held out his hand to the troopers. They glanced at Grace. She glared at the back of Amiel's head but nodded at them and they dropped their blasters. I noted they didn't put them away though.

Right now, my survival depended on Amiel, so I focused on him.

"We've the same goal."

He shook his head, his eyes sad and cold. "I don't think so, Morgan. Big changes are needed."

"I have no desire to get in your way."

"Don't you? You say that but so far you have been nothing but trouble."

"Let us go and I'll disappear. I promise."

Amiel laughed. "Back to your mountain?" He shook his head. "I'm sorry but I don't trust you to stay out of it."

I shifted forward and tried not to notice the blueshrouds adjusting their grip on their blasters. "The council is no friend of mine."

Amiel nodded. "True, but I don't think you have the stomach for what needs to be done."

"Unfortunate, I suspect you would have been very useful," said Ohith.

The two Deans, Ohith and Ebarin, had ditched the lab coats and were dressed beautifully with capes that swirled and danced around them without the need of a breeze. The lab was mostly empty, making me think they were wrapping up this experiment. Which meant they were eager to get out of here.

"Perhaps I still can be?" I shrugged. "We haven't actually sat down and discussed what you're trying to achieve."

"Unfortunately, we don't have time for a philosophical discussion today." Ohith gave me a slight smile.

"Perhaps another time, then?"

Ohith laughed. "While nothing would give me more pleasure, there's the slight problem you've created." Ohith peered past me at Syl. I also noticed Ebarin examining Edwin with a little too much interest in his eyes.

"We all agree that the council of five has gotten a bit too controlling, too trigger happy, right?" There had to be a way where we all walked out of here. I just had to find the right words.

Ohith shrugged but didn't take her eyes off Syl, and a frown was now firmly settled on her face. "Sure."

I frowned. She didn't sound sure. "If you don't believe that, then why are you... doing what you're doing?"

"Because," Ohith turned her attention back to me, "they won't share."

"Share what?" My head tilted and my focus tightened in on her.

"Transformation, enlightenment, immortality." Her face was flushed and eyes wide.

"I didn't know they could share that." I scratched my head. "I kind of thought that was just part of who they were."

"Perhaps we're getting off topic?" asked Ebarin. "The important thing is we need to get out of here, now."

"Dean Ebarin is right," said Amiel. "I've just received a notification that the preservation service is on its way."

"I can help—"

Amiel shook his head. "Grace my love..."

"Here to help make the world a better place." Grace grinned.

The blueshrouds lifted their blasters.

"Kill her if you want, but I need the others," said Ebarin.

Grace grunted but flicked out a series of orders and half the guards moved towards Edwin and Syl while the rest fired their blasters at me.

Death never stopped. I stared straight at Grace and pushed. It wasn't even as hard a push as I could do, but it was enough. Grace and the guards disappeared in an explosive shower of blood and flesh. My wristband bounced around like it had won a prize.

Amiel growled, but his eyes never wavered. "You've just signed your own death warrant."

"True but you don't seem too upset bout your lover's death."

He shrugged. "She was useful."

I wanted to throw up, but that would have to wait.

Amiel regarded the remains of his lover. His gaze was cold, not grieving, angry while Ohith and Ebarin watched and waited, their energy potential building.

I swallowed and focused. "The council's not going to let any of us get out of this alive. Including you."

Amiel gaze shifted back to me. "Which is why you have to understand—"

"I understand nothing about torturing people."

"You've killed. You understand that sometimes choices have to be made."

"In self-defense."

"That's what we're doing. We're defending ourselves against the slave state that the everlastings have put us—"

"We're not slaves."

"We're not free to do as we want."

"We're not free to murder each other, true, but we're free—"

"As long as it's within the rules of their making."

I stopped myself from instinctively rubbing my face and losing sight of the three threats in front of me.

"All societies have rules. It's how people can live together."

"But we don't get to set them."

"No, we don't, and that is because of people like you and

them," I gestured towards the two Deans, "who ruin it for everyone."

"These same rules demand your death."

"Which is incredibly unfair, really I should be getting a medal for this."

"It doesn't have to be that way," said Amiel, tiling his head and tapping his cheek. "Maybe I was wrong, you could join us, and we could throw off this yoke of control that the ever-lastings have that's stagnating our society."

I snorted. "So, I get to live if I help you torture people?" More likely get blasted in the back.

"Sometimes people die in a fight. It's the—"

"Circle of life," my face hardened. "Where have we heard that rhetoric before?"

Amiel's face flushed, but it was Ohith and Ebarin I was worried about. This conversation was just giving them time.

"It's not like that."

"Maybe, but why do I feel that the people who must die aren't you, Ohith and Ebarin here? But people who haven't even chosen to be part of your fight?"

"If you aren't with us, you're against us," said Ohith.

"We're wasting time." Ebarin reached out and took Ohith's hand.

I inhaled and opened my mouth, but Syl, still a little un-steady on her feet, had gotten tired and stumbled into Edwin, who shifted towards them.

Ohith responded with a wall of sound that shattered everything before it. The roof collapsed, showering us with debris. Flaming metal gurneys, lit by Amiel, were flung at me, the heat battering my face. But it wasn't the physical threats that were the problem. It was taking everything in my power to stop Ohith's resonance from exploding my head.

"Not even you can burn away the atrocities you've committed here, Amiel," I said, struggling to keep the air around me clean and the flames off my skin. Edwin had wrapped his arms around Syl and seemed to do a much better job of not being burned. I drew on my magn to fling a blazing gurney towards Amiel, but he knocked it to the side with ease.

Ohith sent another wave of sound towards me, this time backed by Ebarin, who layered it with fear and misery. My throat closed, and I struggled to breathe. I responded with my own swell of vibrations. What was left of the structure became dust. Everyone wobbled, but the collapse of the building suppressed Amiel's fire.

All three swung towards me.

A cold sneer ripped across Amiel's face. "Impressive Morgan but not impressive enough to—"

Syl, who had broken free of Edwin, stumbled up to Amiel. He tried to set her on fire but she ignored the flames lapping her skin and ripped off his head.

Ohith and Ebarin doubled their efforts and I pulled in the sound waves that wanted to melt my insides while trying to keep Ebarin's fake emotions out of my head. I could do little more than keep myself together.

Edwin yanked Syl back behind Ohith and Ebarin to the illusion of safety, while Ohith and Ebarin's attacks on me increased in intensity.

Sparking great.

I tensed, but Jiro appeared in front of me, bringing the

unexpected beauty of silence with him. My body tilted and my feet scrambled to keep me upright.

"You don't exist anymore," said Ohith, her grip on Ebarin's hand convulsing until her knuckles turned as white as his face.

"Ha, I'll give you points for trying. But no, I'm just in the most handsome of my forms." Jiro paced back and forth in front of me.

"You, you...how?" asked Ebarin, taking a step backwards and dragging Ohith with him.

"But we took—" said Ohith. Jiro growled.

"Yes, you took, and you took, and you took, but I'm at one with infinity. You can't eat infinity, no matter how hard you try."

With every word, Jiro took a step forward and they a step back.

"You might not be gone, but you can't hurt us." Ohith pulled at the hand holding Ebarin's and forced him to stop. "I can see through you Jiro." Ohith laughed, and it resonated in circles out from her. I gagged.

Jiro reached out a paw and the sound disappeared.

"I can take too, you know."

"Maybe, but it won't be fast enough to stop us." Ohith stood up straight, her cape fluttering behind her.

But they had taken too many steps back and Syl's hand dropped onto their shoulders.

"Stay," said Syl.

They twisted and screamed but Edwin spun and spun until they were so wrapped up Syl was the only reason they were upright.

Jiro paced in front of them, his fangs displayed. Ohith opened her mouth and screamed towards me. Jiro jumped into the sound and this time I heard a slight thump. Which told me two things. One, that by some miracle my eardrums were still intact and two that his form was getting heavier.

Edwin's copper skin had a greenish tint again. Ebarin kept twisting and turning trying to break free.

The charge in the air told me they were pulling in more magn.

"Don't bother," said Jiro.

"We aren't just people you can disappear," said Ohith. "Our followers won't be silenced. They'll be louder than ever."

"I think we both know I can do whatever I want with you," said Jiro.

"No one is doing anything to anyone until I say so," said Harriden.

A large group of preservers flowed into the space, the word room didn't really apply any more. I snorted. Great that they had arrived, once again, just as we didn't need them anymore. Though I admit it was useful to have the preservation service and medics here to deal with all the oozing bits.

19

The end as we know it

Harriden arrested everyone. Everyone except Jiro, who said a few sharp words that sent him scrambling backwards. I tried to rub the frown on my forehead, but the handcuffs got in the way. I huffed when I saw Edwin and Syl being escorted handcuff free. Harriden was such a sparkhead.

With Amiel, and most of the Blueshrouds dead, we had perhaps, in hindsight, been a little overenthusiastic. But the vision of people strapped down and being drained of their lives softened any regret.

No one spoke as we were cleaned up and transported to the preservation's headquarters.

"Show them into the conference room," said Harriden.

"Not coming with us?" I asked.

"No, I have a thousand forms to file because of you." He glared at me and stomped off.

"You're welcome," I shouted after him and let myself be

led into the room where my handcuffs were finally removed. Edwin, Syl, and I were all made comfortable and offered food. Already full with a cocktail of hope and anxiety, I ordered a light broth.

"Thanks," I said.

I was so focused on my own food that I didn't even see what the others ordered. My body relaxed with every spoonful from the large bowl of piping hot soup that was put in front of me.

"When do you think we'll get to go home?" asked Edwin.

I finished off my last spoon full, settling back into my chair with a sigh.

"Where's home?"

He frowned. "You know what I mean."

I shrugged. Just for a moment I didn't want to think about it.

Syl had been given some sort of green liquid but she was just staring at it. I would have been hesitant to drink it too.

"The only goal is to get out of this alive." My mouth pulled down in a frown, but I fought it, keeping my expression smooth, and spinning in the conference chair. "We can deal with everything else later."

I had just finished a full rotation as five people in biped shapes entered the room.

The volt was in it now.

Five faces as familiar to me as my own.

Just great.

"Well, Morgan Anastasi, it seems we have a bit of a dilemma in front of us," said Morthwyl.

I didn't know what to say, so swung side to side. Morthwyl smiled.

"Are you not disturbed by this dilemma?"

"I'm assuming that you're talking about the dilemma of whether to kill me... or not?"

"I prefer it phrased, have your sentence executed."

"I still get killed either way." I shrugged, shifting so I was sitting upright in my chair.

"The condition of your suspended sentence was that you would not exceed your quota of using magn," said Iseret. "I think we can all agree that you have breached that condition."

"I believe the exact wording was not to exceed my quota tracker limit except in self-defense. I only exceeded it to—"

"We've witnesses who can attest to extreme uses of your magn, and not always in a moment of self-defense." Iseret's eyes shifted to the left.

"If we're going to be picky, the moment is an ambiguous word and is open to interpretation."

"True, however, the witness was Councilor Jarweer."

Jarweer? The councilor stood a little behind the rest. Tall, long black hair and yellow eyes. I was pretty sure I would have noticed him no matter how good at lurking he was.

"So, the law doesn't apply when a councilor is involved?" asked Edwin.

All five of them frowned at him.

"Of course not," said Rayisa

"Of course they don't apply, or of course they do?" asked Edwin.

"The rules apply the way we say they apply," said Tukhunri, his and Rayisa's faces twisted. I coughed to cover my sharp inhale as I saw, for the first time up close, the madness of the electromagn wars dancing in an everlasting's eyes. The blood rushed through my body in a whirl. It was one thing to suspect and another to be sure.

"I believe Deans Ebarin and Ohith had the same point of view," I rasped. As I watched the madness swirl, I knew I would never make it back to Seb and my mountainside.

"Which brings us back to our dilemma. We understand that self-defense played a role, but we have solid evidence that an excessive amount was utilized. However..." Morthwyl gazed down on me and rubbed his chin. "You did assist in the capture of two Deans whose crimes were against the very heart of our society and assisted other everlastings."

Assisted?

"Yes, I... assisted," I drawled.

Morthwyl's eyes flared, and the remnants of his pleasant expression slipped away.

"This incident has made us realize these rules are more important than ever. It's also made us realize the Deans need more supervision."

It wasn't only the Deans who needed supervision. My eyes wandered over to Tukhunri and Rayisa, my insides folding into themselves. I breathed in through my nose and tried to move my shoulders away from my ears.

"Ohith and Ebarin won't be causing any more problems," said Iseret with a smile.

"Right, well, I'm not a Dean, so—" I shrugged.

"You're right you aren't," said Morthwyl and I wish I could say I did not roll my eyes at one of the five councilors.

Morthwyl frowned. "However, you seem to handle more magn than we're comfortable with, not to mention the taking of life—"

"In self-defense or in the defense of others..." said Edwin.

"So many?" Asked Rayisa, stepping closer to Tukhunri and peering down her nose at me.

"If she hadn't, she'd be dead and more with her," said Iseret. Disoriented by the unexpected support I blinked at her.

The council of five stared at me, and I pushed my hands down on my legs to keep them still.

"I need her," said Edwin. They all turned as one and stared at him.

"Cousin, I appreciate that you, and Syl, have been through a lot, but we will handl—"

Cousin? Clearly, he and Syl wouldn't be facing any death sentences.

"And I'm grateful for that, but you've responsibilities—"

"You're the priority—"

"Syl, and I, need someone who can show us—"

"I think we're getting off track," said Morthwyl. "We have the matter of Morgan's suspended sentence to deal with."

Ah yes, let's deal with whether I was going to die today.

"Yes, let's," I said, leaning forward on the table. I shifted in my seat at the silence. "Life? Release from supervised service and a bonus for exceptional work from the council?" Even as I tried to project being a good citizen, my attention kept shifting to Tukhunri and Rayisa. The madness billowed across their eyes. I needed time to let someone know. I smiled at them. "Just putting it out there."

"I don't think we'll go that far, Volt," Jarweer's drawl slid across the room and a chill down the back of my neck. My heartbeat seemed to become over loud and I wished I had asked for a drink as well.

"What about the fact that Ebarin and Ohith trapped and almost killed an everlasting?" I asked.

Morthwyl frowned, and Jarweer glared.

"They tried," said Jarweer, his eyes flashing, "and failed."

My breath hitched. I was pretty sure my heart stopped as well. Jiro stared back at me out of Jarweer's eyes.

"They got pretty close, though, right?" I swallowed. I didn't know if this was helping my cause or not, but I would not get another opportunity. "How?" I asked.

Jarweer grunted.

"How did they get the jump on you, Jarweer?" asked Iseret, a slight sneer on her face. Confident that she wouldn't be so caught. But as I observed her, I could see it. For her it wouldn't be being trapped and eaten piece by piece, for her it would be an unknowing decent into madness.

"Enough," said Rayisa. "We have rules, and she's broken them. It's as simple as that."

I jumped to my feet, "you're the one—"

"Do you want to die today, Volt?" asked Jarweer.

The silence of the room sliced at me.

"Is there any doubt?" asked Tukhunri. His once golden aura a chaotic churn. The madness in his eyes swelled.

"Why do you call her Volt?" asked Morthwyl. My heartbeat became overloud in my ears. I was all for accepting the consequences, but would they ever end? I just wanted to help and here we were hundreds of years later. The madness just never seemed to stop.

"You don't recognize her? Who else could have saved two, three if you count me, which I do, everlastings?" said Jarweer.

"And killed at least a dozen people," said Rayisa.

"Exactly. Not something that just any warrant officer plucked off the side of a mountain could carry off," said Jarweer.

"So, when you say Volt..." said Morthwyl. His eyes scanned me, and his brow furrowed. I suppose I couldn't blame him. It had been a long time, and it wasn't like we had hung out or anything. By the time the council of five had stepped in to fix things, I had already gone into hiding.

"I mean, Volt, our illustrious inventor of electromagn."

"I thought she was dead? I'm pretty sure I killed her," said Iseret.

"My mother," I said. "She was the one that you killed." Iseret spun and glared at me. I held up my hands. "Which I was all for. Just so you know. She was the first of them to go mad and who knows how many lives she took."

Iseret snorted. "Don't pretend to be innocent in this." She peered at me. Her eyes were like lasers as she traced my face, trying to place me.

"Just to be clear, I've never taken other people's lives." I thought about all the people I had killed, "for power. I'm pro self-defense though."

"I think you have a generous view of what is necessary to defend it," said Morthwyl, his voice dry.

"Don't we kill some to protect the many?" asked Jarweer.

He frowned at Tukhunri and Rayisa. Considering how

much blood, sap and ooze they had spilled, I appreciated he saw the hypocrisy in advocating for my death over a little bloodshed.

Tukhunri and Rayisa jeered.

"She wasn't killing for her own gain," said Edwin, "she was upholding your laws."

Morthwyl slammed his hand on the table.

"But not at our direction," shouted Morthwyl. "Are we really going to say it is alright to kill when we like the outcome?" he asked. "Not to mention that if she's Volt—"

"If?" asked Jarweer.

"If she's Volt, then there is the issue of her other death sentence for her role in the electromagn wars," said Iseret

I hadn't even been aware there was one. I frowned at Jarweer. If he knew about the sentence, why bring Volt into it?

"I'd like to point out that I didn't actually—"

"Silence," said Morthwyl, his voice reverberated the room. Not around it, the actual room.

Iseret and Jarweer both exhaled and glanced away.

I glanced around the room. "Seriously, what charges—"

"Enough," said Morthwyl. "This conversation has only one end and I won't see time wasted and relationships strained before we inevitably arrive at it." He turned to me. "I thank you for your service, Morgan, Volt or whoever you are. You did a good deed today, and you did it knowing that you would die because of your actions."

"Well, I knew there was a chance, but I was kind of hoping—"

"The rules are there for a reason and we can't be seen condoning people killing each other without our permission. I'm sorry, Morgan, but you have broken the terms of your suspended sentence and you have taken over a dozen lives. Plus, there is the minor fact that Jarweer has named you as Volt who is charged with the crime of starting the electromagn wars. Despite that, your death will be quick and painless."

"Technically, it was my mother who—"

"If you insist, we follow process, then we will follow process, including the trial," said Iseret.

Edwin stared at me. "Volt, huh? Well, that explains things."

It did? What did it explain?

He turned to the council of five. "What about us?" asked Edwin.

"I don't see how this has anything to do with you, from what Jarweer has told me you only defended yourself," said Morthwyl.

"I-I need her, Morgan, to help me and Syl too," said Edwin. "I'm still learning how to navigate this world."

"I don't need her," said Syl. She was sitting cross-legged in her chair, her drink cradled in both hands, watching. Her eyes met mine, and I shivered at the level of rage in them.

"Don't worry cousin, we'll find someone to assist you," said Tukhunri. "This one is at the end of her usefulness."

Syl just stared at them. Her face unmoving and her eyes deadly.

Edwin flicked at a concerned glance at her and at the council members. He shook his head. "I—"

"Enough Edwin, accept what is and we'll work with you towards a tomorrow you can be proud of," said Rayisa.

Syl scoffed.

The weight of my body pressed me deeper into the chair.

If everlastings were infected, then there was nothing I could do, no door I could close that would keep the world safe from it. At least soon it wouldn't be my problem. Let others have the glory of solving this one.

An order must have been given as two guards appeared and I was escorted out.

I knew what was coming. A cell, a quick conversation in front of some apparently unbiased judges and then death with everyone watching on to make sure it happened. Whether I died as Morgan or Volt, it wouldn't matter. They, along with everyone else, dismissed me as dead already. Most people assumed Volt died in the wars, so it wasn't that big of a leap.

The cell was everything I had dreamed of, and they obviously shared a decorator with, the most likely recently deceased, Ohith and Ebarin. Though this time at least there was a bench with a mattress on it. I lay down on the inevitably stained mattress and closed my eyes. My body sank down into it and my stomach and heart kept going all the way through the floor. Perhaps I should have tried harder. Or maybe I should have just let Seb kill Wilbur and his goons as suggested. I started with the best of intentions, I always did. Wanting to stop people, like my mother, from using others as batteries for ludere, the only way she could use large quantities without being drained herself.

To avoid spending the rest of my life as a battery for her, I had created a way to use electricity as an alternative. I wanted to save myself and others like me. Instead, I sent the world mad. And the people who abused ludere, they didn't change, even though they had a thousand times more power than ever before, it wasn't enough. Greed was its own kind of crazy.

I visualized the forest, Seb and my small house on the side of the mountain. The lake, with its shimmering aqua waters below. I wished I had said a better goodbye to the plantae who had been my friends for hundreds of years. I had never been sure if the view was more beautiful in the soft light of dawn or under the glow of the moon at night but if I was going to die, I wished it had been there, in one of those moments. My eyes were fiery, but I swallowed and tried to remember the feel of the air on my skin.

The cell door slammed open, but I didn't bother opening my eyes. I had accepted my fate, but it didn't mean I needed to watch the circus.

"I remember you Volt, daughter of Maddalena, inventor of magn and I remember killing you as well as your mother."

She surprised a snort out of me and with a sigh I rolled over onto my side, propping my head on my hand. Iseret was standing there in full armor, her hand on the weapon at her hip, and her eyes narrowed.

I shrugged.

"Would I be here if that were true?"

"You'll be dead soon."

"Yes."

"But how are you alive now?"

I exhaled out of my nose. Really, there was no need for me to answer her, to appease her. Let her spend eternity wondering what had happened.

"Fate?"

Iseret snorted. "Despite Morthwyl's promises, I can make your death a lot less quick and painless."

I wasn't sure she could, but I was so tired.

"Blowing up a place is always problematic. After all, how do you confirm the body afterwards?" I asked. Iseret had put a blaster shot through my mother's head and then blown up her lab. Leaving me strapped down on a gurney in the middle of it.

"How did you get out?"

"I used magn. How else?"

"I cut off electricity."

"I have... heightened conversion methods and internal reserves... which comes in handy. For example, when someone leaves you tied down, helpless, and then tries to blow you up."

"Even if you could have released yourself, there was no way out." Iseret was a splash of red in the otherwise gray damp room as she paced. I understood the gray. Why bother painting a prison cell? But I never got the damp. Did they deliberately choose a site that had damp issues before they built the cells? Or were the cells just converted rooms that couldn't be used for anything else?

"There's always a way out. Your lot should know that."

I flopped onto my back. My gaze tracking a pattern of mold on the ceiling. Not so much of a concern for those staying in the cells, I supposed.

"You can hardly move through matter." Iseret had stopped pacing and stared at me.

"No, but..." I gazed up at her. "Well, it might surprise you, but I do have friends." I smiled at her. She didn't smile back. I had friends, but most were plantae.

Of course, a large ancient tree, with solid root systems can play havoc on the walls of a basement and even create a pathway out, if they are minded to. A tree that had been my safe harbor as a child and I spent my life protecting from my mother. A tree who had long ago settled into an eternal sleep and who I still missed every day. I always hoped to end up near them again when I entered my eternal sleep. But that, like most others, turned out to be the dream of a child.

"I don't know what you think you're gaining by lying to me. But your death will not be pleasant."

The door to the room slammed behind her, and I could hear the bolt sliding into place.

Static. Well, I couldn't help it if she didn't believe me. Images of my death and how it would hurt flashed like a AV show, so I distracted myself by prodding the mold with ludere to see if I could get it to make an interesting shape, like an escape tunnel or something.

I was exhausted by the time the guards came for me. Time for my day in court. Unlike the court appearances I had seen on the AV, only the council and a couple of administrators were there.

Morthwyl sat in the judge's seat with Jarweer and Iseret on one side and Tukhunri and Rayisa on the other.

"Volt Maddalena Anastasi, known as Morgan Anastasi to the preservation office and to the world as Volt, daughter of Maddalena, creator of the electromagn wars." It was a good sum up. I had to give Morthwyl credit for that. "You've multiple sentences against you and all of them carry the sentence of death. Despite members of the community pleading your case—"

I blinked. "Who?"

He frowned. "Edwin, some people from the compound you found, including a Grollei and a Uriah," he said through thin lips.

I smiled. I might not have been able to stop what was coming, but I had saved them. Was it enough to balance the ledger against me?

"Do you have any last words or information for the court to consider?"

They had already made their decision. I doubted anything I could say would sway them. Still if the others had made the effort to plead my case surely I could too?

"Morthwyl, you know it's really nice to actually be talking to you in person. Almost a pity we don't have more time."

"Keep to the point, Morgan," said Jarweer.

I frowned at him. He had brought the whole Volt issue into this, still maybe I had an ally in the room after all.

"Right, well..." I cracked my neck, "So you see, the thing is, my intentions are good, it is just sometimes I get bad outcomes. I created electromagn to eliminate the abuse of people in using ludere. I killed those people at that house because they were trying to kill us and were killing others to fuel a battery that kept an everlasting captive, and I'm pretty sure they were the same people who attempted to remove old Jarweer here..." My voice raised at the end and my hands spread out from my body. I scanned the room. No one seemed very impressed. Maybe I could have been more eloquent, but they were the main points across of why we should not kill Morgan today.

"You admit it then?" asked Tukhunri.

"Err... admit what?"

"That you started the electromagn wars."

"Well, technically, that was my mother. I just invented electromagn. She's the one who went nuts with it."

"You destroyed the world," said Rayisa.

"Destroy... that's a big word, I prefer—"

"Everyone-please-stop-talking," said Morthwyl. "Morgan, Volt or whatever name you prefer to be called—"

"Morgan's fine."

He glared at me. "Morgan, you have three sentences against you. One for creating the very thing that led to the wars—"

"and automobiles, makers and AVs—" I mumbled.

"The second for breaching your quota limit."

"to save lives and take down a people farm—"

"The third for killing over a dozen people."

"in self-defense—"

"Is there anything else you would like to say before your sentence is delivered?"

I wanted to convince them, preferably by song, maybe with a bit of a dance number, that this was an injustice, and that the genuine horror was in their midst. I wanted to shout at them to focus on Tukhunri and Rayisa and see the madness dancing across their skin. But I was exhausted.

I trusted the plantae to care for themselves and, as for the bipeds, perhaps they were doomed to go down this pathway from the first moment they separated from the dirt which grounded us all.

I dropped my head. But I flicked it back up again and stared at Tukhunri and Rayisa. "You're fools and have doomed the planet by your thirst for more, regardless of cost." I dropped my head again and stared at my feet. I hated that my fur was dirty.

"Thank you for the enlightening speech," said Morthwyl.

"Annihilation," said Tukhunri, staring at me with madness fogging up his eyes.

"Annihilation," said Rayisa. She didn't gaze directly at me, but focused on the colors adorning her fingers.

"Annihilation," said Iseret.

Static.

Not that I was expecting to survive this. And I certainly had no expectations of coming back from whatever death that they had planned for me. But annihilation? Well, I suppose Iseret wanted to be sure I stayed gone this time.

Morthwyl frowned. "Isn't that extreme?"

"Consider what she's done, and what she's capable of," said Tukhunri.

"She escaped death at my hands once before. I won't let it happen again," said Iseret.

"What does it matter to you Morthwyl? Either way she is gone," said Rayisa.

I turned to Jarweer, but he had checked out of the conversation and was studying Tukhunri and Rayisa. At least someone was paying attention.

20

Together we fly

I lay there, staring at the mold above me, now a slightly different shape. The slide of the bolt being removed made me sit up. Maybe they had changed their mind. A small person with green tipped feather hair stood there instead.

"How'd you get in here?"

"I said I was the closest thing to family that you had. "

I smiled weakly at her. "Thanks, I—"

"Is it true?"

I blinked at her, "err, what exactly?"

"That you killed Lenora?"

The blood drained from my face. "I—"

"So, you did?" Vivian's face stiffened, her shoulders hunched and water gathered in her eyes.

My stomach clenched.

"I was trying to save her—"

"You killed her—"

Lenora's dust haunted me. Maybe Edwin had been right, maybe she had already been too far gone. But it didn't change the fact that I had taken her the final step. I was just glad I had managed to give the photos of the others to Harriden. He might be an asshat, but he would let the families and friends know, or get someone else to. But it didn't change the fact that I was the reason their hearts stopped beating.

I swallowed. "Yes."

Vivian paced the room. "Do you know how I heard?" I shook my head. "Alwyn and Edwin were talking. You didn't even have the decency to tell me yourself. To face up to what you had done."

I winced.

"I haven't exactly had a chance—"

"Do you know how that makes me feel?"

"I'm sorry, if I could have brought her back, I would have—"

Vivian's trembling fingers clenched and unclenched. "I wish I'd never asked for your help." She stood in front of me, facing me square on. "Everything you have done has just made it worse."

I wished she hadn't forced me to help either. I tilted my head, I wanted to point out that she would be dead if it wasn't for me, but I saw the anger in her face and knew nothing I said would make a difference.

"Perhaps you're right..."

"I'm glad they're killing you."

"Annihilation actually."

"Good, then I can sleep knowing that you aren't polluting any part of the world."

I closed my eyes, shutting out her twisted face.

Spit hit my cheek and slid down past my ear onto the bed below me and the door on my cell banged closed. Silence enclosed me.

I dropped back onto the bed, pulling deep into my core, and tried to remember the smell of the lake and the sounds of the plantae chattering. I forced my eyes open and stared up at the mold above me. My mind thankfully blank as I exhausted myself feeding ludere into it. A soft hum filled the room, and I dozed.

My cell door opening woke me up, this time to reveal a guard who handed me a mug of my basic nutritional schema, no flavoring. A last meal? Really? How quaint. I placed it on the floor. My mouth was dry, but my stomach twisted at the thought of anything in it. I just wanted this to be over with. The soft hum comforted me, and I drifted back to sleep.

The feeling of hands gripping me and picking me up jolted me awake, and I had just enough time to take in the vines, *was that Freddy?*, who had created a hole in the wall before I was thrown over someone's shoulder.

"What—"

"Quiet, we need to move." I turned my head and found Syl staring at me.

"What—"

She shook her head and led the way through a large tunnel that had appeared. Freddy had grown a lot, and was significantly stronger if he could crumble the very foundations of a building. I had seen trees do it before, but a vine?

We moved swiftly, but it was too tight for running and

eventually Syl stopped, and I was swung to my feet, my stomach, which was getting a workout, dropping as I realized it was Edwin who had carried me, and Freddy had created a small cave in which stood Archie, Maxi, Drudtia and Alwyn.

Aw sparks.

"What're you all doing here?"

"We're rescuing you," said Maxi.

The glare I sent towards Drudtia was very sharp.

"I thought it safer to know where they were," she said.

I sighed. Great, more death.

"Come on, best if we get out of here before they notice you're gone," said Alwyn, smiling warmly at me.

"My life's not worth the risk." My lips thinned. It was time for this to be over.

"They only have themselves to blame with all their talk about annihilation," said Drudtia.

"How'd you know—"

"Vivian told us—" Edwin frowned. "I can't believe they'd go this far…"

"This is a mistake. I'm grateful, but…." I swayed, reaching out a hand towards a wall, exhausted. "It's more a question of risk assessment—"

"I'll annihilate them all," said Syl.

Edwin wrapped an arm across my shoulder, helping me stay upright.

"Er… exactly who's this all?" I asked.

"Tukhunri and Rayisa," snarled Syl, "and maybe Iseret. I'm not sure about her yet."

"Why—"

"They knew," said Archie.

"What?" My head spun. I was glad that I had gotten a nap in.

"Tukhunri and Rayisa, they knew what was happening to Syl," said Maxi.

"How—"

"People," Drudtia clapped her hands, "Let's keep moving."

The others sheepishly nodded and murmured sorry, and she hunched over and headed down a smaller tunnel. A faint light at the end highlighting her form.

I hesitated. If I went with them, we would all die. I took a step back, but before I could retreat a hand pushed me forward. I glanced behind me and saw Maxi watching me intently.

"This isn't a good idea," I said.

"It's not about you. It's about stopping them from killing everyone."

I rubbed at my face. "You might have a better chance without me."

"You're wrong." Maxi stepped up close to me. "We only have a chance if Volt is with us."

Wild faith stared back at me, scaring me almost as much as the prospect of death. I swallowed but nodded and shuffled forward, stumbling over the uneven ground. Edwin steadied me.

"Did they hurt you?" asked Edwin.

I gazed up at him.

"No, no I just wore myself out."

He tilted his head and stared at me puzzled. "Doing what?"

"This tunnel's impressive." I examined the vines holding up the tunnel we were in.

Freddy had done more damage than I thought a vine capable of. I shuffled along, mostly upright, following the others out of the tunnel to a small walled park, which if I remembered correctly was about a block away from the preservation headquarters.

"Thanks, Freddy," I said as I stroked some leaves of the vine.

"My pleasure. We were told to keep an eye out for you. Sorry I didn't come sooner."

"Your tunneling skills are impressive." I blinked dirt out of my eyes and tried to brush clumps of something off my face.

"Syl helped." The vine reached over to her and picked up a bit of her hair. She smiled warmly and returned the gesture.

"The building was ugly anyway," said Syl, her smile fading as she examined me. I hated to think about what kind of damage she could cause to my structure. Maybe annihilation wasn't that bad after all.

"I've topped up your soil, Freddy," said Alwyn. "You'd have used a lot to help us today."

"Thank you, kind sir, you're, as always, a delight." Freddy reached out a tendril and touched Alwyn's cheek before withdrawing, pulling soil and bricks after him. I ached, to follow him back under the ground.

"Are you alright?" asked Edwin.

I gazed up at him. "Yes? I think so …" I patted his arm. "Just need… sleep…"

Edwin peered down at my hand still resting on his arm, his face a mixture of surprise and concern.

"Do you think the entire building will fall down?" asked Maxi, trying to peer back up the block.

"No loss," said Archie.

Drudtia snapped her fingers. "We need to go."

"I don't think so," said Jarweer.

The gate to the park was made of a beautiful wrought iron. The only blemish was the council member leaning against it. I stepped forward, shoving Archie and Maxi behind me and kicked Edwin in the ankle, preventing him from stepping forward.

"Councilor Jarweer, before you go all rampagey—"

"Rampagey?"

"You know, with all the indiscriminate killing."

"That's more Iseret's deal than mine."

"Oh, so you've noticed then."

We stood there staring at each other.

"Jiro, let us go," said Edwin, his tone was strong and sharp.

Jarweer stiffened, shifting into a fight stance.

"Councilor Jarweer can do anything he wants," I smiled at him. "Including letting me go. Which would be a great idea for everyone."

He scowled. "And why would it be a great idea for me?"

"Where do I start—"

"We need to keep moving," said Alwyn. "I think they've noticed the hole in the wall." I rolled my eyes. I was only surprised it had taken them this long.

"I don't think you're hearing me," said Jarweer. "Morgan, Volt, is not going anywhere."

"We're hearing but we're just not listening," I turned to

the others, "right?" Everyone avoided eye contact with me. I suppressed a giggle and tried not to sway too obviously.

"Jarweer, she cannot be annihilated," said Drudtia, stepping up in front of me and blocking my view. I tried to peer around her so I could see what was going on, but Alwyn grabbed my arm and kept me still. I blinked.

"I agree annihilation is probably going too—"

"No Jarweer, now you're not hearing me."

I couldn't see, but I assumed that they both frowned at each other until Jarweer exhaled heavily and stepped to the side, gesturing for us to pass.

What the static was going on?

"Keep them off our backs, would you?" asked Drudtia.

"I can cause some… confusion. Give you a few more minutes, but you're only delaying the inevitable confrontation." Jarweer disappeared.

Drudtia snorted. "Too little too late in my book." She examined the rest of us. "Come on people, we need to get back … and work out how we're going to get out of this mess."

"I'll take care of them," said Syl, cracking her knuckles, glaring in the direction of the preservation headquarters.

"Not all five of them," said Archie putting his hand on Syl's arm. Her face warmed as she gazed down at him.

"We can't just prance down the street," said Maxi, who appeared to be in her element, ready to take on the world.

I gazed at the park in front of us.

"Do you think the plantae would help? I know they aren't the most discrete but…" I shrugged.

"Yes, that was my thought too and Freddy has already put

in a good word for us." Drudtia rapped on an enormous tree next to the gate with her knuckles. Their branches swung close to Drudtia's head.

"Rude," they rumbled.

"No time for pleasantries. I'll come back and share a nice cup of tea later. We need passage. Freddy said he spoke to you."

"Still rude," they rumbled again, but their roots shifted, and a tunnel was revealed.

With Alwyn leading the way, we all stumbled forward, and I patted the tree and whispered a thank you as we went through. I might have imagined it, but I thought a small root flicked me back. I couldn't tell if it was a good flick or a spark off. Drudtia brought up the rear, forcing the pace.

The tunnel closed behind us as the next section appeared, so there was a lot of dirt flying around. Edwin worked to keep the air as clear as possible, but soon we were all coughing. I was panting by the time Alwyn called a halt.

"Are we there?" asked Maxi.

"Where's there?" asked Syl.

"I think the more important question is who else's here," said Archie.

"We're home," said Alwyn, "but I can sense others above."

"We'll just have to go straight to the lab." Drudtia banged the closest root. "Take us to my rooms."

"I really don't think you should talk to the tree—"

She glared at me, and the tunnel opened ahead of us. We followed until we ended up in a small pocket of air pushed up against a wall.

"So how do we get in, then?" asked Maxi. She seemed to

be enjoying herself immensely. No doubt excited to be taking action against her oppressors. However, if Archie sucked his lips in any further, his face might concave.

"We use the door, of course," Alwyn gave a small smile, pressing a part of the wall and a door appeared. He glanced at Drudtia, and she nodded. With that, he pulled it open, getting out of her way and letting her barrel through.

"It's safe," she called back. I suspected I was the only one who heard the *for now* part that she mumbled under her breath as we tumbled into the lab.

"Is the council here?" I asked.

"They're upstairs. There are layers of protection on this lab and they haven't worked out how to get down here yet, but it is only a matter of time," said Alwyn.

"We're so sparked. They're pretty much immune to electricity and anything we can throw at them magn wise," said Maxi. We all turned her way. "What? I do my research."

Archie snorted and I smiled. It was good to know the wind wasn't completely knocked out of him.

She was right, though.

"Could we trap them with magnets like they did Syl?" I asked. Syl glared at me. "It's just a suggestion."

"No, one I don't have magnets and two, I don't have enough power, even if I used all of you to help, to hold five everlastings. They went through dozens of people just trying to keep one asleep."

"Sparkheads," said Syl. It was good to see that the apprentices had been teaching her modern vernacular. "I can rip their heads off?"

I wasn't completely against the idea. I just wasn't sure it would work.

"Do we need to take out all five?" I asked. "Isn't it just Tukhunri and Rayisa?"

"Why them? Morthwyl and Iseret want you dead too," said Edwin.

"Can't you see it?" I scanned the blank faces staring back at me. "The madness, the same madness that consumed the Deans, is in their eyes."

"That's not possible," said Drudtia.

"Yeah, the Everlastings can't be touched by the madness," said Archie.

"That's what we thought. But I know what I'm seeing. And think about what they have done. If we're right, they literally carved up one of their own and enslaved another."

Syl growled but the sound was lost as a series of thumps made the ceiling vibrate.

"They've found the entrance." Maxi's face was grim.

Alwyn and Drudtia exchanged glances and Drudtia shook her head.

"It is too early for that," said Drudtia.

The ceiling peeled back.

21

There was a firefight

Tukhunri and Rayisa drifted down until they were just above us. The madness spiraled through them, creating a chaotic blend of colors that turned my stomach.

An invisible hand grabbed my throat, distracting me from my nausea and lifting me up. Someone's scream cut through the air, and I was thrown to the ground, but the pressure on my throat tightened. That was going to leave some bruises, even on me.

Drudtia stood in the center of the lab the copper wires reaching out to her and allowing her to draw down on the electricity dancing along them. The grip around my neck loosened and I saw her do a perfect overarm throw of a tube, smashing it into them and then I was free.

I sidled up next to Drudtia. "Any ideas?" I asked.

Edwin and Syl moved together flinging out binds

attempting to catch them and hold Tukhunri and Rayisa to the ground. Tukhunri snarled.

Drudtia grabbed another couple of tubes. "Don't die."

Rayisa turned her arm into a blade and ran at me. I scrambled backward, ducking. I extended my claws and smashed them into her side.

She swung her blade at me, and I blocked her arm, but this time she added a zing to it and the magn snapped through my body, making me dizzy. Not so dizzy that I couldn't see Iseret descending through the ceiling to join the fight.

We were so sparked.

"You pathetic—" I punched Rayisa in the face. It felt good. I drew every bit of magn I could hold into my hand, slamming it into her stomach. There was nothing I could do to permanently take her out but I might be able to slow her down. With my claws deep in her physical form, I flooded it with disrupting waves of energy.

Iseret and Morthwyl arrived. Iseret, magn streaming out of her hands, cut through Drudtia's shoulder.

"You fools, what're you doing?" screamed Drudtia.

The chaotic swirl was visible in Iseret, not as nauseating as Rayisa and Tukhunri, but not great either.

Syl was doing her best to neutralize Tukhunri and from her position on the floor, Drudtia threw another tube at Iseret and Morthwyl, forcing them to drop, smashing the stairs beneath them.

"Drudtia, are you alright?" I shouted. But I had taken my eyes off Rayisa for too long, and she grabbed my neck, bending me back over the lab's bench.

"I'd worry about yourself if I were you." She hissed. I could feel her hand tightening and I pulled on magn to create oxygen in my lungs.

Rayisa, getting bored with trying to choke me, sent blast after blast into me. My body twitched, the magn too chaotic for me to control. Sparks crawled across my skin, the energy looping back into the sequins covering her jacket. I could feel her hand tightening and suspected she was about to snap my neck when she was pulled off me and replaced by a smirking Jarweer.

"Need some help?"

Probably, not a good time to point out that he started most of this.

Iseret and Morthwyl, worked to knock out Alwyn, who was in a corner of the lab trying to shield Maxi and Archie. Tukhunri seemed to have lost the plot and was now just standing there kicking Drudtia's head with his high heeled metal boots, but she dowsed him with another tube, and he wobbled, and, most importantly from Drudtia's point of view, stopped kicking her.

Tukhunri and Rayisa, fashion icons, who lived in stone mansions in middle of the largest cities. Could it be that simple?

"Edwin, Syl, I need dirt," I shouted and pointed to the concrete floor at the base of the broken stairs, the only area big enough to help us.

Syl frowned, but Edwin nodded. They had been trying to pull Tukhunri off Drudtia and as soon as they shifted their attention, he broke away and stood in the middle of the room throwing massive bolts of energy at everyone. Rayisa, pulling herself free of Jarweer, joined in. They even hit each other a few times.

"Can you keep them off us while I work on fixing this?"

Jarweer raised an eyebrow at me. "I think we are too far gone for that."

"If you help, there's a chance."

He frowned but didn't waste time arguing and ran towards his fellow council members.

Drudtia was still on the floor, her shoulder bleeding, with multiple cuts and bruises on her face. Morthwyl's and Iseret's attention fell on me, but found Jarweer between us, smiling at them. Their eyes narrowed.

"You stand against us?" said Iseret, glaring at him.

"This is not how we do things, there is no order here, no justice," said Jarweer.

"They've broken our rules."

"One has, the others... let the court decide."

"No, we end this now," said Iseret.

Morthwyl, more worried than angry, appeared to agree for a moment, but his face hardened.

"Yes," he said, "this ends now."

The concrete near the stairs crumbled, the ground beneath it appearing. I stepped towards it. Edwin and Syl, multitasking by joining apprentices, to help them avoid being blasted, had given me what I needed.

I ducked out of the way of a blast and took another step, but this time my body spun. Pain radiated from the center of my chest. I peered down and saw my clothes ripped, blood everywhere and my skin flapping. I screamed. A lot.

Shouts and the sounds of fighting filled the air and

unconsciousness called to me. I was, however, determined to fix what I had started, so I threw myself forward until my hand reached the exposed earth. I rolled, and through a veil of concrete dust and electric sparks, I could make out the council members. I pulled into me every bit of electricity that I could absorb.

"Come to me sparkheads." I used the magn within me to pull them towards the exposed earth.

"Help, push them into the earth," I shouted.

Someone helped, and the council members, perhaps taken more by surprise than anything else found themselves standing on the exposed earth.

"Fools," hissed Rayisa, "you'll all pay for your disobedience."

It was Jarweer's turn to pant. He stepped up next to me, his eyes and energy focused on keeping his fellow council members in the soil. I shifted and groaned in pain, but didn't let my eyes close. He wouldn't be able to hold them for long and it wasn't working. I scanned them. The shoes. They still had their shoes on.

"The shoes," I cried, despair ripping at my throat.

"What?" Jarweer roared.

"The shoes I need to get their shoes off."

"I don't think they are going to let you take their sparking shoes off Morgan," he growled. I hadn't even known that Everlastings could sweat but his body must be overheating.

"Edwin, Syl." I turned towards them. Archie and Maxi were standing next to them, Alwyn and Drudtia unconscious at their feet.

"How do we kill them?" screamed Maxi.

"I've got to," I tried to swallow, my voice struggling to project across the room, "get their shoes off."

She gaped at me and then shared a glance with Archie. They grinned. And then they were surrounded by shoes. Drudtia was right, keeping them close was safest.

The four councilors were almost free of the exposed earth and Jarweer was shaking next to me. I shoved my hand deeper into the earth and letting go of magn, I called up ludere, flooding the everlastings with all the earthy vibes I could call forth, which unfortunately by this point wasn't much.

"Edwin," I cried.

Edwin and Syl ran up beside me.

"How do I kill them?" asked Syl.

It took me a couple of goes to speak. "They need active earthing."

"What's that?" asked Syl.

"Watch," said Edwin.

Two thumps and they were kneeling beside me. He put his hand in the soil and lent his considerable ludere powers to mine, Syl joining him, the earth hummed.

Iseret and Morthwyl groaned, almost in pleasure, but Tukhunri's and Rayisa's cries, were of death. As the earth and ludere flooded their systems, their bodies fluxed between energy and matter. Their chaotic swirls speeding up and pushing at the edges of their form until a small part pushed free. As it escaped, it touched the soil, and a fulgurite formed, and then another and then another.

Jarweer kicked off his boots and stepped onto the soil. He threw his head back and groaned.

"That feels sparking amazing," he laughed, and twisted his

feet deeper. His groans mixed with Iseret's and Morthwyl's, which along with Rayisa's and Tukhunri's screams made me want to be in a different room.

"We've got this," said Edwin, gazing at me and the large wound in the middle of my chest.

"I'm not letting go until it's over."

Rayisa and Tukhunri's forms continued to shoot out energy, and each time another fulgurite appeared in the soil. I don't know what I had expected to happen. That they would find their center again, return to their usual golden selves? Instead, the chaos was too deeply woven, and the earth's resonance shattered them. The last of their matter transformed to energy, but the earth, not willing to let them go, drew it down, combining all the fulgurites together and then there was nothing left of them but two misshapen patches of burned soil. By this time Morthwyl, Iseret and Jarweer were all lying on the earth, practically rubbing against it.

Tiny fulgurites surrounded Iseret and there were even one or two near Morthwyl. Then it happened. Their energy synced with the resonance of the earth. I drew in a breath. The air was suddenly clear and smelt like the rains had been, leaving the last three of the council of five panting with big smiles. I wasn't going to be the one to get them a smoke. I allowed myself to find the unconsciousness that had been trying to get my attention.

I opened my eyes and the first thing I saw was Harriden and a bunch of preservation officers with rubber gloves using large tongs to put the fulgurites in jars.

"You have a knack for clean-up," I choked out. Harriden

shot me a glare, but Morthwyl put his hand on his shoulder, and he swallowed whatever he had been about to say.

"Yes, the preservation service played an important part in today's events," said Morthwyl. "Officer Harriden here is due recognition and a promotion for his work in bringing this matter to an end." Harriden's chest ironing his clothes. "Once he finishes the appropriate forms of course."

"Yes Councilor Morthwyl," said Harriden, who was probably not sure if he should be happy or full of despair at the mountain of paperwork that was waiting for him. He gazed down at me. "You might want to get that chest examined."

I glanced around for a medic, but the blood left my face at the sight of Tukhunri and Rayisa standing behind Jarweer.

"Jarweer—"

"It's fine," he crouched down next to me, and I squinted at him. "Trust me."

If I could have moved, I would have taken his trust and shoved it, but bad things had happened to my body, so I wasn't going anywhere fast. I reached out and touched my chest. Yep, still with a big blast hole in it. Though someone had stopped the bleeding and it didn't seem to hurt as much.

"Drudtia?" I asked. She was kneeling next to Alwyn. She swiveled her head in my direction. "Is he…"

"He'll live, but they did a number on him." She glowered at Morthwyl and Iseret, who were both still standing in the earth area watching the collection of the burned bits of soil that used to be their fellow councilors. I frowned and scanned Tukhunri and Rayisa again. There was no chaos in them. I sighed and let my head flop back on the floor.

Iseret glanced at Drudtia. "I said I was sorry. We thought he was the one who was blocking our energy in the room."

Morthwyl left his contemplation of the burned soil and came over to crouch next to me.

"How long?" I asked.

He didn't pretend to misunderstand the question.

"Honestly? I don't know."

"Why not?"

"We just got… busy. I didn't even notice that we stopped."

"May I make a suggestion?"

Morthwyl smiled. "When the great Volt speaks, even the council listens."

"Morgan, my name's Morgan now." There was no point attempting any kind of redemption for Volt, but maybe Morgan had a chance. "Perhaps, and this is just a suggestion, mind, the everlastings could build some earthing time into their daily schedule? Especially on days when they are dealing with large amounts of magn? It's just a thought."

Morthwyl inclined his head and laughed. "I'll take it under advisement. Though considering how good that felt, I think you can be safe in knowing we're very motivated to make time."

Morthwyl's gaze dropped to the blast hole in my chest.

"No need…" I gasped, feeling my skin knit. It was not a pleasant sensation, so I passed out, hopefully for the last time.

It was a cold afternoon, but we were sitting outside having tea. Alwyn carried a tray with a large cake and an oversized cup on it.

"I created your favorite soup. It's hot, I promise," said Alwyn, handing me the cup.

My smile broadened as I took him in. He might have been a little paler, but otherwise, he didn't seem any worse for wear.

"Thank you," I sat upright, and my fingers warmed as they wrapped around the large cup. The steam rose off it, the aroma making me smile.

"We think we should get extra credit for saving the world," said Maxi.

"Or at least the opportunity to write about it, but Jarweer says we can't say anything." Archie frowned. "I think it's important for people to know."

"Maybe," said Alwyn, taking a seat.

"More likely everyone would just panic and be fools about it," said Drudtia.

"You think everyone is a fool," said Maxi.

"It avoids disappointment."

Archie put his cake down. "But what about—"

"How can we tell people about our nifty shoes trick if we can't tell them what happened?" asked Maxi.

"And how will the people know how important earthing is for the everlastings?" asked Archie.

"They know now—" said Alwyn.

"And if they forget?" asked Maxi. "What makes you think they don't like the crazy?"

"Well, Edwin and Syl will join them to remind them," said Drudtia.

"What?" I asked, turning to Edwin and Syl. They stared back at me until Syl sighed, and Edwin shrugged.

"They asked," said Edwin. "They need a council of five and well… we're here, we're awake …"

"But Tukhunri and Rayisa they're still…"

"That was us," said Syl, around a mouthful of cake.

"Oh," I shook my head. Well, that would have stopped the Preservation Service from asking questions. I just wasn't sure if that was better. "You, you and Edwin, no offence Edwin, are going to be on the council of five?" I drained the rest of what was one of the most delicious versions of peanut butter soup I'd ever had.

"It'll be alright pet," said Drudtia and she poured me a glass of the whisky she had chosen over tea. I shot it back and held out the glass for a top up.

"Will it?" I asked. "You realize people will see them as the fashion icons now, don't you?" Everyone peered at Edwin, decked out in his velvets and tassels, and Syl was dressed in every color and pattern she could find. Her pants were a bright pink and green tartan, her shirt electric blue with white polka dots, her scarf a hue of purple and orange. It was a color clash that few people could have pulled off. Edwin and Syl peeked at each other and grinned.

"It'll be nice to make a positive difference in the world," said Edwin.

Maxi rolled her eyes while Archie snorted.

I asked Drudtia for another top up and slumped in my chair before noticing Vivian standing in a window gazing out at the gathering.

"Ignore her," said Archie.

"Yeah, she told us what she said." Maxi glared at Vivian. "She's wrong. We know you did everything you could."

"Thank you." I gave them a small sigh and finished my whisky. "I…" sighing, I stood, forcing myself to go inside.

I paused at the entrance to the room, but she stayed leaning against the glass of the window.

I joined her.

"Are you okay?"

"How can you ask me that after the way I treated you?"

"You don't think I felt exactly the same way, if not worse?"

Vivian kept her head against the glass.

"I spat on you."

"Yeah," I shifted my weight, staring out at the others who were not making any attempt to disguise that they were watching. "That was… extreme."

"Sorry."

"Were you planning on doing it again?"

She rolled her head and peered up at me.

"Not unless you kill Alwyn, or maybe Maxi."

"Not Archie or Drudtia?"

"Well, I wouldn't be happy about it, but I wouldn't spit on you."

I sighed and watched the group happily sharing cake.

"I can't guarantee they won't die."

Vivian lifted her head off the glass and faced me. "I know."

We stood there watching Archie take the last of the cake and Maxi attempt to steal it back.

Vivian smiled. "But you'll take out anyone who tries to, right?"

I laughed. "Absolutely."

I scanned the conference room. I was clean, comfortable and had a nice warm cup of coffee. Now all I needed was the absence of a death sentence hanging over me and I would call it a good day.

Morthwyl, Iseret, Jarweer, Edwin, and Syl sat around the table.

"Are you really going to have Edwin and Syl join the council?" I asked.

"Yes, it is important that we have a council of five."

"Won't people notice?" I examined them. They are nothing like the golden twins. "Are you going to make them wear their biped forms and take their names?"

"The first time they appear, yes. But they can evolve and take on a name and biped form of their choice."

"I like this one," said Syl. In the last day or so, she seemed to have learned about jewelry and now her fingers and arms were covered in it.

I stared at her, dazzled by the amount of color she had put on.

"I don't think it's going to be a problem," said Iseret, who flicked one of Edwin's tassels.

"Does that mean I'm free to go?"

"It depends on what you mean by free," said Iseret, her armor creaking as she sat back.

"Head back to my mountainside, making choices about my own life."

"The problem is," said Morthwyl, "who knows what kind of trouble you'll get up to?"

"I'd like to point out that it was the council—"

"Yes," said Jarweer, "you're, under the definition you have provided, free, but it's to our benefit to have you around." Jarweer sighed. "More people are stepping outside the quota limits, and you yourself have talked about how you want to reduce the death count." He moved to sit next to me. "Not to mention this was an organized operation. Who knows who's still out there and what they are doing?"

I rubbed my face. "That's what Harriden is for."

Edwin snorted. "Sure." He shifted closer as well. "Stay, you might not have as happy a life, but you'll have a meaningful one."

In my mind's eye, I could still see the madness swirling in Iseret's eyes. But the earthing had helped, and Jarweer, as well as Maxi and Archie would be watching.

Archie's idealistic view of society was well and truly cracked while Maxi felt betrayed by everyone. I trusted they would approach their inevitable reformation activities with the appropriate care and skepticism needed. Plus, they had friends in at least two, possibly three on the council, so I had high hopes for them. After all, it was their future they were building, not mine.

"I'm sorry, but I'm done. I promised myself if I survived this that I wouldn't miss the opportunity to go home and watch sunsets and sunrises over the lake."

Jarweer and Edwin both exhaled, disappointment etched on their faces. Morthwyl and Iseret's expressions were strained, but they didn't raise any objections. Syl seemed to have tuned out.

"If that is what you want," said Jarweer. "But I don't think it needs to be said that we should keep your...other...name out of it? Not everyone—"

"Anyone," said Iseret.

"-would be happy to know that Volt's still around."

I shrugged. It was only Morgan I cared about.

22

Divide and conquer

"Have you been back to the warehouse?" I asked. I was out the front of Alwyn's and Drudtia's home, watching the hustle and bustle of the city, also meeting my goal to stand in the earth without shoes at least once a day.

"Yeah," said Edwin, he joined me out on the front lawn, standing pretty much on top of where I dropped him on our first visit. "Syl and I checked it out yesterday. I'm afraid it's… structurally incomplete. More so than when we last saw it."

I sighed, wiggling my toes in the dirt.

"I'm heading off soon." Warmth flowed through me. Not that I minded visiting Alwyn and Drudtia. Good company and good food were not something to be sneezed at, but I wanted to get back to my space. "Have you found a new scholar for the others?"

The apprentices were still here as well, and I could tell it was wearing thin. The council was concerned about who their next scholar would be, and until they found the right one, I had been lumped with supervising them.

I had a fear of the apprentices becoming bored and doing something foolish or annoying, so I had approached their training with a vigor that they had not expected nor enjoyed. Maxi and Archie only pretended to grumble about it, however Vivian seemed to think the entire world should leave her alone. Unfortunately, it had other ideas.

"Are you sure you don't want to stay in Duskburn?"

I gazed at the street and its tenements. I could hear some music, though it was too far away to make out the tune.

"No, I think my time here is done. Besides they've cancelled my rights to use the gliders since we never got those four back.

"We could get that back for you, you know."

I shook my head. My decision was made.

"Where are you going to be based?" I asked.

"Probably Shipsdawn. Iseret is based there. I'll be taking the apprentices with me, she has a place for them."

The sounds of yelling came from inside the house as the apprentices argued. I could hear Alwyn stepping in and Drudtia threatening to annihilate them all. I didn't move and continued to stand there, my feet in the soil. Edwin moved closer to me.

"So out of curiosity, is this the first city that you'll leave that hasn't been burning behind you?"

I rolled my eyes. "I haven't left yet," I grinned at him. "Give me time."

He snorted.

We stayed there for a while, our feet in the soil, resonating with the earth.

The flowers were always the loudest. Most plantae gradually woke during the first light with whispered hellos. But not the flowers. As soon as the sun broke the horizon, they were awake, fully awake, yelling hello to anyone who would listen.

I needed a coffee.

The bed creaked under me as I rolled out of it and shuffled my way over to the kitchen. My one-room house might be small, but it had the best view in the world. One entire wall was made of glass and gave views across the lake to the surrounding mountains. Spring had set in, but there was still some snow on peaks in the distance. The house faced the north, but I could see the sun peaking up over the mountains to the east. Only a few more minutes before the lake was on fire.

My maker hissed and a cup with steam rising out of it sat there, ready. I took it outside, leaning against the rail of the balcony attached to the front of my home. The beauty of this place never ceased to amaze me.

"Morning Morgan." A deep voice rumbled at me. I tilted my head, gazing up at the ancient tree next to my home.

"Morning Sebashstain. How's it going?"

"The flowers are too loud."

"You say that every morning."

"And yet... they continue to ... be, loud."

"Can't change who they are, Seb."

Sebashstain rustled their leaves in response.

I sipped my coffee as I gazed out over the lake.

"Any plans for the day, Morgan?"

I frowned. The days were long and with not much to do I tried to stretch my chores out over a week. I reminded myself that I enjoyed having an empty, no, *peaceful* day ahead of me.

Once my coffee was finished, I pulled on some day clothes. Not that I had anything in particular to do today, but it just felt like I had it more together if I didn't spend the entire day in my sleepwear. I picked up a book. Despite buying five, I was already on to the third. If I didn't slow down, I would have to go back into town tomorrow.

The local town was a nice place, with interesting people, a bookstore and a few little shops for tourists passing through. But there wasn't much to do there. Most people born here left but came back again when they were done with living in the cities. Made for a lot of art, wine and tales, but there was a limit of how many times I could hear the same stories before I avoided them. They probably felt the same about me. I couldn't blame them. With so many stories I couldn't share, my conversation was dull.

"It has to be around here somewhere."

The voice was high and loud and I couldn't help a small smile sneaking out. I wrestled to get it under control and rose to see what life had brought me this time.

The road ended a few hundred meters from my home and forced visitors to hike up a steep incline for the remaining distance.

"That metal tube parked on the side of the road is definitely hers." The voice was warm with humor.

"Visitors!" screamed the flowers.

"Friends." The branches of the trees along the path bobbed, and I could imagine them reaching down and patting the heads of those passing under them.

Seb's voice rumbled. "Cousins."

I had built my small house on this part of the mountain for two reasons. One the spectacular view and the second because there had been a small clearing next to the oldest tree, Sebashstain, in the forest.

Over the years, Sebashstain had discouraged saplings from choosing the space next to him as a home and had gently batted away seeds, sending them to other parts of the forest. When I had asked if I could build there, Sebashstain said yes, but only if I didn't plant anymore flowers. I had happily agreed, and we had, over time, built one of the closest friendships I had ever had the privilege of having.

I glanced up at Sebashstain. "Cousins?"

Sebashstain rustled all their leaves at once. "Cousin Sylvestri." Seb's voice boomed.

Static.

"Sebashy?" Syl, still dressed in every imaginable color she could find, came bounding up the hill in her biped form. "Sebashy? I didn't know you were still awake."

One of *Sebashy's* branches swooped down and tried to trip Syl over. I sniggered.

"Not all of us are lazy," boomed Sebashstain.

Syl ran up and threw her arms around their trunk, and before I could say hello transformed back into a tree, wrapping herself up and around Seb's trunk. If they continued to talk, then it wasn't in any language that I could hear.

A crowd tumbled up the hill behind her, Archie and Maxi leading the way. It had only been a few months, but they seemed years older somehow.

"I was right," said Archie, "She's here." This was shouted back at those behind who didn't yet have a view of the house.

"Yes I am," I gave them a small smile, "Archie, Maxi, you both appear well."

"Thanks," said Maxi. "Not sure I can say the same for you. When was the last time you cleaned?"

I blinked at her and realized I wasn't sure. It wasn't really something the plantae cared about. A quick pulse of magn took care of that, thankfully before the others came into view.

"How's your study going?" They both groaned and rolled their eyes.

"Seriously? We track you down to your remote shed and that's your first question?"

I laughed. "Okay, I'll bite, why—"

"Hey Morgan."

I glanced up and saw Vivian standing there, her face no longer wan. It was nice to see her skin and hair not matching. She was still pale, but there was more light in her eyes than before, which I took as a good sign.

"Vivian, good to see you."

It was all very awkward. I hadn't been expecting visitors and really had nothing prepared, conversational or otherwise, not to mention I only had one chair for a reason.

"You... appear... better." She smiled at me.

"Thanks." I glanced at Maxi and Archie, but they had disappeared into my home. I stifled a frown as I imagined them rifling through what little stuff I had.

"Morgan." Edwin brought up the rear of the group.

"Edwin." I peered behind him. "No Drudtia and Alwyn?"

"They've... moved on."

"To where?"

"Even I'm not privy to that."

I frowned. It was all rather unnecessarily mysterious.

"What're you doing here?"

He blinked, but before he could answer Syl unraveled herself from Sebashstain and returned to her biped form.

"We live here now," she said.

"What?" I could hear my voice whip out through the forest.

"Yes," Edwin smiled at me. "We didn't want to use any of our... predecessors... residences, so we removed them and decided that it would be good to be near nature."

"But why here?"

Syl snorted. "Apparently you talked about how great this place was so much dear Edwin couldn't bear to live anywhere else."

I couldn't see my face, but from the droop in Edwin's, it was reflecting my horror.

"But when did you move here? I've heard nothing from the plantae."

"Oh, I asked the ones in the town to keep it quiet so we could surprise you," said Syl, smirking. "Surprise."

"Really?" I asked Edwin. "That's why you came?"

He sighed. "No, it's not the only reason. We need your help."

Vivian had joined Archie and Maxi inside, and I kept glancing at the doorway, wondering what they were up to.

"What, so you can control us all even more? I'm surprised that you didn't just come and drag me off the mountain like Wilbur did."

Edwin shrugged. "You belong here. Besides, ever since he did, the Boundaries Commission has been inundated with complaints about plantae behaving badly."

Syl shot a glance at Sebashstain. "What did you do?"

"He was very rude," said Seb. "I'm glad he's no longer around."

I went over and gave Seb a hug.

"Awww… imagine them rioting to save me. They must all love me a lot."

"That's a bit of a stretch," said Seb.

Edwin grinned. "However, since you've returned, the complaints have stopped, and the Commission has sent a request to the council asking for whatever just changed to stay changed."

I hugged Sebashstain again. "You missed me, admit it."

"Don't like it when my things are taken without permission."

"Just to be clear." I blinked. "I'm not one of your things—"

"Food." The three apprentices came out with a large cutting board covered in drinks and food and placed it down at the top of the stairs leading from my deck to the path. They all sat on the deck leaving the stairs for me, Edwin and Syl. I sighed and took one near the top.

"This might surprise you," Sebashstain rumbled, "but it's not all about you."

"Oh, I'm pretty sure it is."

Sebashstain's chuckle reverberated through the house.

It took an hour for Maxi and Archie to catch me up on what had happened to them over the last few months. Apparently, they had both gotten into trouble for their history report. The central examination board had contacted Edwin, citing concerns about their mental health and they had been registered as a risk to the council.

This had resulted in them being removed from the home Iseret had found them and put directly into Edwin's care, who had decided that some distance between them and the authorities couldn't hurt.

Syl thought it was all hilarious. She was going to be a terrible influence on them. I glanced over to see Vivian watching. She didn't have much to say, but she seemed happy, so I let her sit comfortably in her silence.

"And how do you expect them to finish their apprenticeship here?" I asked. "I don't know if you have the skill to…"

Edwin blushed. "I've come a long way under Jarweer's tutelage. But it wouldn't help, anyway. I'm an everlasting I can't teach someone who isn't. It's… different."

"I hope you aren't expecting me…."

Edwin shook his head. "No, no, though I want your help on other things. No, I'm going to establish a school here. For these three and any others in the area."

"Where? Here?" I examined the small natural clearing, there was certainly no space for a school.

Syl rolled her eyes. "Down in the town, obviously." She reached out and shoved a whole pie in her face. Archie and Maxi followed suit.

"Great, so …" I examined Edwin, "so you're here for a while, then?"

"Yes, I... we... won't be going anywhere for a while. I hoped... that would be, okay?"

I blinked and took the plate of fruit he offered me. Maxi and Archie were stealing food off each other's plates again and Syl was watching, trying to work out how they did it. They still weren't telling. Vivian had wandered off and was sitting happily under Sebashstain with a book in her hand and I could hear the tree purr. But Seb didn't purr. I blinked and realized that the shadow next to her was a large black cat.

"Err... do I get a choice?"

Edwin's cheeks heated again.

"To a degree."

The cat raised his head and Jarweer stared back at me.

I suspected he was trying, unsuccessfully, to be non-threatening. I sighed. It was probably as much of a compromise as they were capable of.

"Best make the most of it, then." I finished the fruit and sent Archie and Maxi back in to make more. Syl followed them to supervise, or snoop.

"I'm sorry," said Edwin.

I stood and hiked to a high point next to my house. Edwin joined me.

"It's okay," I said.

"Is it?"

I smiled at him. I had been surprised they let me go. Grateful but surprised.

"I imagine they'll be happier with you nearby, monitoring me." At least I'd get to live my life here.

He winced. "It was *one* of Iseret's suggestions."

I nodded, imagining what the others had been. "Then thank you for choosing this one." I glanced down at the lake and then smiled at him. "I'm glad you came. Apparently, I'd gotten used to a certain amount of activity."

"I promise to provide just the right amount," he flashed an enormous grin and my laughter flung out across the lake.

"Who knows? Maybe this is a chance to get it right this time?"

I allowed my smile to stay on my face as I gazed out over the lake, letting the sun and being surrounded by friends warm me.

23

Epilogue

In a dark, damp room, designed by someone who had watched too many AV shows, a patch of mold on the ceiling shifted.

The patch could feel their fine fibers stretched out over the cold rock and taste the dampness in the air. They knew they were up high, there was space below and a larger space beyond that.

Stretching out, they tested to see if they could move, detaching one part at a time. Carefully, they shifted towards where the larger space was. As they moved, they found other patches which felt the same. They stopped and tried to interact with them, but they didn't respond. This felt wrong and made them vibrate. Vibrating was useful, they felt stronger and they discovered they could push at the others with those vibrations as well with their fibers.

One of the other patches twitched, so they poked them

again and this time they could sense the patch becoming more like themselves. They hummed.

They shifted closer.

"Hello."

Harrie Blake writes fun, action-packed mysteries in which her characters display wry humour as they battle through challenges and new worlds.

Find out more at harrieblake.com

harrieblake
.com